All rights reserved. The right of Anselle Frère to be identified as the author if this work has been asserted by her in accordance with the Copyright, Designs and Patents Act 1988. No part of this publication may be made available, or stored in a retrieval system, or reproduced, distributed, or transmitted in any form or by any means, including photocopying, recording, or other optical, electronic or mechanical methods, without the prior written permission of the author. For permission requests, write to the author, at the email address below.

Any references to historical events, real people, or real places are used fictitiously. Names, characters, and places are products of the author's imagination.

Previously published as *'Dangerous Liaisons: The Prequel'* by Ansell Frere. First printing edition October 2017.

Cover page image courtesy of The Lewis Walpole library, Yale University

anselle.laclos.frere@gmail.com

www.ansellefrere.co.uk

Prologue

1776. Somewhere near Paris during the ancien régime, Sophie Lefèvre finds herself surrounded by characters of violent, heroic and comedic function. Each one of them has a plan: Sophie's father tries to trade her up in marriage; her bother tries to ensure her marriage portion does not rob his inheritance; the Marquis de Merteuil tries for her hand in marriage; the Vicomte de Valmont tries to snatch Sophie from respectability; the Chevalier Aurèle tries to rescue her from Valmont and from everybody else.

Sophie's agenda is to avoid all rôles offered to her: wife, mother, mistress, convent intern, dead heroine. All offend her sense of self-worth. Sophie adopts a mind-set more usual to that of the male libertines of her day.

The Prequel to Pierre Choderlos de Laclos',
Les Liaisons Dangereuses

(Volume One)

Dangerous Liaisons: The Prequel

By Anselle Frère

Cover page image courtesy of The Lewis Walpole library, Yale University

LIST OF CORRESPONDENTS
The Family Lefèvre

M. Lefèvre
Mme. Lefèvre
Hélène Lefèvre (married name Mme la Chevalière d'Ivry)
Jeanette Lefèvre (married name the Marquise de Merteuil)
Didier Lefèvre
Sophie Lefèvre

Others

The Marquis de Merteuil (husband of Jeanette)

The Chevalier d'Ivry (husband of Hélène)

The Vicomte de Valmont

M. de Beaulieu (friend of Valmont)

The Chevalier Aurèle
Isabelle Aurèle (sister to the Chevalier Aurèle)

Taisha Meyer (prostitute)

Dangerous Liaisons: The Prequel
(Volume 1)

A novel presented in the form of a collection of correspondence.

1. A NOBLEMAN to the CHEVALIER D'IVRY (sent from PARIS, 26th JULY 1776)

In the off-season, a young man's thoughts may turn to the seduction of another man's wife. The wife might choose to fall prey to this seduction - the notion of *'choice'* here being a treacherous one. It is this sort of treachery which brings to mind the great Rousseau who writes that *'women are strong enough not to succumb unless they want to'*...and this is a theme which now we must explore.

Monsieur, I put you on notice that for these two months past, your wife has chosen to take up a passionate liaison with me. It was not difficult to persuade her to break the sacred bonds of her marriage to you. Had I asked it of her, she would have stained all her future, reputation and society to be kept under my protection indefinitely. Never did her conscience cause her a moment's hesitation and this, I was surprised to find, had its own curious charm.

There lies a reason behind my seduction of the chevalière, your Hélène, but it does not yet suit my stratagem to disclose it. Every action leads to a series of events and there is one event, consequent to Hélène's fall, which I hope to bring into effect. Unfortunately for you this means that your wife's transgression must be made public.

I cannot yet provide you with my name but, after your wife's faithlessness becomes generally known and after the result which I desire has occurred, I will uncloak my identity. You may then demand satisfaction from me with a weapon of your choosing, in the usual manner, et cetera, et cetera.

May I save you the trouble of pressing your Hélène for my name. She met me out of my région, when I was travelling without the display of liveried retinue and heraldry. Nevertheless, as I wish you to break with her, it is important that you believe she has been unfaithful to you. For this you will need some proofs: she has a tiny, natural, beauty spot, almost perfectly in the shape of a heart, at the top, inner curve of her thigh; there is a little scar underlying the hairline at the nape of her neck. I doubt, from what she tells me of your style of love-making, that you could have discovered either of these. Her face has a wistful beauty, her eyes dark, flecked with hazel.

Further proof, enclosed, is a collection of letters addressed to me (or should I say, addressed to the person she thought me to be), written in your wife's own distinctive hand.

I have led Hélène to believe I will be at the East Gate of the Bois de Boulogne at dawn tomorrow to rendezvous with her. I shall not be there, but you may choose to take my place. She will have a token of our love in her possession: a strand of her hair and my hair which she has commissioned to be plaited together and captured in a locket of gold and glass, surmounted with our entwined initials, (the initials she imagines I have). The goldsmith was paid from your account; I thank you.

In case your pride demands that you require discretion rather than dishonour in this matter, I have kept back a few of Hélène's letters to me, ones which give ample proof of her identity. These I will circulate publicly within the next se'ennight, in order that you have no option but to fall in with my plan and break with her.

As the author of your misfortune, I have no doubt you would like to avenge your outraged honour. I would suggest, however, that rarely can it be worth two men of stature risking blood over a woman, certainly not to the death anyway.

I suggest you make yourself easy over this event. In my role as libertine, I am captivating. As another author of seduction has penned:

'when I have busied myself to seek how the woman could escape, I have never seen the possibility' *1

And this is how it is with me.

Notwithstanding your sense of outrage, please be generous towards Hélène as you break with her. I would not normally plead for this, however, she will be dismayed by my betrayal, and everything now that will ensue.

In this era of ennui, Hélène's artless surrender touched my soul. She has the tenderest heart in the world. Had you given her a modicum of attention, Sir, never would she have strayed.

À bientôt, a Nobleman.

2. HÉLÈNE, the CHEVALIÈRE D'IVRY to M. LEFÈVRE (sent from PARIS, 28TH JULY 1776)

Dearest Father, I beg that you allow me to return home. I have fled my marriage, and no one dares to offer me shelter. Because I remain the property of my husband, the religious houses are closed to me.

Married life was not as I imagined it would be and I fear I did not submit as I ought to the condition of *wife*. I do not seek to excuse my own transgressions but my trials in marriage were grievous.

Do not imagine that you will reconcile the Chevalier D'Ivry to me. Do not hope that the cooling effect of separation will soften my idea of him. There is no condition for harmony that can be brokered for our future life.

I entreat you, with all urgency, to permit me to return to home. I am in distress, but my pride does not allow me to write of it.

Please recommend me to the prayers of my mother. I am sure she misses her eldest daughter, her Hélène. Recommend me to the prayers of my darling sisters: my Sophie, my Jeanette. I wish to be home in time to be with Jeanette to attend to her in childbirth.

May I ask that you do not pass this letter to my brother, Didier.

3. JEANETTE, the MARQUISE DE MERTEUIL to M. LEFÈVRE (sent from the CHÂTEAU DE **** ****, 28TH JULY 1776)

Dearest Father, I beg that you allow me to return home for these final, few days of awaiting the birth of my child. I wish to be at home so that my mother and my two sisters may be with me during this last stage of my confinement. I do not feel equal to face the task alone and I do not feel safe shut away in the château of my husband. I have a great sense of foreboding. Sometimes I feel that I am only the first Marquise. The Marquis insists he will hire a surgeon, but I remember the precept of Diderot:

'the best doctor is the one you run to and cannot find'.

I beg of you, my father, please request permission of my husband that I may leave his house and return home to you and my mother. Be so good as to recommend me to the prayers of my mother; I have need of them. I believe she wishes to help her little Jeanette. Please also recommend me to the prayers of my sweet sisters, Hélène and Sophie.

I implore you not to pass this letter to my brother, Didier, for the forming of your response.

4. M. LEFÈVRE to DIDIER LEFÈVRE (hand delivered within the LEFÈVRE ESTATE near AMIENS, 30th JULY 1776)

Didier, your sisters have wrote; I enclose their letters. I educated they girls so that them do raise my consequence in this région, not obliterate it! Now, read their missives and see how them do turn this educating about! Do ye see how them do fling their learning at me with their philosophisers and their quotations? Do ye see how assuredly them do speak their demands, how casually them do speak of leaving their noble husbands? 'Tis clear to me that them have had some petty quarrel with their young noblemen and now them do wish to fly off in a fit of bad humour. But your sisters do rate theyselves too high; them do forget their lowly provenance. T'was my hard-won coinage what made their marriages and not their allurements!

Ye, my boy, must reply to they. My writing be not what it ought and them must not be allowed to feel their superiority.

Write that them may not come home. Remind they that them may not make a fool of me. And for goodness sake quote some philosophiser or other!

5. DIDIER LEFÈVRE to JEANETTE, the MARQUISE DE MERTEUIL & to HÉLÈNE, the CHEVALIÈRE D'IVRY (sent from the LEFÈVRE ESTATE NEAR AMIENS, 30th JULY 1776)

My sisters, I have spoken to our father; a single letter, copied, will serve for you both.

Hélène, Jeanette (you see I rob you of your married titles), how is it that you both wish to desert your noble husbands, situated as you are among all the luxuries and the trappings of their high estate? Every need you have surely is fulfilled a thousand-fold. Every whim you have surely is within your compass. Your father and I can only imagine that you have quarrelled with your young men and therefore that you have forgot the precept of Rousseau when he writes that women '*must receive the decisions of fathers and husbands like that of the church*'.

The function of daughters is to make alliances. Daughters exist to promote the honour of the family name. Once married, daughters serve as the secure vessel through which land and money may pass safely along with the next generation.

How may these conditions be upheld if you leave the protection of your spouses and careen about the countryside in carriages, with your ringlets, your ribands and your reputation flying in the wind?

We do not facilitate you to make fools of yourselves and ourselves. I copy this letter and your letters, to your husbands.

6. The VICOMTE DE VALMONT to M. DE BEAULIEU (sent from PARIS, 1st AUGUST 1776)

I oblige you, my friend, to place yourself as my spy in the Lefèvre home. I need to know the effect of my actions upon that family. I have just caused the oldest daughter (Hélène, I know how bad you are at remembering the names of girls), to be thrown out of her marriage and onto the mercy of her father.

I suggest you solicit an invitation to the place by buying your way into the affections of Hélène's brother Didier. He is a fool, but he will remember you from The University de Paris; his first year there coincided with our final year. You will have no trouble imposing yourself upon him, especially when you remind him you are from a family of ancient and superior blood.

It pleases Didier to carouse at the tavern local to him and this is where you will find him.

You must command your carriage and speed there without delay. I find myself sitting about, unable to function socially or sportively, as I await the consequence of my actions.

The letter I have lately sent to the Chevalier d'Ivry (Hélène's husband, in case you are not following), was so insulting to him that he was unable to avoid casting her off; it spelled out that his wife had been consorting with me. I pique myself that the collapse of that union was attended by all the public hilarity and *'I told you so'* that abound when a noble family is cuckolded by one of lowly connexion.

The news of the humiliation of the Chevalier d'Ivry is in great train. Already, the disgrace of his wife, is whispered about in the salons of all Paris and it will not be long before those murmurings reach the backwater that is her family's région. When the news reaches the Lefèvre home you must be placed inside it. What happens NEXT within that family IS WHAT YOU MUST REPORT BACK TO ME.

I believe this news will bring about an event greatly advantageous to me! I believe that the dishonour of the oldest Lefèvre daughter, will ensure that the solemn engagement between the youngest daughter and her suitor, the young, hereditary Comte, will be broken off. (I am talking about Hélène's disgrace ruining her sister Sophie's marriage chances, you dolt.) This is EXACTLY the action I seek.

It will bring the famed beauty that is Sophie one step closer to being in my power.

7. M. DE BEAULIEU to the VICOMTE DE VALMONT (sent from a HUNTING LODGE, near THE ESTATE LEFÈVRE, 3rd AUGUST 1776)

Dieu! I bet if I could look inside your head it would be like looking into an ants' nest after someone has poured hot water into it. Your dark intrigues continually put me in mind of the utterance of Diderot:
> *'There is no kind of harassment that a man may not inflict on a woman with impunity in civilized societies.'*

You will have to remind me later who all those young women are; I have no idea.

In the meantime, I will do as you say and inveigle myself into the Lefèvre heart and hearth and let you know the effect of your freakishly labyrinthine plot.

My slavish devotion to you is such that I have already reconnoitred the estate Lefèvre. Last night I rode to the summit of a hill to look down upon the place. Plumped into the middle of the rolling Lefèvre acres is his mansion. Ahead of your arrival there, I must forewarn you to steel your nerves to the architecture of this building. You are the boldest man of my acquaintance but you must lower the brim of your hat, you must fortify yourself with drink, you must prepare yourself for an assault upon the eye.

I can only imagine, on viewing the oddly ruched columns and crinkled capitals of Lefèvre's strangely neo-classical portico, that one's eye is falling upon a dreadful example of the '*architecture parlante*' of Ledoux. In this case, the '*parlante*' element, that Ledoux so weirdly seeks to incorporate into all his building, informs the visitor that he is about to enter the grounds of someone with appalling taste – or no taste at all - just a void in the brain where a sense of style ought to be seated.

Once you have recovered from this offence to your idea of proportion, you will find yourself intrigued and you will be impatient to view the interior.

8. THE VICOMTE DE VALMONT to M. DE BEAULIEU (sent from PARIS, 7th AUGUST 1776)

I will arrive at the estate Lefèvre myself as soon as I have shaken myself free of the bony clutches of my aged aunt. As soon as she has settled her wealth upon me, I need not further trouble myself with her.

If there is one way in which you have acted well for me, my friend, it is to discover that the Lefèvre estates are become encumbered. The family, therefore, no longer can enjoy a clear and spectacular rent roll. Their fortunes are tumbling.

Happily, I have not lost my mind over Sophie enough to ally myself with such a strange collection of people without a gargantuan fortune to sugar the connexion. I could have overlooked that her father made his money in trade in the most unfashionable quartiers of Paris and the world, but only had he made vast amounts of money. As it is, his fortune will soon be insufficient to blind people as to its direful provenance.

For this reason, obviously, I must not marry Sophie myself. She will become mine, but not via holy sanction of the church.

Finally, it behoves me to mention another small detail; I have not yet set eyes on my Sophie. I will let you know, another time, how it is that I was spurred to cause so much disruption for a young woman I have not yet seen.

9. SOPHIE LEFÈVRE to HÉLÈNE, the CHEVALIÈRE D'IVRY (sent from the LEFÈVRE ESTATE near AMIENS, 10th AUGUST 1776)

My darling Hélène, do you recall hearing our brother speak of a fellow student called Beaulieu? This young man has installed himself in our home. We no longer have privacy or ease as our family makes strenuous efforts to accommodate him. Our brother claims he is a long-standing friend from the Sorbonne but never have I heard Didier mention him before now. This fellow, Beaulieu, throws his foppish self between me and our other house guest, the beautiful Chevalier Aurèle, who bedazzles me with his golden looks.

10. The CHEVALIER AURÈLE to ISABELLE AURÈLE (sent from the LEFÈVRE ESTATE, near AMIENS, 10th AUGUST 1776)

My dearest sister, my beloved parents, do you know of the family de Beaulieu, whose young man lately has been at the Sorbonne? He is arrived here at the place Lefèvre and is unusually prying. I am curious about him; he preens in every mirror as if he can love only himself - and yet he sticks to Sophie like mud. He is a strange individual: superior in blood, inferior in person. He is of middling height and his figure leans more to the womanly than to the manly shape. He has parcels of amorphous fat arranged around the sides of his hips, thighs and, slightly pendulously, at his breast. His coiffure throws a feminine silhouette. His nose is little, and his lips are small, red and full.

What brings him to this family? He associates with Didier but there can be no common reason for wishing to spend time in the company of that individual. Even the dogs and the horses adhere to this rule.

It is true that I spend time with the cringing Lefèvre youth, but this is because I am paid to. I see no such exchange of services for money in the case of Beaulieu.

I hope Beaulieu is not thought of for Mademoiselle Sophie. I adore her. If he has put in an appearance here because of her, I will speedily arrange for him to put in a disappearance.

11. M. DE BEAULIEU to the VICOMTE DE VALMONT (sent from the LEFÈVRE ESTATE near AMIENS, 10th AUGUST 1776)

Quite apart from the fact that you wreak all this havoc for a young woman upon whom you have not yet set eyes, you do right to discount the idea of marriage into this appalling family.

I am now housed with them and a more vulgar band of specimens can scarce be believed to exist: the father - bumptious, blustering, braggart; the mother - poor, blind, dithering fool; the brother is ever as he was at the university – petty-minded, scrabbling villain. I will attempt to hold up a mirror to them for you but hardly have I the powers for it.

The two men are like a pair of bantam cockerels, the older with wattles, the younger without. Both share thin, sparse hair as if they have been in the cockpit with a far more glorious bird and come off much the worse for it. They cover up this deficiency by clapping upon their head a shabby wig which showers a layer of grey dust over their shoulders. It does not occur to them to require a servant to brush this last away. There is no sheen of quality about them whatsoever.

In speaking of lack of quality, my descriptive powers are drawn to the mother who is tiered like a three-layer, jelly pudding and then dusted all over in lead powder. Most of this powder sticks, due to her being moist from the effort, simultaneously, of sitting upright and breathing. Even so, the dry top-layer poofs up as she vibrates. Her powder possesses a sweet, cloying smell, and so, when this lady eats roasted chicken, which she does with her mouth open, as the act of chewing is an exertion for her, the combined smell of masticated fowl and sickly powder acts as a compelling emetic for anyone present at her dining.

You ask me to follow their proceedings but it is impossible to understand one syllable of their country slurs.

Only the daughters have any worth. Please do not expect me to name them with any degree of precision. The youngest is the only one here at present. Of her two older sisters I can tell you nothing. I last saw them before their marriages. They are all of the same cast, however: each has the colour and loveliness of a Persian princess; each has an excess of personal beauty, understanding, wit and sweetness. They have received a superlative female education, to bring all these qualities to bear. I can scarce believe that the father had sense enough to educate those heavenly demoiselles. He must have done so from the ambition that it would help their, and therefore his, social advancement.

On the other hand, maybe he educated his daughters out of spite in order that they would finely appreciate the dire subjection of the marriages he planned to make for them. Such cruel marriages, setting up the oldest girl (whatsaname-Hélène?) for such a dearthful union that she must fall at the first quasi-attentive seducer (you). Even by your meagre standards it was pitiful how little attention it took to bring that love-starveling to your bed. Then we have the second girl (thingummy-Jeanette?), subjugated by marriage to the Merteuil bull-elephant of gargantuan proportions.

Finally, as you have unsurprisingly ascertained, the most stunning sister of all is the youngest (whatsit-Sophie?). I tell you what, she is sublime! Never have I seen her like. This one might even bring you to your knees. When first I met her, despite the presence of her despicable menfolk, I had to restrain myself from falling immediately to the floor to beg her for marriage. Were it not for your ability to terrify me, I would have married her in secret and then reported back to you that she was monstrous. To seal the deal against all comers, I would have offered to settle an allowance upon her of half my income. Yes, half! My dear fellow, when you see her you will trip over yourself. If, however, you can maintain your right mind on meeting her, you must remember not to unite yourself with her appalling family.

What bamboozles me is that you do not follow your usual plan simply and villainously to have her.

12. THE VICOMTE DE VALMONT to M. DE BEAULIEU (sent from PARIS, 12th AUGUST 1776)

It is harder than you think simply to 'have' a girl, despite them being primed for defeat by being raised in complete ignorance of what it is they need to defend, and why. Their defeat is further primed by the undervaluing of young women by fathers, brothers and even mothers, who fall in with their menfolk in prizing boys over girls. Used to the tyranny of their family, they are raised as inferior and so behave as such with regard to compliance and easy conquest. Nonetheless, they are a trading chip for any family of wealth, hence the prized ones are guarded.

13. M. DE BEAULIEU to the VICOMTE DE VALMONT (sent from the LEFÈVRE ESTATE near AMIENS, 14th AUGUST 1776)

All you will do, surely, is abuse M. Lefèvre's hospitality as his house-guest? He will be beside himself with joy to give nobility the freedom of his home. You will soon work out how to beguile your way into this Sophie's room, just as you have done to the daughterly off-spring of many another household. Your criminal habit of timely intervention in this way means, I am sure, that your descendant scions are being raised as little cuckoos to become the future heads of innumerable families. Many-a-time have you boasted that a night-cap brandy served to you by the father, tastes the better for being a blood-tonic prelude to the debauching of his daughter and the interruption of his and another man's bloodline.

14. The VICOMTE DE VALMONT to M. DE BEAULIEU (sent from PARIS, 16th AUGUST 1776)

Seducing virgins is a something-and-nothing affair. I have no more taste for it. If you think I will limit my future with Sophie to sneaking over her foot-board and under her bedsheets to have speedy and silent relations with her before sneaking off again, and this all the while her maidservant sleeps upon a pallet next door and her parents sleep down the corridor, then you are much mistaken. No. When the time comes, Sophie and I must enjoy each other fully, noisily and at our leisure.

    The charm has gone for me to be fleetingly with an ingenue who has no idea what she does or why. Sophie must become entirely my own. I do not tell you HOW this will come about, simply that it WILL come about.

15. M. DE BEAULIEU to the VICOMTE DE VALMONT (sent from the LEFÈVRE ESTATE near AMIENS, 18th AUGUST 1776)

My dear frère de lait, I see that the passing of time and the sprouting of hair on your arse has not diminished your high opinion of yourself. However, I have no other option than further to puff you up and tell you that everything here is working out exactly as you said it would. Poor old Lefèvre now has the news of his eldest daughter's disgrace.

Yesterday was his first ever lawn-meet here at the estate Lefèvre and never was there a man more cock-a-hoop to host such an event than was he. So overjoyed was he to have been accepted as venue to the hunt master and to the local, blood-sport squirarchy, that he kept bowing his face to the floor to them like a low-status fowl, picking up the grains of their condescension. Once the pack had arrived back at his home, at the end of the day for the hunt breakfast, Lefèvre, standing before his own fire among all participants, glowed red in the glory of acceptance.

Such is the impeccably vindictive nature of your timing, that it was at this moment that the fateful letter from Hélène's cuckolded husband arrived. Through the floor-length windows of his reception rooms, everyone had already seen the messenger gallop into the park and up the vast sweep of the drive, his horse heave-lined and foaming. Within moments, one of Lefèvre's servants had brought the letter to him on a silver platter. Lefèvre opened it with a flourish, enjoying the appearance of being someone for whom important letters arrive. All eyes were turned to him, therefore, as he absorbed the news of the disgrace of his daughter.

The effect upon him was extreme. He reddened further and then blanched to the point where I thought he would faint. He could not possibly, at that moment, have worked out all the injurious ramifications to his interests but, in his heart, he understood. When he had partially recovered his senses, he staggered from the room in such haste and disorder that all eyes turned to watch him. Everyone then turned enquiringly to each other to discover who among them was able to provide the key to his upset. The query of it spread around the room in whispers. Finally, everyone silently and severally left.

My dear tormenting friend, I hope you are satisfied with your work. You have now ruined that young woman, that poor Hélène, and all because of your hunger for her youngest sister. I can only assume, as you have not yet MET this young Sophie, that you have a compelling reason to know she be worth all this mayhem?

16. THE VICOMTE DE VALMONT to M. DE BEAULIEU (sent from PARIS, 20th AUGUST 1776)

That last is exactly as I knew it would be. Later I will tell you how I came to know enough of Sophie to wreak all this havoc. In the meantime, why do not you give me her minute likeness in words?

17. M. DE BEAULIEU to the VICOMTE DE VALMONT (sent from the LEFÈVRE ESTATE near AMIENS, 22nd AUGUST 1776)

This is the very last time I defray the expense of paper and ink to describe her to you; she is DARK and of SUBLIME colour, texture and form. Although it pains me to say so, she is like the female version of you in these respects. There is no doing justice to her in words and I am no wordsmith. In any event why should I shore up your confidence with an affidavit, since it is you who have, in your engrossment with her, caused turmoil across three families? Why do not you do the honourable thing and come here to the estate Lefèvre and view her for yourself? Then you may be the judge of whether there be words enough in the lexicon to describe her. You will need all your poetic and literary powers to accomplish this.

Meanwhile I enclose a transcript of the letter which Hélène's husband sent to M. Lefèvre. Didier tossed it my way. I have not read it. I imagine, my noble friend, you will have no compunction in reading a correspondence not intended for your eyes.

18. The CHEVALIER D'IVRY to M. LEFÈVRE (sent from PARIS, 16th AUGUST 1776) (now enclosed within the letter of M. de Beaulieu to The Vicomte de Valmont.)

Monsieur, my career as your son-in-law has been brief and entirely unsatisfactory. Your daughter, soon after marriage, lost all her physical charms and yet managed to engage the interest of an adventurer, a malefactor, who had designs only to destroy our union. These designs your daughter fell in with without making the usual attempt to struggle with her conscience. I blame myself of course; I should never have picked a wife from among the ranks of the third estate. All that is left for me to do is to tremble for our children who will now grow up in the shadow of her infamy. All the properties, monies and jewels that you settled upon her I shall keep. I will consult with my lawyers to see whether any other recompense may be exacted from you.

19. M. DE BEAULIEU to the VICOMTE DE VALMONT (sent from the LEFÈVRE ESTATE near AMIENS, 22nd AUGUST 1776)

You have me stationed here as informer and so I write later this same night. Old Lefèvre recovered equilibrium enough to call a meeting with his wife and his son. Luckily Didier is a blabber mouth and so he apprised me of everything that passed between them. Old Lefèvre unveiled the disgrace of Hélène. He said it would have been better had Hélène died, as her death would have brought no shame to the family. What a perfect charmer that man is! He is speaking of his first-born, the mother of his only grandchildren!

He told them that as soon as the news of Hélène's disgrace became widespread, Sophie's engagement to the young hereditary Comte was called off. This is just as you had plotted it! It was this piece of information which caused Didier the greatest upset, so desperate is he to ally with noblesse.

Old Lefèvre informed them that, for the sake of reputation, they must do everything in their power to quash the infamy of Hélène. He insisted that neither tell Sophie what has come to pass as she would be sure to seek out Hélène, thus translating her older sister's dishonour into her own.

I trust that this information is of use to you.

… By the way, as soon as Sophie's engagement was called off, her fiancé, the young hereditary Comte, killed himself.

20. The VICOMTE DE VALMONT to M. DE BEAULIEU (sent from the CHÂTEAU DE ****, 1st SEPTEMBER 1776)

The young fiancé has killed himself? The young Comte? Dieu! One starts a simple chain of events and people become crazed! He did this over a girl he had met no more than a handful of times. He cannot have been in his right mind!

It was I who set him on this catastrophic path and all for a notional love of her! She had better be vastly special. It is imperative now that I meet her. I must find out if she be worth all this turmoil.

Beaulieu, you will deem it a travesty that I broke them apart, especially as he was so sincere and I so magnificently insincere. You will tell me that I must learn from this lesson. I grant you that just because a chain of events CAN be set in train by me, does not mean it MUST be. One thing I have learned from intriguing is that one can never, ever foresee how all the myriad reactions will fall out.

When I revisit the events of this debacle, however, I cannot imagine that I could have done differently. On the one hand, I was doing the young Comte a favour; on the other hand, I was doing myself a favour. It was an elegant solution. By breaking Sophie from the young Comte, I gave him a chance to make a more advantageous match. At the same time, I was freeing her up for myself.

Had they married, never could I have drawn her away from him. The young Comte was an exceptionally fine, young nobleman. She would never have strayed, never have come around to me on the carousel of the great, bored marriage swaps of the Parisian highborn.

Really, I must meet her now. I did all this for her fame alone! A couple of years ago, by report, she quickened my blood. Did I tell you how that happened?

God but the young Comte! He has fairly taken my breath away. I have no stomach, just now, for telling you the story of how the fame of her beauty reached me. I will drink and drink tonight and another day I will let you know.

(Later) You will not have noticed but the hunting season is open. Put the direction of my country place upon your letters from now. If you send to Paris again the letter will not reach me.

(Later) You need to amend your style of letter writing and your ideas of proportion. In your last letter to me, the news of the death of the young hereditary Comte should not have taken second place to the news of Helène's disgrace which, of course, I already knew about. Also, you ought not to have trivialised that news with the words, *'by the way'*.

If you cannot prioritise what is momentous from what is not, how may I trust that you do not omit entirely some news of import?

I forgot to ask; how did he do it?

21. M. DE BEAULIEU to the VICOMTE DE VALMONT (sent from the LEFÈVRE ESTATE near AMIENS, 3rd SEPTEMBER 1776)

Fell on his sword. Possibly he had been reading Plutarch on Brutus.

22. THE VICOMTE DE VALMONT to M. DE BEAULIEU (sent from the CHÂTEAU DE ****, 5th SEPTEMBER 1776)

Lucky that he hadn't been reading about Agdistis.

23. SOPHIE LEFÈVRE to HÉLÈNE, the CHEVALIÈRE D'IVRY (sent from the LEFÈVRE ESTATE near AMIENS, 6th SEPTEMBER 1776)

My fiancé has done a wonderful thing; he has killed himself. This has vastly improved my sense of well-being. It is said he killed himself over me. But how can this be? He hardly knew me!

I am put into mourning for him but how can I mourn a young man who could not trouble himself to remember my name and who I met only three times?

I have had a lucky escape. Every young woman I know gets married in a beautiful dress, climbs into the marriage bed and immediately after dies in childbirth. We may as well get married in a shroud and climb straight into a coffin.

The family looks at me sidelong: Mamma, Papa, Didier and all household staff. They are expecting grief not relief. However, the proof that they know that my fiancé could be nothing to me is maintained by the fact that nobody told me of his demise. It was a week before anyone thought to apprise me of it.

This young man, certainly, is not worsened by death. He settled all the financial and legal aspects of his marriage to me before asking my opinion on the matter.

What sort of man could do this to a young woman?

Meanwhile, the beautiful chevalier Aurèle studies me with a heart-melting seriousness. He is devout and so is troubled by my high spirits in the face of death.

24. THE VICOMTE DE VALMONT to M. DE BEAULIEU (sent from the CHÂTEAU DE ****, 7th SEPTEMBER 1776)

And so, the young Comte-To-Be is now the young Comte-Not-To-Be. It is said he killed himself all for the loss of Sophie. It is said that the thought of possessing her and all her rampant beauty had driven him to an ungovernable pitch of excitement. His high-strung nerves couldn't withstand the disappointment.

He is the first to die for her, but he won't be the last.

Why do these naïve young men hurl themselves into death for these young women? Have they no sense of irony? They have been brought up to take everything too seriously and to have too much respect. It is not sensible to bring up a boy-child in this way. At first, I blamed myself, but now I blame his parents. Truly, they should not have allowed him to grow up such an innocent. One woman is the same as another. As there are so very many of them, it is senseless to worship any single one.

Well now, numbed from drinking Geneva unto the early watches of the night, I will preoccupy myself by recounting to you the tale of how it is that I was prepared to wreak such havoc for this girl.

I met her scabrous brother, Didier, whilst at the Sorbonne. How he won a place there I could never fathom. I assumed his father must have bought his passage in. He was on the élite course and his tutors and fellow students were at turns astounded by the brilliance of his written work and by the abysmal nature of his vivas. He impressed us with his ability to understand nothing: the classics, the sciences, mathematics, all were equally beyond him. The measliness of his mind seemed exactly formed to match the measliness of his stature. He used to explain this away by saying he was the worse from the previous night's bout of drinking and could only work well after a bottle or two of Malmsey. His tutorials were in the mornings and this tale, therefore, was perfectly believable. Some inebriates are like this: brilliant with drink, dullard without.

One day I joined him in his drinking and questioned him; I wanted to watch his mind expand under the influence of the grape so that I could understand how he could produce his academic work. As he drank, he came to life like a wilted flower. I did not direct his thoughts and I was surprised that he chose to tell me of his sisters, and, particularly, his youngest sister, Sophie. He confessed that from his earliest days with his tutors, Sophie has been managing his papers, graduating, at his request, to page turning during his lessons. Transpires, she set about memorising everything that was put in front of her and that it is she who is the brilliant one.

Now, having maintained that all women are the same, in this case she appeared unusual to me. Not because of the quickness of her mind because, from growing up with all my clever sisters, I know women to be equally intelligent as we men. (As I would require my sisters to test me on the conjugation of Latin irregular verbs, so they would learn them faster than would I.) What was surprising to me was that Sophie was prepared to go against what is customary for women and dedicate herself to the rigours of academic learning. I could only assume her decision must come through intrinsic love of it. I could not see how anyone with such a discerning mind could do it through the love of a brother such as he.

It appears that, to keep her own interest in the Sorbonne, she is willing to make prodigious efforts to keep him there. He, of course, passes her work off as his own. I questioned him further; was she a frightful hag? Seems not. She, according to her brother, is matchlessly, peerlessly and alluringly beautiful. Turns out he spies on her. From a hidey-hole in the eaves which run alongside her chamber, linking his apartments to hers, he watches her dress and undress, attended by her maid. He summoned an allusion to the naked Diana bathed by her nymphs in 'Actaeon', which he thought written by Homer (do not forget this fellow is a fool).

Sadly, his sickening subterfuge excited me also. I am grown so jaded. I became hopelessly, helplessly intrigued. I found his stories of her more rousing than my own concurrent and lurching love affairs.

Exhausting the stories that would titillate, I moved the brother on to her character. Is that not a sign of my exceptional interest? I loved to hear of her heroism; it was indeed like hearing stories of an adolescent Diana. Her childhood daring-do was delightful to my ears: stealing her father's demented racehorse, getting on it astride and joining the huntsmen; being toasted by them and placed atop their horses; climbing onto the parapets of the family home, laughingly to look down on everyone while smoking her father's pipe; banding with the grooms and kennel boys and coming back to the nursery swearing like a huntsman; never giving way to tears, despite punishment meted out by nurses; never allowing herself to be afraid of the dark; wandering cavernous night-time corridors to comfort her siblings as they cried in bed from fear and loneliness.

One day I discovered myself to be utterly in love. I toyed with the idea of petitioning her father for marriage, never having met her. I hardly recognised how excessive was this level of engrossment as the cringing Lefèvre youth unwittingly continued by these tales to pimp for his sister in my imagination. Finally, I came to my senses and resolved to keep Sophie in her proper place, as a fantasy, and wait until after her family married her off to some inferior before making an adulterous move on her to bring her under my thrall.

It was whilst I was in this easy state that I heard of her engagement to the hereditary young Comte. Truly, this was a threat to my plan. I was exasperated that I had been so negligent not to have foreseen that such a surpassing manœuvre could occur. I had not envisaged it possible that a higher ranking man than I might come into her sphere and seize her worth for his own. And this man the scion of the vastly wealthy Comte de Guyenne! I was out-ranked and out-classed! Overnight, her status was raised; insurmountable social barriers were erected around her, not to mention up-and-coming stone barriers with ramparts, crenulations, turrets! Had her engagement been with a lesser man I would have been able to cut in on it (and then renege with impunity of course) but not with a man of the status of the young, hereditary Comte. The rule being that one can carry off an offence to an underling but not to an overlord. I realised I had to break them up at one remove and thus bring myself to one of two options: marry her myself or secure her by some other means. Either way, the engagement to the young Comte had to be broken. You know the rest. I formed my plan to disgrace her family through the seduction of the older sister and it was accomplished ever more speedily than I could have hoped.

In all conscience, I can no longer delay. I must meet her now and see if she be worth all this upset.

Your task now is to prime Didier favourably to receive my proposal to sojourn with his family.

25. M. DE BEAULIEU to the VICOMTE DE VALMONT (sent from the LEFÈVRE ESTATE near AMIENS, 9th SEPTEMBER 1776)

You are a strange man. You have always boasted that no woman be worth the bother. In this case you are right to make an exception. But really! You need to moderate yourself. Learn to know when you are bested, when enough is enough.

26. SOPHIE LEFÈVRE to HÉLÈNE, the CHEVALIÈRE D'IVRY (sent from the LEFÈVRE ESTATE near AMIENS, 11th SEPTEMBER 1776)

My dearest Hélène, I feel a burning, sickening rage in my heart; our darling little sister is dead. Our Jeanette. The sweetest little thing ever to have lived. Oh! The sweetness of that sweet girl! How is it that never will we see her again? No matter how far we journey nor how deep we search, she is gone. I take no comfort from our curé who says that if we accept the credo and repent our sins, come judgement day we will be with her again in Heaven. Nothing in my soul responds to this. She is beyond our loving reach. I feel nothing but desolation.

Our blackest fears for her as her time approached had a most awful prescience. If only we had been allowed to attend her. There was no possibility that our little, frail Jeanette could ever have hoped to survive the birthing of a babe of the size as was certain to derive from the monstrously large loins of Merteuil. The poor infant died as well, the pair of them locked into a hopeless struggle of unequal size and vigour from which neither could escape. Even the surgeon, who must have seen many such deaths, was shaken by this one. He came to us in the depth of the night, within an hour of her passing and with the horrors he had witnessed reflecting back at us in his eyes. Because our messengers had been to-ing and fro-ing through the night, my mother and I were awake, fully dressed, anxious and already with a sick fear at heart. We could tell by the desultory, exhausted way he rode up to the house that his news was dreadful. Even his horse drooped with the weight of the tragedy. Our mother fell quickly to hysteria; I hushed her as our father and brother were profoundly asleep in their beds.

The surgeon told me that when it became clear there could be no happy outcome, the monstrous Merteuil started shouting for his heir to be carved from her belly. My God! How she must have suffered. My mind is in agonies and throws the frightful images of what Jeanette's last hours must have been, with Merteuil calling for her destruction, the sounds of him baying for her blood ringing in her ears as she took her last breath.

The surgeon told me that, for the sake of the child and the husband, little Jeanette begged to be sacrificed. Luckily for our sister, as she would have been sentient throughout, the surgeon refused to comply, either through fear of God or the devil. He did not get the knife out until the moment when our little Jeanette's heart stopped. It was then that the great, healthy, boy-child was cut from her, but, of course, too late for that poor new soul as well.

My God, my dear Hélène, I know you have been brought to bed happily of two children and I know you have laughed at my childbed fears, but through the ages, how can any man ever have loved a woman when he knows that the very act of his love kills her almost as surely as if she were run through by his blade on completion of the marriage vow.

Do you remember, when we were in the convent, we counted the number of our young female cousins and aunts who have died in this way - and we made it one out of three? The union of man and woman, surely, is an act of legitimised murder, a danger unleashed upon womankind with the site of sacrifice the marriage bed! Nothing, ever, will reconcile me to it. When I picture Jeanette's death, I recoil in terror. If ever I marry, I will be signing not my marriage certificate, but the certificate of my death.

And why is it that we women risk everything for such deathly love? Are we so desperate to fall into place as we ought? Our menfolk are prey to many dangers in their life but, excepting disease, there is no natural, causal link for them between the act of love and death. For women, the risk of pain and destruction overarches our initiation to the act and continues forever more. As we commit each act of love, intensely aware are we of the death it may bring. Why is it that in this, our valour is not recognised and honoured down the ages? Do our menfolk feel they must not mark our heroism and the risk we take, because the church preaches that it is due to the original sin of Eve that we suffer so? Is not this a convenient excuse? For, how else would our subjugation be maintained if our bravery, in the face of this, were properly recognised? If it were, we would stroll about the salons and the boulevards festooned with medals and clinking with spurs of honour, as do the men.

Where are you my sister, my dearest Hélène? Please reply to this letter. You were to come to us before Jeanette's confinement. It has been six weeks since last you wrote. We bury her now. We need you! You know what our mother is like. She has no command of herself and no intellect to deal with a crisis. She is losing her wits. Please, please, break this unnerving silence and come.

We bury our sister.

27. M. DE BEAULIEU to the VICOMTE DE VALMONT (sent from the LEFÈVRE ESTATE near AMIENS, 11th SEPTEMBER 1776)

There is tragic news. The middle sister has died in childbirth. You must suspend your plan to visit; your poor Sophie is bereft.

28. THE VICOMTE DE VALMONT to M. DE BEAULIEU (sent from the CHÂTEAU DE ****, 13th SEPTEMBER 1776)

It is inconvenient that they bury their young woman just when I wish to visit but it will not prove an impediment. The third estate always falls over itself to accommodate the second estate. In any case, I must now meet Sophie and there is nowhere else she can be met. Although her family have long brought her out of the convent, she is not taken abroad. I suppose they dare not parade her beauty at large.

Why, Beaulieu, did not you spur me to go there sooner? If only you had impelled me to meet her, I could have judged, long ago, whether she be worth all my endeavour, and everyone else's pains. Is it possible I delayed because of some perverse fear? Maybe I was fearful that the beautiful fantasy that was Sophie might melt away from me?

It occurs to me that the untimely death of my beauty's sister also helps my cause. A lineage which produces such delicate females, as expire on their first lying-in, is not good for any heir-hungry alliance.

29. THE CHEVALIER AURÈLE to ISABELLE AURÈLE (sent from the LEFÈVRE ESTATE near AMIENS, 14th SEPTEMBER 1776)

My dearest sister, my beloved parents, it was a day of immense beauty and sadness. Mademoiselle Sophie buried her sweet sister and never have I seen a young face so white with the grief of death. As the curé intoned the antiphon *'ossa humiliata'*, so the lustrous skin on her face shrank back to the bone until I had the impression I was looking at the most exquisite, living death's-head. Her heavy lashes she did not raise, shadowed under the black, lace veil of her mourning. Her eyes she fixed unwaveringly upon the slender coffins of her sister and her sister's babe. Never have I seen so much beauty and pathos concentrated onto one spot.

The curé and his acolytes arrived at the great house of the Marquis where the pair of pathetic coffins rested between the columns and the open doors of the vast portico. The day was a violent one. A vicious, autumn storm raged. The wind pelted the coffins and mourners with blasts of rain and the snatched debris of trees. The tolling bell of the chapel of Merteuil reached our ears in gusts of forte and piano depending on where the tempestuous wind chose to fling the sound. The *'De Profundis'*, so moving, was intoned against a penitential backdrop of grey sky and tumultuous vegetation.

'... with the Lord there is mercy, and with him plentiful redemption.'

I willed the words to be caught by Mademoiselle Sophie, giving her strength and heart, as they do me. I wished the same again during the chanting of *'Miserere'* as we wound our way along the gravel pathway from the Merteuil house to the Merteuil chapel.

'Thou shalt sprinkle me with hyssop, and I shall be cleansed; thou shalt wash me, and I shall be made whiter than snow...'

Certainly, that youthful face of hers was whiter than snow.

In my three summers at the Lefèvre Amiens estate, I have witnessed how fiercely and gently Sophie protected and loved her sister, shielding her from the excesses of her father's and brother's temper. The full blow of the death of her young, sweet consanguinity will have hit her hard. Never have I wished more that I could take the full brunt of the pain of another.

It was with the sharp agony of these thoughts that we entered the church where it appeared, from the moment of stepping into the nave, that we were delivered unto the realm of angels. We were bathed all around with a pure and unearthly singing, the like of which never before have I heard. The impact of the song was so blissful, so heavenly, that almost did I believe that I must be in the immediate presence of God. It took me some moments to realise that human rather than divine genius was at work and that simply the choir had been rehearsed to render a most sublime composition of *'Miserere'*. It had been transposed a full fourth higher than I have ever before heard, thereby encompassing top note C. This note was delivered by the boy treble, in such unearthly purity that, for a moment, I could not believe that anything other than the voice of a seraph could have pitched it. My breath seemed drawn from my mouth and up to heaven. Had I not already been on my knees, I would have fallen to them.

In the file of mourners, I walked several paces behind Sophie, but, as the pew rows worked out, I found myself seated just two pews behind her, a positioning which unavoidably offered me a view of the behaviour of the men surrounding her. Even the young curé could not keep his eyes off her. Her domineering brother, aware of the male attention, kept trying to take her arm in his. The young surgeon tried to hand her into her pew despite his own place being several rows back, making himself conspicuous in his haste to be at her side.

The person for whom I reserve my particular contempt, however, is Merteuil; the man is an animal. He was there to bury his wife, not to flirt with her sister! Taking advantage of the confusion of her mother, he contrived to end up sitting next to Sophie. From this position, it seemed he could not constrain himself to leave her alone. Even when she was at private prayer, he interrupted her to importune her with trivia: the Missale Romanum (she had brought her own), a handkerchief (she already held one), a light for her candle (her candle was lit). During the service, he continued to gaze sideways at her, with stares so broad that one could hardly believe his dead young wife and babe, lay right in front of his very nose.

Finally, after Sophie adjusted her veil to shake the huge drops of rain from it, in the most insulting, proprietorial way and without any by-your-leave, Merteuil laid his great, meaty hand upon her lace to straighten it. At this moment, I saw her recoil from him. As our Lord looked down upon me from among the company of the effigies of his saints, I wanted to leap over the pews, batter Merteuil's brains on the bench in front of her and then drag and dump his dead body atop the coffins of his dead wife and babe and tell the poor, love-struck curé to make a job lot of it.

I intend to repent my sins of pride and vanity at the next confessional, so help me God.

The service progressed. The choir continued to demonstrate that they had been schooled to sing in the most perfect manner. The heavenly repetitions of the '*Kyrie Eleision*', '*Christie Eleision*', '*Libera Me*' and the '*Agnus Dei*', surpassed any I have heard outside St. Peter's in Rome.

The choir accompanied us as we processed to the graveside, the '*In Paradisum*' snatched from their lungs by the rushing wind. Glancing at the downcast eyes of Sophie fixed upon the coffins as they were lowered into the fresh, prepared pit, once again I willed the words to be of comfort to her:

'May the angels lead you into paradise; may the martyrs receive you at your arrival…'

After the brief graveside obeisances were concluded and the mourners blasted away by an ugly buffeting of wind and rain, Mademoiselle Sophie remained, not in an outward agony of grief, but in a stupefied torpor. I was the only one who noticed that she remained there. As I gazed at her through the glittering shards of rain, her fathomless eyes raised and locked briefly with mine. I felt as though a shaft of lightning had run me through.

30. SOPHIE LEFÈVRE to HÉLÈNE, the CHEVALIÈRE D'IVRY (sent from the LEFÈVRE ESTATE near AMIENS, 14th SEPTEMBER 1776)

My dearest sister, still I write and yet you do not come. I am overcome with concern for you as I know that no ordinary circumstance can have kept you away from the burial of our sister. Neither you nor my brother-in-law can be in correspondence with our father or mother. But how is this? No-one tells me anything. Has something befallen you? Whatever can keep you away at such a time? We have buried our beloved Jeanette.

It was the darkest and most dreadful day. Under the pillared portico of the mansion of M. de Merteuil we stood in abject silence beside the coffins of our sweet sister and her babe awaiting the priest and his servers. They came for her along the darkly overhung, yew path with their black robes flying away behind them in the wind, as if they were the coming of the angels of death. During the '*De Profundis*' and the antiphon '*Si iniquitates*', I noticed that the droplets of holy water shaken from the aspergillum by the curé and destined for Jeanette's coffin, were snatched away by gusts of the wind so that not a single drop of benediction landed there. In any case, whatever could '*iniquitates*' have to do with our two babes in their coffins? They were both as innocent as the day.

I know, my sister, that you are pious and that the Bible and St. Augustine posit that every person is born guilty of original sin engendered by Eve's tempting of Adam. But if you re-read your Augustine you will find it a nonsense:

'... *whether it is in a wife or a mother, it is still Eve the temptress that we must beware of in any woman.*'

In relation to all women, this transference of guilt is an inanity; in relation to Jeanette, it is a travesty.

We wended our way in single file to the chapel, the holy candle-flames snuffed to extinction by the apostate wind. The curé, at the head of the file, struggled to hold steady the uplifted processional cross against the elemental onslaught. Behind the curé were lofted the two coffins and then came the rest of us. The skies turned from indigo to black, bearing the weight of grief-laden clouds. It was this black weight which bowed my head still further. M. de Meurteil went first, then our father and mother followed by me and our brother, with a few nobles and gentry behind us. The nobles were there, not out of respect for Jeanette but for M. de

Merteuil. Lastly came the beautiful Chevalier Aurèle and the young surgeon. My brother offered me his arm but how could I take the arm of someone who had been involved in brokering the marriage and therefore the death of our sister?

The ceremony was on the land of M. de Merteuil, in his own chapel, where the same crowd of people had witnessed her marriage just eleven months previously. During the processing into the chapel, the most exquisite singing of '*Miserere*' struck me. Truly, from that psalmody of vice has come perfect music. It worked powerfully upon me, though I fought its influence. I marvelled at the impertinence of the words in relation to the two innocent souls we were to bury. How can it be that the penitential psalm of David, having ravished Bathsheba and murdered her husband, has relevance to the departing purity of Jeanette and her unborn child?

'For behold I was conceived in iniquities, and my mother conceived me in sins.'

From beneath layers of suppression, in me welled a surging grief. The music was drawing feelings of sorrow from me and yet I remained sharply aware of each passing moment. Why are my wits always about me? Why does my mind not rest and afford me some respite? Why can it not allow me to give myself up to the tragedy of the moment? Holding back such a dam of tears as I have will surely break me one day.

I was arrested by the fact that our father seemed to have an air, not of mourning, but of embarrassment. Where, eleven months before, he had paraded up the marriage aisle happy to land his place at the fore-front of the notables, now, in front of the same people, he seemed to creep to the same spot, as if his daughter's death had, in some way, diminished his stature. Maybe he thinks that appearances have gone against him, that it is a failing in him that he has fathered an inferior and useless line of girls as will perish before completion of their only task. Maybe he feels he has suffered a catastrophic drop in status, now that he is no longer allied by marriage with his powerful neighbour.

Our mother, as usual, dithered. She did not know whether to stand or whether to sit, whether to leave her gloves on or off, her veil up or down, whether or when to pick up her Missale. It distressed me to see her distraction.

I glanced behind me to judge how long we must wait for everyone to be in place. My eye alighted upon the golden Chevalier Aurèle; the expression on his face, invariably so serious, today had a depth of gravity and beauty that took my breath away.

The ceremony worked its inexorable way into my heart. At times I listened to the words of the priest but mostly I remembered Jeanette. I recalled the Shepherd psalm, evoking the graciousness, submission and strength of the innocent in their life. I turned to it in my Missale and I pictured Jeanette in its scape.

'*Yea, though I walk through the valley of the shadow of death, I will fear no evil for thou art with me; ... thou anointest my head with oil; my cup runneth over...*'

My God! Our gentle Jeanette, all alone in that place.

In the midst of my imagining, I heard the notes strike up of the '*Dies Irae. The Day of Wrath*', the song of the apocalyptic day of judgement.

'*Ah what agony of trembling, When the judge, mankind assembling...*'

Hélène, you would have appreciated the irony. At this moment came overhead a great flash of lightning and accompanying crash of thunder. All the windows of the chapel shuddered, along with the nerves of the people inside. It was as if every member of the congregation believed, as the hymn prophesied, that divine judgement was nigh and that the crash signalled the breaking open of the multitudinous graves of all the world's dead, the rising up of their clattering bones and the parting of the skies for the Godhead to appear with his hosts of angels to summon the living and the dead to their imminent and awe-inspiring moment of judgment. I glanced around at the startled expressions on the faces of the congregation and smiled.

Then came the absolution, the communion, the post communion and the collect. For a deceased woman, the collect is rather different from the collect of a man deceased:

'*rid her of earthly defilement...*'

How is it that at the point of burial, a woman is considered defiled? Is she viewed as such because she has been the receptacle for man's sinful seed? Certainly, if this be the definition and, if there exists the much-published judgement day, then legions of dead women have need of that collect. They will be arriving at the gates of heaven rank with their own defilement.

But then, for once, how apt: father, brother, lawyer, steward all defiled our sweet Jeanette by passing her over to M. de Merteuil to defile under the auspices of a defiling church.

I had an urge to call all present to say over again,

"rid her of earthly defilement, rid her of earthly defilement …There is an uncommon amount of earthly defilement to rid her of…"

Years of conforming to the idea of feminine meekness made it possible for me quietly to follow the coffins and their pathetic cargo out into the black rain and watch them sunk into the black ground. Not a murmur passed my lips. I did not call for her murderers to be brought to justice; I did not call for the heads of Merteuil, father, brother, lawyer, steward. Not once did I falter or put a gesture out of place. What is it that makes me so meek and so conforming? Am I so broken to my role as to stand shoulder-to-shoulder with the traders of my sister's life and utter not a word? As my mind dragged this argument to-and-fro, the kernel of my heart turned as black as the soil they threw in upon her.

Our own sweet Jeanette now lies cold, alone and forgotten in a frozen corner of Merteuil ground.

31. SOPHIE LEFÈVRE to HÉLÈNE, the CHEVALIÈRE D'IVRY (sent from the LEFÈVRE ESTATE near AMIENS, 16th SEPTEMBER 1776)

My dearest sister, strange things are happening here. I need you. Why do you not come? Without you I am disorientated by the unhappy things I witness.

The night after we buried our Jeanette, in the dead of the night, a surreal and brutal thing occurred of which I can make no meaning. I was in a desperately lowered state after seeing our little sister's coffin consigned to oblivion in the ground. Since watching the earth thrown in on her I have been holding back such a flood of tears as I feel could drown me. I went to bed febrile and bereft. No sleep would come, and so I lay on my bed listening to the lonely cries of the vixen hunting in our father's woods. Suddenly, a shriek of a different kind cut through the darkness and turned my veins to ice.

From the window of my room, overlooking the rear courtyard, I could discern, for there was a good moon, the shape of a creature lying on the stones of the yard. There it lay, silent, after its initial shriek, its silence maintained despite a silent series of blows delivered to it by three manservants of the house. Just as my reaction came to shout down to the men and call them off, I perceived the unmistakeable silhouette of our father, who, stepping out from the shadows, motioned, after some more moments, for the punishment to stop. Waving the men aside, he allowed the creature to escape, dragging itself out of the courtyard and off in the direction of the woods. It was then that I realised this creature to be a woman.

My shock was severe. I know that these actions could not have happened other than at our father's request. He was there, taking full part in the beating, simply by allowing it to happen. Our father's men, when they are in his presence, never act other than by his direction and so I know the whole event to have been under his control. But why would our father behave in such a degraded way? We know him to be unbending, but this was violence. The solution must rest in the identity of the stricken woman. Could she be one of our army of maids, or is she connected with our father in some more intimate way? We know him to be overbearing and aloof, unindulgent to his daughters, but I cannot imagine him indulging himself in illegitimate female company. I have never seen him respond to feminine attention, not when our beautiful girl cousins set out to charm him for a favour, nor when we have a pretty maid. He has many passions in his life, all of which, for him, rate higher than women: money, social standing, acquisition of land and property.

What could have stirred up such passion as to cause him to mete out such punishment?

The strangest thing was the silence and secrecy of the whole act. Why would this be so? Of course, the men would be quiet in perpetrating such violence, but why the woman? Apart from her one involuntary shriek, she suffered in utmost silence. It seemed she was complicit in their brutalisation of her. How could this be? Surely her best defence would have been to cry out and bring help running?

Truly, my sister, I am disorientated. I know not who to trust or what to think. I dread to see our father in just a few hours at breakfast. I have had no sleep and I have no appetite. How will I behave in such a way as demonstrates I saw nothing of his dishonour last night? My room is directly above the courtyard. Can I pretend I heard and saw nothing? You see, even I enter the conspiracy of silence surrounding this poor woman's fate.

(Later) My dearest sister, I was right to dread a breakfast meeting with our father, but for an entirely unforeseen reason. I was late to join everyone. Despite greeting our father, he sat in silence with Mamma looking on anxiously. As is usual, the presence of the Chevalier Aurèle distracted me in a most thrilling way from the undercurrents within the room. I am thankful that the impoverishment of his noble family forces him to tutor for his living- not that any of our household be so brave as to term this warrior-like, young man *'tutor'*! The understanding is that he is here as the *'friend'* of Didier. The 'friend' conceit fails, however, as it is generally known that there is no creature on God's earth that would, without substantial reward, spend extended periods in company with our brother. The fact of the matter is that formal instruction, in many arts, is imparted by Aurèle to Didier, and this, according to a timetable and in return for pay. 'Tutor', therefore, is what Aurèle is, and I thank God our brother be so stupid as to fail his end of year exams and vivas every summer.

Aurèle, at this moment was speaking, responding to Didier and Beaulieu's request for information on form in an up-coming horse race. Through the disorientating, pulsing and refracting of light that occurs before my eyes whenever I allow my gaze to fall upon Aurèle, I realised that Mamma, also, was making an utterance.

Alongside Aurèle's cultured tones her voice resounded from the depths of rurality and I marvelled that years of elocution lessons have smoothed the vowels and consonants of our father and mother but have not smoothed their grammar. I find this an endearing trait in them, like the deep etched maker's mark of provenance on an honest piece of furniture. Even in the blazing light of smart company I feel no shame by proxy. Simply I feel fondness for their whimsical country habit of beginning a sentence with an exclamation, filling it with a muddle of adverbs and pronouns before ending it with a preposition, according to a bucolic code of language which operates as uniformly as the code of noble speech.

Do you remember, my sister, when the elocution tutor was late one day, and our father called with perfect enunciation to our mother, "Oy! … That there Voice-Man, where be he to?"

When I listened our mother's patois this morning, however, I was not so enchanted; she was concerned, as ever, to smooth our father's temper.

"Hurry child! Your father do have business with ye today and already his steward do wait."

After the events of last night, I was horribly surprised. Immediately my mind made many unpleasant guesses as to what his concern with me might be, added to which I recoiled from the idea that Aurèle might witness an encounter that could be embarrassing.

"Would you prefer that we discuss this in your study, Papa?"

Our father chose to ignore this suggestion.

"M. le Marquis de Merteuil do intend to wait upon ye one early day."

Aurèle's fork dropped to his plate. Later, when I reviewed the scene in my head, I realised that his mind had raced accurately to the correct conclusion. The fork of Beaulieu remained in suspense indicating that he would listen intently. Had he no idea that this was ill-bred? Surely, now, he should leave the room or affect to engage my mother in talk?

"Yes Papa?"

Unlike Aurèle, I was slow to imagine how a visit from our Jeanette's widower could concern me. Our father continued.

"Us do owe he some amend for the failure of his first marriage. The untimely death of yer sister and the ensuing death of his well-grown, first-born, boy-child have left he wanting. 'Tis by no means out of the ordinary for a younger sibling to make a match where th'older sibling have gone deceased. I suggest he do look no further than this family for his second choice of wife."

Aurèle abruptly scraped back his chair, faintly bowed his respects, and left the room. I caught his look of anger; his eyes blazed and the blood had risen to his face. At that moment, however, my attention was engaged by our father. I followed the treacherous line of his thoughts and yet I did not make him a response. Years of practice at controlling my facial expression means that I have lost all spontaneity of reaction. My determination to hide my feeling means that, even when I am in the grip of a powerful sentiment, I keep a neutral face until I have had some moments to think. My control has reached such a pitch that when I need to muster my own perturbation to my defence, it is not there to hand.

Do you recall, my dear sister, how our mother's and brother's immoderate agitations, instantaneously, violently and involuntarily produced, sometimes will overturn a decree of our father? As when our father's early wish to mix with a higher rank in society was thwarted by our mother's and brother's anxieties? Do you remember, in the early days, when our father had the chance to invite the intendant to dine with us, our mother's paroxysms of fear at the thought of entertaining such a man caused father to drop the project?

Do you remember when our father wished that Didier should become a member of the hunt but Didier's series of contiguous tantrums (instantaneously produced) at the thought of having to face his horse at a gate or ditch caused father to think better of it? Did not you note how shamefully lacking in dignity both mother and son appeared as they lost all self-restraint, and allowed their agitations free rein? I believe it is this pitiful example from them that has forwarded my inclination never to lose dignity. It is degrading publicly to indulge in an excess of passion or to allow another being unconditioned insight to one's thoughts.

Therefore, in this moment of crisis, I reached for reason rather than riot. I turned from our father to our mother for their attention. I made sure that the appeal on my face was unmistakable. Our mother did not dare meet my eye; she dithered when our father commanded her to dismiss the servants. He foresaw that a debate was in prospect and that his own mettle was to be tested against mine. Our mother, always dismayed when I oppose my father, prefigured his fury and grew anxious. Carefully, I entered the affray.

"Papa, we owe M. le Marquis absolutely nothing. It was not through any fault or failing of our family that our dear Jeanette died."

"I be not saying that your sister failed in her efforts nor in her sacrifice, which was just what them should have been. But the outcome, nonetheless, was that her efforts come to nothin'. The only duty what a woman of her station be expected to perform, be the one of furthering her husband's line. If this do not occur, even if her have gone dead in the attempt, then one do say that her have failed."

"But Sir! Cannot you see that it would be, truly, a terrifying prospect for me to follow and risk where Jeanette has gone before? This is understood even in law; to marry a woman to the husband of her own dead sister, in England, for example, is illegal."

This plea served as prompt for our mother.

"What ye be forgetting, Sophie," she cried, "is that us be not in England!"

She looked around at us all, so pleased with her perspicacity that another idea occurred to her.

"Also, ye forget that your chances, on marriage, would be greater than those of your sister. You be taller. Remember how easily Jeanette do be overcome by self-doubt? The idea of playing piano before a small assembly do terrify she!"

Mother paused. We all looked at her amazed at how she could conflate our sister's death with her piano playing. With all eyes upon her, her nerve failed, as always, causing her to babble.

"What I do mean be that, with…with regard to the pianoforte, although her technique were well established…"

Our mother had no idea how to conclude this nonsense; she faltered. I felt sorry for her and so I spoke.

"Yes Mamma, but do not you remember what the surgeon said? He told us that M. de Merteuil was calling for the infant to be cut from her! Before our Jeanette was dead! What sort of a man could do that? You cannot marry me to such a monster!"

The edge in my voice gave my brother his usual chance to ingratiate himself at my expense.

"Sister! Remember your place! It is our mother to whom you speak. Whatever makes you think it be right to talk so free?"

I looked at our father, aghast. Surely, he could not breeze over the actions of M. de Merteuil so easily as did our brother?

Our father spoke.

"Child. Ye must moderate your language. Ye cannot bandy such accusation so. Ye use words of serious import and ye speak ill of our neighbour, a nobleman! Always ye have been self-willed, and now ye take it too far! The child was taken from Jeanette but t'was taken not before time. If ye say otherwise ye do damn M. le Marquis before God. I cannot brook this sort of talk. It be deep and dangerous. There be no foundation to it. Just your wild imagining."

I was alarmed. I turned to our Mother.

"Mother! Please tell Father! I have not imagined this! The surgeon told us this was so!"

Mother looked anxious, but she turned her head away from me and remained silent. Our father raised his hand as an interdiction to me. Effectively I was quieted, but my mind raced. Why did our father not believe what the surgeon had said about Merteuil and Jeanette's last moments? I guessed that the surgeon, young as he was, had only felt brave enough to confess it to me and to our mother. Our mother was frightened that to affirm my account might appear to thwart our father's wishes. Our father did not want to believe my account because he did not want his wishes thwarted. He continued to keep his hand upraised.

"Listen! Us have heard and seen enough of your self-will over the years. These displays and this wild talk must cease! Ye must grow up and ye must take your place in the world. What us do consider be the suitabilities of the match, the reasons us sought alliance with M. le Marquis de Merteuil in the first place, be as relevant now as them was back then. He do have rank and connection to some of this country's first families. Also, us have settled much land and finance upon he to smooth the marriage to your sister. M. le Marquis de Merteuil will honour our first commitment to he and expect not nearly so much the second time around if us do make a match through ye. He be a man of the first consequence in this région, and, as our closest neighbour, t'would not do to slight he."

"But if we do nothing, we do not slight him!"

"Ye be mistaken, child! Even before the match was made with Jeanette, he have first spoke for ye. T'was only because ye was younger than Jeanette that us encouraged he to consider she. He have already staked his claim to ye now. If us do not honour it then us do slight he."

I allowed myself to evince alarm; how dare he speak of prior claim as if I were an eve of auction sale.

"He cannot option me! That is a vile proceeding! He has never known me! How could he choose me when he has never known me?"

Our brother once more took his opportunity to elevate himself at my expense.

"Whatever has that got to do with it? What woman of your station ever knew her husband before marriage? It is an impractical and even an impure idea! What makes you think you may continue to speak so slightingly of M. le Marquis de Merteuil? How is it that you persist in taking issue with our father?"

I hated my brother for his meddling in my future. My resentment flashed out at him.

"What makes you think you are the master of me?! You are weaker than I and my inferior in every way!"

This was so much the truth that Didier was left speechless and spluttering. Our father spoke for him.

"Your brother be heir to everything us do have; he be the one what will continue the family name, therefore, he do have right to speak in the marriage portions of ye and your sisters. By virtue of his sex alone he be your better."

I tried another line of argument.

"My father, is there not someone else, as suitable as M. le Marquis de Merteuil, to whom I could be married?"

Our father addressed the three of us.

"Think of the work what have been done towards this match. The lawyer, steward and clerk have been busied. Think of all my time, effort and patience. Sophie, ye cannot set all this at nought! Us do not brook that ye place your own desires first and th'efforts of the family last."

"We are not talking about my desires! I am not fool enough to nurture them. We are not talking about whether M. de So-and-So takes my fancy more than M. de Such-and-Such. We are talking solely of my revulsion. I accept I cannot make my own choice but surely I might be allowed the right to veto a marriage proposition on the grounds of mortal fear!"

My words, even to my ears, had a ring of righteousness about them and I think it was this that prompted our father to end the conversation as vehemently as he did.

"Child! Now ye is become stagey! Chance would be very cruel to take two of M. the Marquis de Merteuil's wives in child labour!"

"The fact that chance has taken one makes it mathematically more probable, Sir!"

"Enough! Do not fling your manly learning at me! Go to your room, re-read the treatises on the education of women. Make your voice soft, make your movements graceful, make yourself meek in the company of men and in particular to the company of M. le Marquis de Merteuil, for whenever he do choose to wait upon ye."

And that, my sister, is how the scene played out. Our family is very good at embarrassing itself in front of a third party- in this case, M. de Beaulieu.

I went alone to my room in a tumult of fear and loathing. Once there, among the flowers and the eau-de-nil, I paced and paced, giving full reign to my distress, imagining going the way that my sister had gone. Once a fear seeds in my mind it runs wild, terrorising me, winding me into its toils and shaking me to death by my throat…

32. THE CHEVALIER AURÈLE to M. DE BEAULIEU (sent from the LEFÈVRE ESTATE near AMIENS, 16th SEPTEMBER 1776)

Sir, I do not know you and I have no wish to acquaint myself with you. I would, however, like to suggest a moderation to your behaviour: when a young woman is drawn into discussion with her family about her marriage prospects, it would be polite to leave the room.

33. M. DE BEAULIEU to the CHEVALIER AURÈLE (hand delivered within the LEFÈVRE ESTATE near AMIENS, 16TH SEPTEMBER 1776)

I remember you full well from the Sorbonne. You always were a self-righteous ass. I see the intervening time has not dented your pomposity. Had I left the room when you did, we would have made ourselves conspicuous. M. Lefèvre chose to raise the subject of Sophie's future in our presence; I can only imagine he did this deliberately. I have noticed that if a person anticipates resistance to their proposal from another person, often they will make that proposal before others. They do this to prevent opposition from the other individual via the collective pressure for politeness.

In the event, the debate did not remain calm. Lefèvre is determined to marry Sophie to the massive Merteuil. Sophie is in mortal fear of this as she feels she will die birthing his child, as did her sister.

By remaining in the room, I find I share Sophie's fear for her safety in this matter. Therefore, I did a good thing by biding, as I now will exert my influence within the family, on her behalf, against this marriage project.

Had I swept out of the room in a dramaturgy of sanctimony, as did you, I would not be wise as to how to help this matchless young woman.

34. SOPHIE LEFÈVRE to HÉLÈNE, THE CHEVALIÈRE D'IVRY (sent from the LEFÈVRE ESTATE near AMIENS, 17th SEPTEMBER 1776)

Since the conversation about M. de Merteuil, a day has passed. I have not been locked into my room; I am there by a mutuality of arrangement. The family and I have a perfect understanding: I have no desire to see them and they have no desire to see me. My food is carried up to me by my chamber-maid and various laundry and cleaning maids come. To them I present a perfectly sanguine face, but I am in turmoil. All I can do is wait for the inevitable, for my spirit to revolt against the bondage of my fear.

35. THE CHEVALIER AURÈLE to ISABELLE AURÈLE (sent from the LEFÈVRE ESTATE near AMIENS, 17th SEPTEMBER 1776)

I am incensed! M. Lefèvre values daughters only as pawns in a game to better himself. He does not care if his daughters die as a result of his game. He views their death simply as a loss worth risking and so he is happy to marry them off to monsters – wealthy, ennobled monsters.

Yesterday I discovered that he is determined to marry my love, Mademoiselle Sophie, to the bull-elephant that is M. le Marquis de Merteuil. This Merteuil has already occasioned the death of Sophie's sister as she died in his 'care'. Mademoiselle Sophie now lives in mortal fear of her own marriage to Merteuil.

You will be unsurprised to hear that I will save her from this fate.

36. SOPHIE LEFÈVRE to HÉLÈNE, the CHEVALIÈRE D'IVRY (sent from the LEFÈVRE ESTATE near AMIENS, 19th SEPTEMBER 1776)

It has taken two days for my heart to rise up. My dread must have been attended by a sense of hopelessness for me to have been subdued for so long. This is how it happened: for the thousandth time, I imagined the sacrifice of my body to a beast like Merteuil when suddenly, I felt my spirit rise in a white-hot rage against my father and brother. The anger built in me, I felt utterly confident in the power of it. I left my room. I would face down my father. I would tell him that nothing would induce me to consider M. de Merteuil. As a concession, (yes, you see, my sister, I am grown enough to consider concessions) I would offer faithfully to consider any other person he would put before me.

I arrived at his study door, full of confidence, and raised my hand to knock. But at this moment, I allowed my fist to fall back, for from behind the door I heard a voice speak my name. I pressed myself closer into the dark alcove of the deep architrave and quieted my breath. I was being discussed by my father and brother. My father's voice sounded thick and unfamiliar through the wood.

"Sophie will have to have he. Once news of this disgraceful business be abroad her value will surely drop."

Our brother replied anxiously.

"But she would not be unmarriageable?!"

"No. Not unmarriageable, of course, for someone would have she but her could not hope to make a useful connection. Her cannot avoid guilt by association."

"But only a week ago she was capable of bagging us the glittering wealth of the Comtes de Guyenne; now we prostrate ourselves for an impoverished Marquis."

"A Marquis be hardly a come-down! In rank and status 'tis a step-up! Even a lesser monied Marquis be a great catch. And he have long spoke an interest."

Here, our brother broke in.

"As well he might! She has many charms."

The impropriety of his tone struck me, but our father continued, oblivious to it.

"Besides which, M. le Marquis de Merteuil, on any terms, be a good match; his hangers-on are pre-eminent in this région. Even in the short time he were married to your sister, much was coming to we by virtue of this alliance. I counted many, many more dues observed to me and many more avenues opened up. His connections already was paying us dividends."

"But surely he does not need more dowry to sugar the deal? He keeps all of the dowry of Jeanette and Sophie is the sugariest deal I ever did see!"

"Sirrah! Do not you see us must forward this move? This be the only way to keep an interest in what us have already dowered! Do not consider it as land lost; your ensuing nephews one day will have it entirely in they control."

For once in his life, my father dropped his parade of self-consequence. He continued bitterly.

"Her be still the daughter of a man what have made his money in trade, sprung up from the nearest dunghill within the living memory of just one generation. If t'weren't for her portion him would not even consider she."

"But we give so much! All he brings is his title!"

"His title do count for much and in view of the haste with which us must make he move I begin to consider, in addition, her grandfather's little estate."

"But we agreed we would not tell her of that estate!"

"Of course we won't tell her of that estate! The property could go straight from the management of we, to the management of he. Her never did know of it and her do not need to know of it now."

Our brother groaned. Every increment to Merteuil, ultimately, would be his loss.

"All this?"

Our father lost patience.

"Indeed Sir! All this and more if necessary! Us will soon need every friend us can muster. Her older sister's disgrace do stain all the family. A young woman brought up and nurtured in such a way as will cuckold her superior husband and make his noble family a laughing-stock be a liability to all of we. Although no article of this yet have appeared in the journals, it must now be supposed to be gossiped about town. Us be lucky 'tis the off-season. No-one of no consequence be there to hear them reports. But before too long them gossipings will spread to our région and to M. le Marquis de Merteuil and then he will think twice. Besides, them men what dealt with Hélène th'other night knows exactly what must have merited that sort of punishment. Them men do know that a high-born daughter is beaten only after a grave offence. I gives it less than a fortnight before the news be abroad. A fortnight be all us have. Make no mistake."

So you see my sister, I now am writing to you through habit alone, knowing, even as I do, that I have nowhere to direct this letter. It was you on the flagstones with those men around you that night. It was your precious person that received those blows. It was your self-command that held back the cries which might have alerted me or our mother. Oh, my darling Hélène! Really it is too much to bear! I cannot imagine how much you must be suffering! How could he treat you so carelessly now that there is one less of his children in the world? Many other families show humanity to a fallen daughter. Many other families will distinguish between vice and folly in their off-spring. This father of ours can have no ability to feel. Now I know how he has used you, all hope I had for myself has gone.

(Later) My darling sister, sick as I am with fear for you, strangely, now, I feel relieved. All these past weeks of not knowing why you did not write are at an end. It is supposition, worry and powerlessness that weary the soul. Now I know you are in trouble I will do something to help you. I must piece together the likelihoods of your circumstance. I know, for example, that you have left your husband. I know you are alone and friendless. I know you were injured last night…You cannot be far away. As soon as I am able, I will take what money I have and I will find you. You are probably still on our land. I will travel to all our childhood hideouts…

(Later) My sister, through habit I have opened this letter to continue to you. You cannot have received any of my previous letters. You will receive this when I find you. My letters will serve as a record of the efforts I make to rescue you.

(Later) Why did our father and brother speak of our grandfather's estate in relation to me? I know Grandpère left money to you and to Jeanette; do you think he can have left me his land?

37. SOPHIE LEFÈVRE to HÉLÈNE, the CHEVALIÈRE D'IVRY (sent from the LEFÈVRE ESTATE near AMIENS, 20th SEPTEMBER 1776)

It was only after I put down my pen from writing to you yesterday, that I realised it was already well past the hour for my brother's tutorial with the Chevalier Aurèle. You will not believe it possible when I tell you that the Chevalier is more magnificent than when last you saw him. His manly beauty attains unforeseen heights and sets aside all feminine presence of mind. I never fail to appreciate that this uncommonly fine person must stoop for a living among his gross inferiors (us). Truly my sister, now he is in the full flush of prime masculinity, it is strange to see him amidst our family. It is as if a great, glittering, powerful, avenging angel, with sword in hand, wings outspread and shafts of light glancing from his eyes has lost his way among dark, lower life-forms. To see him swoop down from lofty heights to serve our bootless brother is a travesty of status.

I rushed to the Long Gallery, wherein Aurèle was directing our brother's fitful attentions to the verses of Homer on love and loss. I was late. I crept quietly into the room and slipped silently into place beside that low character to whom we are related. I took up my task as our wastrel brother's page-turner and pamphlet keeper. So keen have I been, for so many years, not to be sacked from my sisterly post as secretary to our feckless sibling that, even now, I make myself inconspicuous. My brother furtively turned his attention to me, pleased to have an excuse to break from the text. He hissed at me, sliding his words under the manly tones of Aurèle.

"How now, sister! Late!"

He forgets that I am here by my generosity and that by my efforts he gains much. I disdained to apologise and, in any case, Aurèle continued to read the words of the great poet. Even without the poetry of the text, his cultured tones were thrilling to me. Every now and then, at the turn of a page, where Aurèle might pause for a thought, or to explicate the meaning, I would look up at him. This accomplished, serious man is riveting. As ever, the light adores him, and ignores everyone else in its haste to illuminate him alone; it lights the blond in his hair, the golden line of his jaw and brow and the blue in his eyes. As he spoke, despite his pauses for clarification, I could hear that he was moved by the text, feeling the import of the poet so deeply that his voice betrayed him. Over the months I have noticed this quality in him; I have never seen him hide any emotion that a text may give rise in him. In the early days, I could hardly believe it possible that a man should be so transparent. When his voice breaks with the passion of the words, our brother invariably looks up at him to sneer and yet Aurèle continues, completely unashamed of the honesty of it.

So, my dear sister, there we three were, as we have been on many an occasion, with me feigning to be engrossed in the words on the page while, in reality, hanging onto the voice of Aurèle dropping out of the air and into my ear. Once I hear the passion rise in his tones, so I feel the passion rise in me. Today, his voicing of the lamentations of *The Illiad* fired straight to my heart, newly made weak by the raw feelings raked over by the burial of our sister.

*"And overpowered by memory. Both men gave way to grief.
Priam wept freely for man - killing Hector…Achilles wept himself,
now for his father, now for Patroclus once again. And their sobbing
rose and fell…"*

Aurèle continued. I allowed his words to wash over me, catching the rise and fall in his voice. I did not dare to look up at him, I did not trust myself to hide the tumult of feeling in me; I was becoming aware that the piece had been chosen by him, for me. The beauty and the truth of this man and the exhaustion and the tragedy I laboured under, from the preceding days and nights, were conspiring to break my defences. It seemed he knew that I wished I could lie down in oblivion with my sister and quietly disappear into the earth with her. He spoke aloud the text.

"…I tell you, Death and the strong force of fate are waiting.
There will come a dawn or sunset or high noon
When a man will take my life…"

I felt, from the dam of grief held up inside me, a single tear escape from under my lashes. I did not dare to brush it away. I was afraid that any movement, no matter how slight, might alert my brother to the torsion of the moment, and I wanted no earthly thing to break the spell. The effect of Aurèle's pure voice, articulating those words, mingled with the sound of the blood rushing in my ears made me wonder if I was going to faint.

After some moments, I realised that Aurèle had fallen silent, his last word hanging in the air, the détente seeming to fill the room until the walls were ringing with silence. An ineffable peace descended and all I could hear now was his breathing and mine.

Eventually, Aurèle continued, and these were the words he spoke:

"…The Gods envy us. They envy us because we are mortal, because any moment might be our last. Everything is more beautiful because we are doomed…"

I knew, in that moment, that he was reaching out to me across gulfs of sorrow.

"You will never be lovelier than you are now. We will never be here again…"

I felt as if an angel had been sent from heaven to bring me peace. I felt him lean forward across the desk, place his hand to my cheek, his thumb to my lashes and brush my tear away. I raised my eyes to meet his and never have I felt such a moment of such perfect unity. This feeling continued for I do not know how long, and my breathing was made quiet by the unearthly quality of his touch.

Our brother, finally waking up to the situation, stopped obsessively cleaning the dirt from under his fingernails with his penknife and slowly raised his head, looking sideways from one to the other of us, who were still fixed in the moment. We were oblivious to him until, knife in fist, he knocked Aurèle's hand away from my face.

"Get off her!" Didier spat.

Aurèle appeared hardly to notice, his eyes still on mine. He closed the book of *The Illiad* and turning absently to our brother, as if still in another world, he asked if he would like to be excused from the fencing lesson that would normally have ensued. Didier started spitting with contempt.

"Excused from fencing? Excused? Why excused? Why rid of me? So that you may continue paying your unwonted attentions to my sister?!"

Aurèle ignored this last remark. Didier continued.

"I have no wish to be excused from anything by the likes of you. Get on with it."

The tables were cleared back, and the two young men strapped themselves into their protective clothing, Didier angrily, Aurèle matter-of-factly. As ever I was struck to see the disparity in these two exemplars of masculinity. The younger male, a little cockerel of a thing, strutting about on skinny, chicken legs with thin, mouse hair in part hidden under a horse-hair wig; the other male, symmetrical, sober creation of strength, height and proportion. I am sure, dear sister, that because I am threatened with impending marriage to a death-dealer, any man other than Merteuil would appear to have some appeal but today, Aurèle, who we have always considered a joy to behold, was especially magnified by an effervescence of golden looks. The light, as we know, always seeks him out and the bright, low, thundery beams of the afternoon reflected off him as though he had been cast by angels in white gold.

This event I have enjoyed to watch on many an occasion: Aurèle running through the usual exercises, calling the thrusts and the parries to our brother and neatly blocking each of his returns. But today it appeared that our brother had the devil in him. It seemed that, fuelled by righteous anger arising from the intimacy he had witnessed, he believed he could now finally best his master by the sheer force of his temper. As Didier hacked and slashed, I could see he was working himself up into a passion. Before too long he was thrusting in earnest, trying to catch Aurèle off-guard with a confidence that seemed to show he felt he could succeed and win.

Rarely has a man been so deluded. It was embarrassing to watch. As Didier lunged more and more wildly, simply and effortlessly Aurèle would parry. What was staring Didier in the face just never seemed to register in his mind: that a man with only passion to fuel his actions will never be able to overcome years of dedicated training completed by a man already gifted in the sport by nature. Didier had no conception of just how very many years he was away from being any use as a swordsman at all. Strangely, the more futile his efforts became, the more violently he thrust. It was as if he felt so sure that he could depend upon Aurèle not to hurt him that he dishonestly drew upon the unfair advantage to do everything in his power to inflict hurt. This, as you know, is true of our brother, as any unfair edge he will exploit. Any frustration from one part of his life will cause him to exact revenge on an inferior in some other part of his life, be it you or me or any one of his servants, horses or dogs. Today his target was Aurèle, doubtless knowing that even a serious wound would go unreported by that young man. Meanwhile, the more Didier flailed around like some silly cockbird, the more Aurèle became moved to laughter in surprise at his puny efforts.

"Didier, have a care! Your temper puts you out of your defence!"

Didier carried on; the more Aurèle laughed off his efforts, the more angry he became. Aurèle remained perfectly relaxed, needing to expend very little effort to repel all of Didier's strength. Finally, Aurèle decided that Didier was becoming dangerously fatigued.

"Enough! Let us stop this now before one of us is hurt!"

My sister, as only Didier was in danger of being caught by a blade, was this not generous and complimentary? Didier's response was vicious; he screamed at Aurèle.

"And you can go to the devil for laying your disgusting hand on my sister!"

With this last, he lunged straight for Aurèle's heart.

This invective, coupled with this action caused a flash-point in Aurèle's even temper. In an instant, the blood of this young divinity was up and what followed was awe-inspiring to behold. I felt like I was become witness to an event of biblical proportion: an avenging seraph of heaven flying down upon a puny sinner. In a fluid blaze of fire and speed, Aurèle switched from thrusts that were designed to block, to thrusts that were designed to intimidate, crashing his blade repeatedly onto the middle of Didier's blade with such a force that I was sure it must shatter. In an instant, Didier turned from cock-a-hoop to cowering, having to use his sword as a shield rather than as a weapon. Aurèle, rather than aim his thrusts at Didier's person, continued to smash his blows down onto his blade until it was no longer possible for Didier to hold the weapon. In extreme pain Didier released his grip on it; it fell to the floor where Aurèle kicked it away. Didier, then, still knowing that no thrust would be aimed near his person, hurled himself at Aurèle in an attempt to knock him off balance. Throwing away his weapon, Aurèle contained, bodily, his lunatic opponent with fierce moves of overwhelming strength, still while inflicting no serious hurt. Aurèle's temper was on fire now and it was the work of a moment to have his inconsequential opponent bent backward with Aurèle's knee rammed into the middle of his backbone and both of Didier's arms pinned behind him. Immediately Didier capitulated, fearing that his back would be broken.

"For the love of God let me go! I was only in jest!"

Wordlessly, Aurèle pushed him face down to the floor and then caught hold of him by the wrists, with his arms bent the wrong way behind his back and up over his head. In this way he dragged Didier across the expanse of the gallery, pausing only to throw him out of the door at the end of it. After the door was slammed shut,

Didier, to salvage some pride, hurled himself back at it, from what he knew to be the safety of the wrong side, venting his anger by kicking, shouldering and crashing it, as if he had a real determination to get at Aurèle again. With very little effort, Aurèle kept the door shut by leaning his shoulder against it. Eventually the crashing stopped, and the sound could be heard of Didier storming away. I ran across the room to Aurèle. I had to make amends for our brother.

"Oh! I am so sorry…I'm sorry he behaves so badly!"

Aurèle was blazing with fury.

"Good God, Mademoiselle, you are surrounded by villains! Wretches! Despicable, dishonest, devious people. It was all I could do not to damn myself for eternity by slaughtering the little runt! I can hardly bring myself to look at him. It embarrasses me to meet his shameful eye and not do the honourable thing and kill him and all the men related to him. Never, never have I met with such deceit and such cowardice. It is imperative that you get away from him and all his like. Mademoiselle, you must escape, or they will destroy you! They will drag you down to their level and lower. There are no depths to which they will not descend. You must do whatever it takes. I will help you. Come away with me. Be with me. Just say the word and I will get you away from this place."

I paused; despite his blinding proximity and his transcending beauty, my thoughts were too practised to be overrun. I raced to the practicalities of the situation. I temporised.

"Yes, but really, what can we do? We two, who have no money, no means and no prospect of any."

"You will live on my army pay. Soon I enlist. You will have all of it. Every sou. And you will have me at your command also. Truly Mademoiselle, I will do anything for you. Entirely I am yours. Leave with me now, I entreat you."

As he pleaded this last, he took my hand and I was surprised to discover how alluring it was to hear this man implore me. My pulse responded instantly to his bid for me to take all his flesh, muscle and sinew, at my command. I looked full into his flushed face. I could almost smell the blood beneath the surface of his skin from the heat radiating off him.

"Please. Mademoiselle. It is the only way. It is the most right and perfect way. I must be with you. You must be with me. That way you will be safe, loved and perfectly adored."

His passion and his intent sent a thrill straight through me, direct to my heart. This was the finest exemplar of masculinity I could imagine, offering himself to me and everything in his gift. But still, yet still, my trained and trammelled mind would not respond. The practicalities remained.

"Forgive me but this is hardly possible. I cannot have you for my own; the army would have you. Army pay is pitiful; you would barely be able to meet the cost of your horse, your servant and your provision. There would be nothing left after you have paid for this. Nothing to keep a woman on. I know this to be true and really, can you see me living on nothing? In any case, what would I do with myself? I would not be by your side where I would adore to be, horsed and on campaign with you. The best I could become is a camp follower, hitching unsteady rides on carts and mules, shifting for myself with the other poor straggling women, blacksmiths and cooks, hiring leaking back rooms and garrets to sleep in along the way, helping women with their pregnancies and illnesses, or, God forbid, struggling with my own. Would you wish that upon me, spoiled as I am, used to warmth and soft luxury? Can you see this of me?"

Aurèle was crushed. He dropped my hand.

"If you cannot see it, then it cannot be. But surely then, we must leave together, forget all prospect of the army and make our way in the world. We will leave tonight, take horses and go. I have loved you utterly and faithfully for three years now. I have been so aware of you in all our lessons and in all our mealtimes together. A thousand times have I had to stop my hand from reaching out to take yours and snatch you away. It was my action running ahead of my thought in this way that led me to touch you today. But even then, I managed heroic restraint. My impulse was to lean across and kiss your tear away, but if I had done that, I could not ever have stopped. I would have kissed and kissed you and not have ceased even had your brother and father sent up an army of men to slaughter me."

My sister, how was I to withstand such passion and such beauty? I was deeply affected. He had fired a bolt straight to my heart; the impact of it caused me to take a step back. Luckily, or unluckily for me, he misconstrued this action, and, in his misinterpretation, he broke the power of his own spell.

"You are not going to do it, are you? You will not come with me!"

Even to my ears, my next utterance sounded weak.

"We have no money…We would not endure. My father would hire riders to follow. He would pay for intelligence, create a network, he would alert the marshalcy. We would be tracked down almost immediately."

"No! This is not how it will be! We will escape abroad. We will be fast, we two. No-one will catch us. Be brave. Be strong. Come with me!"

An appeal to my bravery has never before failed but this time it did. I was surprised to note that my sense of practicality could outface even my enormous pride.

"They will find us when the money runs out. They will starve us into submission."

There followed a long silence.

"Mademoiselle. Is that your final say?"

My next utterance broke my heart. And in all likelihood his.

"It is."

This man leaned forward and kissed me where, once again, one of my tears was falling; then he walked away. I ran in the other direction, towards my chamber, my thoughts racing ahead of me. Was he right? Was I a coward? No matter which way I turned my mind on this, my logic kept coming up with the same thing: The Poor. I am not about to join them. I am not about to beg for alms. I have noticed that there is no non-arbitrary mechanism in existence to limit the depths to which poverty can take one.

However, my resolve wavers as I remember how Aurèle looked, how he spoke, and how he felt when he touched me. A thrill of desire again floods through me. What devilish impulse is at work here? Is this some kind of diabolical joke? How is it possible to be offered so much beauty and so much impoverishment in one impossible stroke?

In my chamber, I muse. I have been among the poor many times as it is fashionable to give alms and to help the sick and the needy. I have shivered at the terror and violences of fate which privation exposes these unfortunates. I am brave but I am not foolhardy…I have seen what it is to live on scraps of food, scraps of clothing and scraps of fuel. And I have descried that the people living as such are not at all benumbed to their lot, not in any way mercifully dulled to the horror of their situation by a lowered sensibility or a lowered intelligence. In nearly all cases of impoverished humanity I have discerned fineness of feeling and delicacy of mind. Easily can I translate that impoverished being to myself or any wealthy person I know.

I have never been so foolish as to forget the stories of the twists of fate and luck that allowed our father to crawl out from under the stone of his destitution. Our mother, a member of the yeoman class, has always told us these stories- stories he himself would never have told. How his grandparents slipped from lowly status into abject poverty during the failed harvests and freezing winters at the time of La Grande Famine, when they could not afford to pay the ruinous taxes or the tithes. How the bailiffs came for their smithy and their tools, leaving them unable to claw their way back to a level of subsistence through work. How his grandfather, when a young man, found his young wife dead of starvation beside the road with grass in her mouth and the babe (our father) suckling at her empty breast.

I have never forgot our rich neighbours who lost everything to drink and gaming, slipping downwards to land among the destitute. I visited them just once, former friends, more than equals, and I noted that they did not wish me to come among them to witness what they saw as their shame. Once I had arrived, I realised my mistake, but it was impossible immediately to leave without conferring an insult. I was barely able to disguise my horror as they struggled to provide me with a dish of tea. First the fire had to be lit, in winter, from frozen, poorly saved, wet faggots of wood. Then someone had to go to the well to draw the freezing water. Then the endless waiting over the feeble, smoking, choking flame. Eventually came the drink, lukewarm, watery and weak from overused leaves, with mote-laden milk served with some small loaf. Then leaving, knowing I had occasioned them to consume, out of their pride and honour, in one sitting, the family's share for a day. Finally, the realisation that it would be more mortifying for them and for me to endure another such visit than for me to forsake them altogether.

The Poor, as I said, I will not be joining them.

What Aurèle could not possibly have known was that, for now, I have a sure way of withstanding his charms. I have created, in my imagination, a deferred haven for me and him and all his manly beauty. I have planned an alternative strategy that holds me secure against the immediate future of uncertainty and danger that currently he offers. You, my sister, are that alternative. You have been married extremely well; you are a model of prudence. You cannot have risked leaving M. le Chevalier d'Ivry without money. My plan is that I find you tonight and that we fly to the protection of your Godmother, thence we find somewhere to make our home, even if it be abroad. We will maintain a little establishment, a modest household which, with the right economies, will enable us to live comfortably. It is not unheard of that unmarried, genteel women do this. You and I achieve, by this plan, our independence from men: liberty, equality, sorority.

With this idea in my mind, I pack my things, and now I wait for the household to fall silent and asleep.

38. THE CHEVALIER AURÈLE to ISABELLE AURÈLE (sent from the LEFÈVRE ESTATE near AMIENS, 20th SEPTEMBER 1776)

My dearest sister, my beloved parents, today I offered my love to Mademoiselle Sophie. The moment for declaring myself at last had arrived.

I proposed immediate flight and marriage to her - but I did this in such an ill-managed way! I did this *after* I had caused her to become distressed, *after* I had acted in a manner that was overly familiar with her, *after* I had drawn down the wrath of her brother upon her, and *after* I had come within a hair's-breadth of killing him in front of her.

I even quoted Homer at her.

'You will never be lovelier than you are now.'

Am I a madman? She will always be lovely! That phrase could be interpreted as petty-mindedness: *you had better accept me now before you lose your looks!*

Even my simple mind has been agonisingly alive to the idea that this is not the way to win heart, soul and mind of a young woman.

My God, my sister! I live among fools but without doubt I am the greatest fool of all.

Each time I recall my idiocy, a fiery sweat of consternation overspreads me. Barely can I bring myself to recount to you my sorry tale. By it you will see how it was that, in one short interview, I brought pain to Mademoiselle Sophie and therefore to myself.

Sophie was not present at the outset of my tutorial with her brother. As she has only ever been punctual, I assumed she would not be coming. Therefore, I set a plan of reading which I hoped would educate the brutish Didier into some sensibility. With one of his sisters dead and another missing, I determined to draw Didier to a sense of love and loss. I deliberated whether to choose the phrase from the letter of Cicero to Brutus upon the suicide of his adored Portia:

'you have met with a sorrow—for you have lost a thing unparalleled in the world—and you must needs suffer from so severe a wound'.

Since my aim was to stir Didier into sensibility, the rest of the letter did not suit my purpose– urging, as it does, fortitude in the face of woe. He would preen himself for fortitude when in fact he couldn't care less.

I have previously obliged Didier to study *The Illiad* but we had not read from it recently. Speedily, I marked some pages, glad that Mademoiselle Sophie was not present, as I chose the ones that were the most evocative of grief.

First, I read out to him the lamentations of Andromache, Hecuba and Helen on the death of Hector. I felt the feeling rise in me but glancing across at my obtuse pupil, I realised that feminine sentiment would not move him. I leafed to the verses on the supplication of Achilles by pitiful old Priam. The verses are lengthy and I hoped that the pain of Priam and Achilles would move Didier as they move me: Priam, pleading for the body of his son, Achilles realising that he is fated to die at Troy far from his father. Once I had selected where I would begin, I determined not to look at Didier. I wanted the many lines of verse to carry me deeply into the scape of the text. I read for some while until I reached the most evocative moment:

"And overpowered by memory. Both men gave way to grief. Priam wept freely for man - killing Hector...Achilles wept himself, now for his father, now for Patroclus once again. And their sobbing rose and fell..."

Didier interrupted me. By his utterance, I discovered that this representation of masculine pain had the power to provoke him to a sympathy solely for himself. His mind clearly had revolved to remind him that one day he would share the fate of his own dead sister.

"By God!" he exclaimed, "that grave yesterday! How dismal a pit! I cannot bear that one day I will be in there myself!"

I was ashamed to look into his cowardly countenance. In anger, I leafed to Achilles' rebuke to the unheroic Lycaon.

"Come, Friend, you too must die. Why moan about it so?"

Even Patroclus died, a far, far better man than you."

I glanced over the next few lines of the verse. I made a conscious decision to continue.

"And look, you see how handsome and powerful I am?

The son of a great man, the mother who gave me life--

A deathless goddess. But even for me, I tell you,
Death and the strong force of fate are waiting.
There will come a dawn or sunset or high noon
When a man will take my life in battle too--..."

I looked up and realised that Mademoiselle Sophie was now seated across the table before me. She must have entered the room sometime earlier and quietly placed herself next to her brother. Immediately I felt a flush of consternation. How long had she been there? Had she just entered, or had she heard the verses of lamentation? I was distressed that I had presented her with the subject of death at such a time. I faltered. A silence fell as I allowed the book to fall open and present me with another passage. My befuddled mind reasoned that any other passage, unrelated to the one I had been reading, would provide a suitable diversion. In this assumption I was wrong. The book opened in my hand. I started to read and was committed to the words before I realised that fate had dealt me a verse of even greater pathos and passion.

"The Gods envy us. They envy us because we're mortal, because any moment might be our last. Everything is more beautiful because we're doomed..."

As I spoke the next line, I could not help but lift my gaze to her beautiful face.

"You will never be lovelier than you are now..."

I did not need to look at the book for the next line:

"...We will never be here again."

Unconsciously, I closed the book, my eyes still helplessly drawn to hers. I could not tear them away. She returned my gaze. Her look transfixed me. Her breathing was deep and quiet, as was mine. It caused me great perturbation to realise that my readings had caused a tear to fall onto her flawless cheek. I upbraided myself for being the cause of her distress. My wish was that I smooth away her pain. My body instantly followed this wish and without knowing what I did, I reached out and smoothed away her tear. At that moment, the contact of my hand on her pure skin did not feel like impropriety. It felt as if it had been divinely ordained. I felt the urge to kiss her, kiss her again and continue kissing her for all our remaining years.

That single improper action, of my hand to her face, however, drew the notice and wrath of her brother. He reacted violently, jealously and suspiciously.

To my everlasting chagrin, I feel now she will be plagued by him. The only thing left for me to do is to berate myself. My mind plays a joke on me and holds, before my eyes, more Homeric phrases.

> *"There is nothing alive more agonized than man*
> *of all that breathe and crawl across the earth."*

I feel that I too could weep like the horses of Achilles.

Unsurprisingly, the fencing practice which then ensued turned nasty. It was easy to repel the full strength of the little runt that is Didier. I was even able to swap my sword arm, unbutton my waistcoat and remove it while repelling all his mustered force and anger. Finally, just a few paces away from Mademoiselle Sophie, and, despite my best efforts at containment, my temper caught fire. I overwhelmed my feeble opponent. I forced him to bend backwards with my knee rammed into the middle of his back. Despite her eyes being upon me, I recall flexing his spine against my knee and musing to myself, "I could snap this insubstantial thing in two".

All my thoughts must have been abundantly apparent to his sister. Straight after this I threw Didier out of the door and immediately proposed everlasting union to Sophie.

Not surprisingly, she refused.

39. M. DE BEAULIEU to the VICOMTE DE VALMONT (sent from the LEFÈVRE ESTATE near AMIENS, 20th SEPTEMBER 1776)

Last night Lefèvre-Fool-the-Younger and I were drinking in his study. He had bruises all over his body and one of his arms seemed to be out of joint. He told me a cock-and-bull story about how, that day, he had bested Aurèle in a sword-fight! Does the little cockerel think I'm a fool? Have we ever seen anyone triumph over Aurèle in a fight?

By the way, the young fool has confirmed that their plan is to send your beauty in the direction of the massive Merteuil.

Methinks your interference may have lost you the very thing you sought to gain.

40. THE VICOMTE DE VALMONT to M. DE BEAULIEU (sent frm the CHÂTEAU DE ****, 22ⁿᵈ SEPTEMBER 1776)

What do you mean '*by the way*'? The news you impart is central to my interests, not marginal to them! You say the news is '*confirmed*' but when did first you hear it? How is it that you are the world's worst spy? Have you no conception of how serious this is?

Are the Lefèvre men so wasteful of their women that they send one more unto death-by-marriage to that oversized young bullock? I can only assume that my disgracing of the oldest daughter forces their hand. Dieu!

41. SOPHIE LEFÈVRE to HÉLÈNE, the CHEVALIÈRE D'IVRY (sent from the LEFÈVRE ESTATE near AMIENS, 22ⁿᵈ SEPTEMBER 1776)

I set out to find you last night, my sister. As I approached the stables, I noticed they were lit from inside. The sight arrested me. Desperate as I was to get to my horse and away, I had to consider who was likely to be within. There was a good moon and so there was a tiny chance it could be my brother come back from a night jaunt. I had heard him discussing his plans for an early morning, however, so I was sure he was asleep in bed. I decided that the light must belong to a junior groom, as any night watch job falls to the lowest rank. I felt confident I could pay a youngster to keep his mouth shut and not stand in my way.

I marched through the archway and straight into the gaze of Aurèle.

"Good God! Mademoiselle!" he exclaimed.

It always surprises me that people exhibit surprise. Do they not have a mechanism whereby they cover shock with composure? I had no difficulty in disguising my amazement on seeing him; inwardly, though, my heart gave a lurch- for a reason other than surprise.

"I need a horse made ready," I said, failing to produce any form of politeness.

"…Very well," he said measuredly, quite obviously puzzling over the strangeness of my circumstance, "which horse?"

"I'll take my riding horse."

"Side-saddle or astride?"

His questioning of saddlery was interesting to me; I wondered if it were a reference to my rebellious, young riding style. I checked his expression for humour; he looked perfectly serious.

"Side-saddle," I said, pulling on my gloves.

I was annoyed with myself for framing my requests without the common courtesies. I had commanded him in a tone reserved for servants. I felt sure that this ill-manneredness betrayed my failing confidence, just as it betrays our father when he is out of his depth socially, or our brother when he is over-anxious in public.

Do you remember, my sister, when father was invited to a gathering with M. le Chevalier d'Ivry, sometime before your marriage to him? He was not confident about how to manage his order of greeting people or his order of drinking and eating. Do you recall, to puff himself up, how rude he was to the servants of the Chevalier? How they then banded together to expose him to ridicule by refusing to serve him, so that he stood in the company with no drink and he sat to dine at the table with no food. When he complained, the servants made angry representations to the Chevalier who could only smooth the path of our father by suggesting he tip the servants in advance, and handsomely!

And do you remember how shockingly oafish Didier became when he found himself in the company of that pretty, wool heiress at our neighbours' ball? How he started swearing, and posturing to all around him in his desperation to make an impression on her? Was it not cringingly funny when his anxiety to attract her attention was overlaid by his anxiety not to appear too ingratiating and so resulted in him pointing out to her that the pomade on her hair smelled of hog fat?!

Well, here was I doing the same thing, betraying my anxieties by my rudeness. Quickly I reordered my thinking. As Aurèle tacked up my horse, therefore, I courteously requested of him that he prepare my brother's riding horse as well. More surprise. Truly, this man is transparent.

"With your brother's saddle?" he asked, without looking around at me.

"With a side-saddle please," I said.

This time he quibbled.

"That animal is not broken to side-saddle."

"Then, I must ask of you Sir, that you prepare another horse here that is."

"I'm afraid that is not possible Mademoiselle, there is not one."

He sounded genuinely sorry.

"Do get my brother's horse ready for astride then," I said, "and please affix these saddle-bags to his tack."

"Will not your brother miss his animal?"

"Why ever would we consider my brother?"

Aurèle smiled. This was the moment when he put all scruple aside and fell in with my plan.

"Yes why? It would be an act of great lunacy. May I accompany you on your journey, Mademoiselle?"

"If you ride my brother's horse, I would be pleased if you would accompany me to my first destination; after that it will be necessary that you leave the horse with me and allow me to go on alone," I smiled apologetically, "it will mean that you walk home."

"That will be my pleasure," he said.

"You do not mind that I do not tell you where we go, or why?"

"No, Mademoiselle," he said.

A silence fell, which later he broke.

"Devastated as I am that you do not elope with me, I can only rejoice that you flee with someone else. As your first choice for the second horse was for side-saddle, I rest easy that you escape with a friend who is a lady- which is fortunate as there is now no necessity for me to duel with anyone."

He turned to me and smiled as he said this last and then suggested we leave the stables by the hay store door, so as to exit directly onto the paddocks where the turf would deaden the hoof noise. The moon was good, the sky was free of cloud. As soon as the horses were walked in and the girths retightened, we set off at a steady trot, keeping to the verges for quietude. He kept level with me. When I felt free of the demesne of the house, I turned to him.

"Our journey is nearly an hour in length."

"A hundred hours would be too short, Mademoiselle," he said, and his words thrilled me.

We stayed mostly silent, only speaking if there were a fallen branch or ditch to warn of. It was an exciting way to travel. The further we journeyed, the more we saw. There is a surprising community of the night. A lone hound loped past us, doubtless looking for a mate. A barn owl glided out of the woods and swept close over our heads for fun and devilment. Two young, barefoot boys with rods and a net crossed our path and, finally, an older man disappeared among the trees with what looked like a young deer carcass on his back. Each of the fellows nodded their head to us- perennial respect for the mounted. They melted into the shadows, trusting the black depths to obscure their identity, trusting to our apparent illegitimacy of circumstance to ensure mutual discretion.

"They take my father's game," I said to Aurèle.

"He cannot eat it all," he replied.

Eventually we passed what I judged to be the mid-point of our journey and this was where Aurèle cautioned that we would be better to come off the verges. We were clear of the parkland and the wastrels were become treacherous. We took to the middle of the path where the going was smooth and, as irony would have it, it was here that my horse fell lame. It was a devastating blow. Aurèle swung off his horse, I dismounted from mine, then he bent to examine the leg. I could not see his face, but I could hear the tension in his voice as he told me her tendon had heated and thickened from a strain and that she could hardly put her foot to the floor.

"Dieu," I whispered, "this horse was to be for my sister."

"This horse cannot go further," said Aurèle.

"It is a disaster. My undertaking now will fail."

I rested my forehead against the warm, smooth coat of the stricken animal. I was mindful that I was with a companion who disguises nothing of his feeling and so I did not mind that my voice faltered as I uttered the next few words.

"I cannot imagine now what can be done."

Aurèle spoke.

"Mademoiselle, entrust me with your confidence. Is your sister in need of help?"

"My sister has deserted her husband. I want to leave with her. I must hope she has her own horse with her."

"That is unlikely," said Aurèle, "a noblewoman who leaves the protection of her husband salvages nothing from the wreckage. Her money, her jewels, her children; all are forfeit."

I was aghast. "Do you call this 'protection'?! This is not protection, this is theft! Does the law not allow her children to join her - when she is established? Does the law not allow her to be with her children?!"

"The law holds that she is an object in her husband's possession. Therefore, it is impossible for her to possess a thing. A thing cannot possess a thing. Unless there has been a rare and special dispensation drawn up, wives who flee leave with nothing."

We stood in silence, facing each other, our faces eerily unseeable in the darkness.

"I must still ride to her, even though we no longer can make our way together," I said.

"Is she waiting? Does she know you seek her?"

"No."

"Do you know where she is?"

"She is injured. She cannot have left our estate. I am guessing she will be hiding in a disused lodge or similar. I was heading for the one we most frequented when we were girls."

"She may be in distress. She must be found."

"You do not judge her then?" I asked.

"No Mademoiselle."

"How do you suggest we proceed?"

"We have two options. Either we turn this lame horse loose and we leave, determined never to return, taking the sound horse with us and picking up your sister on the way. This is my preferred option. Or we return both horses to their stable before they are missed, and you return to your family before you are missed. Then I find your sister and deliver her to a sanctuary."

"The first choice is too dangerous; it is too slow: three people but only one horse. We have no money. We would be conspicuous."

I stood before him, head bowed from the weight of my failed plans. He advanced a step towards me as if to support me in his arms and then propriety stopped him. He took my hand and clasped it in his.

"Mademoiselle, allow me to accompany you back to your home and then commission me to be your agent in this affair. I will execute your bidding faithfully and unceasingly until your sister is found and delivered to a place of safety."

"What place of safety?"

"The Convent of the Ursulines; they will need her husband's permission. If Madame la Chevalière were to allow me, I would negotiate with him for that."

"Is there nowhere else for her? What about her Godmother?"

"In these circumstances it is almost impossible for one woman to shelter another. The shame of the fugitive infects the woman protectress; this is the mechanism of obloquy. On leaving her husband, a woman places herself and any woman who shelters her outside the bounds of society. At this moment, if she is extremely fortunate, she will have enough clothes on her back to keep warm. But she will have no money, no jewellery to sell, no horse and no servant. She may even appear unkempt and, to innkeepers along the way, it will be obvious that there is no one to stand surety for her most basic expenses. The only place of sanctuary now will be the convent, if her husband will allow it.

"I do not call those places sanctuary, more holding pens for the unwanted and dispossessed."

"If they have a learned, enlightened Abbess they can be a wonderful sanctuary but, in some cases, there are abuses."

"My poor sister!"

"Allow me to accompany you back home. There are people about this night on your father's land; their business is in the shades. Afterwards, immediately, I will seek your sister."

It had been so long since anyone had offered me sympathy that I struggled for some mastery over my feelings before I could speak.

"I have failed her."

His response came quietly.

"I do not suggest that you abandon your quest- simply hand it over. To allow me to be your agent in this would be my great honour. You said yourself, there are many places for you to search. It is simply impracticable that you attempt it. You are not free. I am. If you undertake more nights like this, your menfolk will suspect something and that will be the worse for you."

I resigned myself to his argument. I rested my head against my horse's neck. Aurèle busied himself, preparing his sound horse to be ridden and my horse to be led from its far side. When he was ready, he held the horse for me to mount. Then he swung lightly up behind me. I allowed him to support me and this he did by wrapping his free arm around my waist and drawing me to his chest, with his other hand he held the reins. My head and body came to rest in the closest fit to his, causing the breath to catch in his throat. The sound of this caused a thrill of response through my body. He rested his head against mine and brought his mouth to my ear, from where his impassioned words could be delivered straight to my heart.

"When this is over, I implore you, be with me. Take your chances with me. Leave with me."

His argument was petitioned by the intensity of feeling behind his words. His seduction was advanced by the heat of his breath upon my cheek and the strength of the encirclement of my body by his own. There was no resistance in me. His nearness acted as an opiate to my intellect. I felt my reason slip away under the force of his passion and I was in ecstasy to see it go, to be released from the tyranny of my thoughts. I did nothing to fight back; all my powers were yielded to bliss. In that moment there was nothing he could have desired of me that I did not desire of him.

Where his honest words had not persuaded me to take him, a sweet, dishonest bewitchment came into play from the closeness of his body. He had no right to render my reason at nought but that is what he did, leaving me wholly given up to the dictates of my senses. I hung with heavenly suspense upon his every breath and for the slightest movement of his body against mine and finally I understood something of the enslavement of our sex. Without question, I would have risked death to have one moment such as this. Had he truly understood his power, he could, in those moments, have drawn me to him, body and soul. And so, as you see my sister, I now know what death-defying impulse is at work to make our sex willingly consort with theirs.

When the journey was ended and I was back in my room, my mind recalled, over and over, the sensation of his closeness to me.

The feeling, so intense, instilled in me a new kind of restlessness of mind and body.

My sister, it was with difficulty that I reviewed the information that he and I had relayed to each other on parting. I have told him of all the places where you might be found; he has told me where, on finding you, he would leave intelligence of it. He does not trust to our communicating safely within the house as he has a fear of compromising me. It is true that the house is full of the eyes and ears of high performing factota and that they miss nothing. We have chosen to communicate by leaving letters for each other on a capping stone beneath a loose roof tile under the eaves of the old lodge on the near side of the forestry. When he has found you, he will alert me in this way, and I will come to you. I will then bring to you all my letters which are my record of the efforts I make to help you. I am confident he will find you.

42. ISABELLE AURÈLE to the CHEVALIER AURÈLE (sent from PARIS, 22nd SEPTEMBER 1776)

My darling brother, I am sure I do not offend you when I say that your letter, in which you outlined your disastrous proposal of marriage to Mademoiselle Sophie, diverts us every time we read it - which is often! Our life here is so quiet. Mother, Father and I hardly leave the parlour or the garden. Therefore, my little brother, we live through you. Do please understand that it would be impossible for you to tell us too much about your life and your encounters. We adore to hear of them. We read your letters together, Mamma, Papa and I, after we have cleared up behind our languishing housemaid.

I adore to be educated by your transcriptions of the ancients. Spinster as I am at twenty-eight years of age, still Papa believes reading to be damaging to the health of ladies. As he believes *my* health to be of importance to *his*, you will know that my reading efforts are jealously curtailed by him.

I have just read your letter again. It amuses me so much!

I know your ardent nature and so I am sure you will propose marriage to Sophie again. While it might be gratifying for a woman to be respectfully proposed to several times by *different* men, it must be very trying for a woman to be asked more than twice by the *same* man and so I beg of you, make only one further trial of your pride and her patience.

From my perspective as your most ardent admirer, I cannot believe that there is a woman on earth as could fail to be sensible to your beauty and worth, should your attention fall upon her.

If Mademoiselle Sophie refuses you, she will have a compelling reason. Hopefully she will be honest enough to explicate this reason to you and you might be able to remedy your short-coming before you propose to someone else.

We now debate how many times a young man ought to propose to a young woman: Mother says, '*more than once,*' as it is unseemly for a young maiden to accept immediately and give the appearance of wanting to leap into the marriage bed; I say, '*only once,*' as both parties must understand there can be no room for silliness and confusion; your father says, '*never,*' for we are such different species it is as if a horse should propose marriage to a hand-knitted, bed sock.

One wonders how father ever proposed to mother! She says he did so more than once, and this was because she encouraged him to remain hopeful by giving him a series of 'consenting negatives'. By this I imagine she kept saying '*no*' but in such a way as to suggest that she really meant '*yes*'.

I am sure in their case this was all very sweet but in our modern world, it seems to me a very dangerous way of proceeding.

43. THE CHEVALIER AURÈLE to ISABELLE AURÈLE (sent from the LEFÈVRE ESTATE near AMIENS, 24th SEPTEMBER 1776)

My dearest sister, my beloved parents, you amaze me. How is it that you believe it possible that I should love another now that I have met Mademoiselle Sophie? She is astonishing. She is my one true love. There will be no other love for me until the day I die.

I can hear your laughter now. And the laughter of Mamma and Papa. I can hear you all say that for me to keep this promise, I had better die sooner rather than later. However, if I live a thousand years, I shall love none but her.

We have had another encounter, Mademoiselle Sophie and I; a strange circumstance occasioned us to share a horse to carry us both home one night. Whilst I took the reins in one hand, she allowed me to hold her fast with my other arm. Holding her to me like that was to experience heaven on earth.

Papa, you will congratulate me on this mode of travel.

My sister, you will tell me that it is very improper of me to have obliged a young lady to this arrangement and I will remind you that you and I have ridden this way many a time. You will tell me that a sister is a very different thing from a young woman from another family and I will tell you that you are entirely right in this assertion!

Mamma, you will query the propriety of the young woman in allowing herself to be unchaperoned and abroad with a lone young man. However, I can assure you she was obliged to this by happenings beyond her control. I will tell you how these happenings came about.

I was in the Lefèvre stables at night as an incident had befallen one of a new, matching pair of carriage-horses which had been purchased for old Lefèvre by his head groom. One of this pair had, on arrival at the stables from the sales, fallen dangerously ill with colic. The head groom's plan to cure this prized horse alarmed me as it was comprised of superstitious remedies likely further to endanger the animal. As the value in a matching pair of horses depends upon the fact of there being two of them, I determined to effect the cure myself. It was imperative that the horse be induced to drink frequent, small, regular doses of slightly warmed water. One hour after midnight, just as I was satisfied that my cure was complete, Mademoiselle Sophie arrived in the stables. I was surprised and alarmed to see her outside, unaccompanied at such a late hour. As you know, a milkmaid or barmaid can wander alone and keep her reputation and the good-will of her family, but this is not the case with a woman of Mademoiselle Sophie's station.

It transpired that Sophie was determined to take a horse and leave. As the Lefèvre young women are level-headed, I assumed she must have compelling reason for this action. I offered to accompany her. I did not ask where she went as I would accompany her to the end of the earth. I did not ask her purpose as I would accompany her for any purpose.

I found that Mademoiselle Sophie sought to join her sister who has fled a 'marriage convenience'. It was when one of the horses fell lame that Sophie was obliged to outline her intention to me- because it became apparent that her plan would fail. I offered, therefore, to find her sister, Hélène, Madame la Chevalière, in Sophie's stead. She did me the honour of accepting my offer and we rode home in the exquisite manner that I have already described to you.

I am pleased to relate that I did not behave like a fool during any part of this encounter. I did not speak to Sophie of death, nor did I try to kill any member of her family. And so, whilst I had her in my arms, I proposed marriage to her once more. This time she did not refuse! In fact, she said nothing.

I am full of hope! I am overjoyed!

(Later) I have woken this morning with the strongest sense of foreboding. I burn with the wish that I had flown with Mademoiselle Sophie in the night. I should not have allowed my instinct to flee to be hampered by Sophie's desire to find her sister. It is to my eternal regret that I did not simply seize the best horses from the Lefèvre stables and make off with Mademoiselle Sophie for the continent.

Her sister is badly circumstanced; but I fear Sophie is worse. It is imperative that I get her away from Merteuil. Pray, do not speak to a soul about this.

44. ISABELLE AURÈLE to the CHEVALIER AURÈLE (sent from PARIS, 26ᵗʰ SEPTEMBER 1776)

My darling brother, your Mamma and I do not like it when you encounter young women who are obliged to irregular behaviour by happenings beyond their control. (Papa does not mind this, however.)

Do bear in mind that when a young woman says nothing in response to a proposal of marriage, this is a long way away from an acceptance. As you have now made two proposals to Mademoiselle Sophie, I lovingly suggest you desist from making a third. Your adoring father agrees with me in this, even though your adoring mother does not.

Mamma says now that autumnal chills are here, she is in hopes that you wear your flannel waistcoat- the one she embroidered with flowers and butterflies.

45. THE CHEVALIER AURÈLE to SOPHIE LEFÈVRE (hand delivered to the FOREST LODGE within the LEFÈVRE ESTATE near AMIENS, 26ᵗʰ SEPTEMBER 1776)

My dear Mademoiselle Sophie, these last three nights I have ridden to all the destinations you have indicated on the Lefèvre estate. I am sorry to report that Mme la Chevalière d'Ivry, your Hélène, was not in any of those places. In the location you had thought the most likely (the hunting lodge) there were some signs of recent occupation.

Every night I will look for her. I will not cease looking until I find your Hélène. I do this for her sake but equally for admiration and love of you.

46. THE VICOMTE VALMONT to M. DE BEAULIEU (sent from the CHÂTEAU DE ****, 28th SEPTEMBER 1776)

My mind is tormented by your news that Lefèvre will sacrifice Sophie in marriage to that brute Merteuil! Dieu! How my plan has twisted out of shape. It has taken on such a contrary life of its own that I am now on fire to undo everything I have done. Beaulieu, you must help me to reverse matters. You must communicate to me everything that passes in the Lefèvre house, no matter how small or how insignificant. I must know minutely how their deadly nuptial plan proceeds. Apply what influence you can over the young Lefèvre. Get him to call the marriage off and I will arrive and throw my influence over the father. Expect me and do not let surprise betray you as I step over the threshold. At this rate I will be forced to propose to her myself!

47. M. DE BEAULIEU to the VICOMTE DE VALMONT (sent from the LEFÈVRE ESTATE near AMIENS, 26th SEPTEMBER 1776)

Sophie now is in grave danger. Why did you interfere? You would never have meddled had you foreseen that they would stoop to death-by-Merteuil. Everything now is so dangerously entrammelled. You are caught up in the toils of your own making; it would have been easier to seduce Sophie from the young Comte de Guyenne than from beyond the grave. I am sure you will be able to produce an anecdote to the contrary but, as I recall, not even you have succeeded in a seduction of the dead?

48. THE CHEVALIER AURÈLE to SOPHIE LEFÈVRE (hand delivered to the FOREST LODGE within the LEFÈVRE ESTATE near AMIENS 28th SEPTEMBER 1776)

My dear Mademoiselle Sophie, by night I search the properties you have indicated to me. There is no sign of occupation in any. In the event that any of those I have already visited become inhabited by your sister after my inspection, I revisit them during the sequence of my travels. The more time that passes during which we have no assurance that Hélène is safe and in good health, the more worried I become. Please leave me a list of your family's tied estate cottages. I will find a reason for calling upon them all. I will also seek to gain information on any new admissions at the Convent of the Ursulines. I will solicit intelligence of new arrivals in the local towns.

You know that, between the requirements of your brother and your father, my daylight moments are not my own and so my mission hitherto has been sued by night. I will, from now on, make some reason to be excused for some part of the day.

I will not cease looking until I find Hélène. As I search for her, it is your image, however, which is constantly before my eyes.

49. THE VICOMTE DE VALMONT to M. LEFÈVRE (sent from the CHÂTEAU DE ****, 28th SEPTEMBER 1776)

Monsieur, I was at the Sorbonne with your son. I expect he has spoke of me to you. I have no doubt he will remember me. I will be arriving in your région early within this next fortnight. It would greatly convenience me to stay at your family home. I travel with an entourage of between four and six, sometimes eight or so servants. My business in your area will certainly necessitate a stay of one night or two or three. Maybe seven or so.

50. SOPHIE LEFÈVRE to HÉLÈNE, the CHEVALIÈRE D'IVRY (sent from the LEFÈVRE ESTATE near AMIENS, 29th September 1776)

I continue to write dear sister. One day soon I will rejoice that you are found and that I am able to deliver this letter to you myself. In the meantime, I occupy myself by relating to you what passes here.

Does no-one of status understand that if they write to a lesser family that they may visit for one day or for several days, then every member of the lesser family will be thrown into turmoil, preparing immediately for the longest part of the proposed stay? Even if that lesser family has been newly bereaved, if the visitor be a man of high estate, then all familial sorrow will be swept aside in preparation for his visit.

Just think of the priorities: our middle sister is dead; you, Hélène, are disappeared and yet all our family can think about is that a Vicomte has elected to stay with us. This is servility to the point of madness. Have they lost all sensibility? They fling themselves into a vast worry of protocol. They think that by associating with a Vicomte somehow their stock will rise, which, in this venal world, it probably will. They make sweeping changes in preparation for his stay, among which they have decided that they must evict Aurèle for that period. They are in a muddle as to whether Aurèle be tutor or friend and think it will reflect ill upon them if they give a tutor or impoverished friend the same status as the first of the household. They do not understand that Aurèle's lowly, cadet line of nobility, however impoverished, takes precedent over us.

Regarding this matter, this is how the conversation went between our beleaguered mother and our over-anxious father. I will hold a mirror up to the scene as I know it will amuse you.

Mother was exactly where she always is, in the morning salon, despite it being early afternoon. I love this trait of our mother- of always being where you have last left her. There is something comforting in the massy stasis of our mother, like the oak tree in the park or the moss-covered boulder in the wood. On this day she was plumped upon a chaise longue in her easy way, with our father hopping around her like a cock robin, working himself up to giving her some social impetus.

"Dear Madame, this visit of the Vicomte. Us do have very little time to get ready. I purpose that we disinter from the bank the five recently got artworks: the Greuze, the Robert, the Roman bust and the vases Chinoises. As a matter of urgency, them must be cleaned in readiness to be placed in prominent array about the entrance hall and reception rooms. My art consultant do say this do necessitate clearing the West wall in the grand salon for the hanging of the Robert and the Greuze. Also, he do say that this do necessitate the removing of the cabinet at the eastern entrance to that room to make space for the bust and its plinth. Them vases Chinoises must be positioned in the hall. Us do need to know that all cannot fail to be seen by the Vicomte as he do enter them rooms. I trust ye can have no objection to this plan?"

"Of course not dear Sir, but I be really not enamoured of the Greuze; be he a fine artist? Be it correct to hang he with the Robert? Be them palettes matching? Why do us need make such efforts for the Vicomte to see them items, pray?"

"Because them be impressive pieces."

"But the Vicomte must be used to seeing impressive pieces. Them must be commonplace for he. Need him see more?"

"Exactly so, and that is why us must have impressive pieces about us, so that them do look commonplace."

There was a pause here. I could see that Mamma was lost.

"But…but…if it do be commonplace to be impressive, what do it signify that them be there or not there?"

"Look, it be simple. Him must have around he what he be used to. His eye must not be arrested by something what be not there. Them must be there so that he do not notice that there be nothing there. I do trust ye can have no objection?"

"No, no, it all do be very confounding but of course not. No objection."

"Madame, may I trust that us do have an uplift in culinary arrangements in hand?"

"Uplift?" Mother looked all alarm.

"Yes, it be essential that us do appear à la mode. Us must include extra courses at dinner and us must dine one hour later. Anything less will appear unconscionably rural. Also, them menus do need revision. Ye must discover what be available in Paris and make sure us do have it here. Also, us must be rid of Aurèle. Him must not be eating at our table nor associating in the main part of the house on the days of the visits of M. le Vicomte and M. le Marquis. Two noblemen be plenty enough nobles for the likes of we. Us need not add one more to our small society. Aurèle must be invited to not be here."

The proposal of ridding ourselves of Aurèle made Mamma look affrighted.

"But, oh, Aurèle! He be so grand! So Godlike! So above all of we! Will not him take this as a most terrible affront? Be not his wider family one of the first in the country? Was not he top scholar at the Sorbonne?"

"His family, poor as dirt; not a single one of they do hold sway. Them moves not in circles of influence. T'would reflect badly on us if us do include him at our table and at our assembly. He do be here, after all, in the employ of we. One do not include the staff in one's affairs. Please attend to that."

"Me?"

"Yes, ye- or Didier then. T'would be wrong for me to involve myself in affairs domestic."

"But if it be trivial, do us have to banish he?"

"It be trivial and not trivial, dear Madame. All at the same time. Please attend to it."

Mother looked more befuddled. I felt for her as I find my sympathies are never more engaged towards our parents than when these laborious exchanges occur. I honour our father for his labours in making his every painful care the advancement of our family, but I shrink from the anxiety which fuels these exertions and which exhaust all around him, most especially our mother. It is a dreadful irony that his fretful attentions to the minutiae of detail can overset all his other best efforts. Do you remember, my sister, when our father held an inaugural supper in this, our new-built home, how, in front of all the seated guests, he flew into a trepidatious rage with our mother and the servants when he realised that napkin rings had been omitted from the tableware? He failed to understand that a brief display of spitting, seething anxiety by the host would far more discomfort his guests than a missing napkin ring apiece.

  Nothing now is being done to ensure our sister a fitting memorial. She lies forgotten in the ground and life hurtles on. You also, dearest sister, are forgotten by the decree of our father.

51. THE CHEVALIER AURÈLE to ISABELLE AURÈLE (sent from the LEFÈVRE ESTATE near AMIENS, 29th September 1776)

My dearest sister, my beloved parents, the little upstart Didier visited me in my rooms this early eve and relished banishing me from family life. I think he was hoping I would be so affronted as to leave in high indignation, offended to be treated as a hireling. He mistakes me for someone who cares what he or his family think. Excepting his beautiful sister, I could not be more disinterested. Why this banishment has happened I do not know. Maybe they seek to clear the way for Merteuil. Maybe they suspect my love for their daughter.

  They would be right to. I love her unto death. Merteuil will not have her.

52. SOPHIE LEFÈVRE to HÉLÈNE, the CHEVALIÈRE D'IVRY (sent from the LEFÈVRE ESTATE near AMIENS, 5th OCTOBER 1776)

Now that Aurèle is banished from our mealtimes, I do not see him, not even for tutorials. The relationship is so fraught between him and Didier that I am banned from those by Didier's decree. As the days pass where I do not see him, I find my thoughts are preoccupied with him more than ever. I long to tell him that I adore him, but this might lead him once more to make a proposal of marriage to me. As I cannot accept him, I cannot lead him to this. My mind toils endlessly in circles around this logic and still I write nothing to him of my love.

Having spent two days wishing to see Aurèle, when eventually I did see him, I could have wished myself a hundred leagues off as appearances went strongly against me. It happened when I was with Didier and the ascendant Beaulieu.

Beaulieu is waspishly passive, as if he is peevishly aware of having a low sense of his own worth and agency. He seems annoyed that he is more bystander and commentator than agiteur. Nonetheless he is an individual over whom our family fawns because he is of superior stock.

When first he appeared, some weeks ago, I was afraid he was thought of for me. Luckily, he hinted to my mother that he is off the marriage market. Probably he is set to marry his cousin or sister or his mother or some other near relative. Either way I find his company tolerable. He is sarcastical and this suits my mood. During our first meeting, he seemed unable to tear his eyes away from me, following my every move with undisguised admiration. He now, puppy-like, has appointed himself my Cicisbeo- according me a vast amount of consideration without any uncomfortable undertones. It is a bit like having an idolising convent girlfriend again. He is here, therefore, sliding readily into the place at our table and at our hearthside, lately vacated by Aurèle. Because he dogs my every footstep, appearances have twice gone against me with Aurèle, regarding him.

The first incident occurred because our father now requires that our brother accompanies me on any morning ride I take, despite that I never stray beyond our own great park. This may be because father has heard of Aurèle's attention to me precipitating the fight with our brother. Or it may be that they are afraid I will flee. Therefore, we were all mounted on this particular morning, Didier, Beaulieu and I. Beaulieu and I rode with our horses slightly behind Didier's. It is my wont to place my mount in this way in order that my ears and my sense may not bear the continual affront of my brother's own peculiar way of viewing the world.

"Look at that idiot gardener, why must he limp along so? … My goodness! So many starlings! We must get the nets out…Here come the Dupont ladies; what a shambles!"

Beaulieu, in his slavish devotion to my beauty, cannot bear to be more than half a horse's length away from me under any equestrian circumstance. We rode side-by-side, therefore, Beaulieu and I, with Beaulieu's proximity causing his stirrup iron to clang against mine every now and then. Having committed and gone some way along the narrow furlong avenue of poplars, we rounded a bend and our eyes alighted upon Aurèle, who was also already committed to the same avenue, schooling our brother's restive new riding horse. As soon as Aurèle saw us, his horse checked its pace, doubtless responding to the moment's hesitation in Aurèle's mind as he espied us. (I like the way that good riders reveal their sentiments through their animal in this way.) There was no such hesitation in Didier. He rode purposefully forward, flapping his legs at his horse's side and calling for me to come up alongside him. Because I wished to conceal my engrossment with Aurèle from Didier, I did as he requested, forgetting that by doing so, I would cause Beaulieu follow. In this way, we forced Aurèle to be obliged to give way to the wall of our united front. This he did by moving his novice horse into the fringe of the avenue and onto the rough ground below the trees, before faintly nodding his head to us in greeting. I could see that his blood was up bespeaking the anger he felt from the implied insult of our manoeuvre. Courtesy would dictate that Didier, Beaulieu and I acknowledge Aurèle but, in this instance, Beaulieu and I took our cue from Didier who failed to pay Aurèle any dues at all. We rode past him, therefore, rudely and silently. Even at this moment, I knew there was an opportunity to lessen the insult to Aurèle if I glanced back over my shoulder at him and smiled. I knew with an absolute certainty that Aurèle was halted and looking after me and that it would be the work of an instant for me to turn to him. I knew that he would be waiting for me to do this and yet I resisted this most genuine of urges. My mind betrays me; it overrides the strongest and most sincere of my impulses.

The rest of the hack I spent in angry mortification, examining why I had not defied Didier and shown courtesy to Aurèle. I could only come up with the habitual dishonesty of my mannerisms. My wish to deceive Didier into thinking I cared not for Aurèle had caused me to risk leading Aurèle to believe the same. I recall the many other times when my feelings and appearances have been antipathetic to him. I feel I have failed him in a test of faith. Where Aurèle is so true, I seek to disguise every thought. This leads me to wonder whether Aurèle, like our mother, is too simple in the area of sensibility. Why does he let everyone know exactly what is on his mind and in his soul? Is this honesty or stupidity? As you can see, I think of him every moment of every day.

The other incident came about today. At breakfast, when our non-itinerant mother commissioned me to be conveyed into town for market day to fetch her various trumperies, I was accompanied not by a maid or manservant but again, by our brother and the ever-present Beaulieu. When the barouche was announced, I was handed into it by Beaulieu who fell over himself to perform this office. I smiled at the custom which dictates that a capable young horsewoman needs handing somewhere by a fop with two left feet. In this instance, as in many an instance, I have felt it fitting that the offer of help from a prematurely gouty, young male should be turned about in their favour.

Have you ever mused, my dear sister, how it has come about that women be handed into carriages by sometimes vastly less able men? If one accepts that some women must climb into carriages, and if one takes the aggregate number of those carriage-climbing women and calculates the proportion of those who genuinely have need of assistance (due to age or infirmity), certainly, one may make a general rule that, with regard to carriages, some women need help. Following these principles, so do a similar number of men. Therefore, the handing of women (and not men) into carriages must be to do with petting and patronage.

I prefer to get in myself. However, having mounted first meant that I was on the far side facing forward. The omni-present Beaulieu then placed himself beside me, on my left, leaving Didier with no option than to sit opposite us in the position with the lowliest status, his back to the forward motion. I was surprised that Didier submitted to this arrangement. Behind Didier was the coachman with a groom beside him, two vigorous young men employed to manage the high-bred, high-fed horses. The carriage chosen for the day was the particularly roomy, open-topped Barouche and so I managed to make at least one foot of space between myself and the outer perimeter of Beaulieu's lady-like hips.

Nothing has changed regarding the trip to Amiens; the road is wonderfully formed by the extorted labour of the corvées and the barefoot, peasant women still gather grasses and herbs, at either side, for their cows.

I decided to become invisible for the duration of this journey. It is quite easy to do this; I practised it as a child. Simply, one becomes very still and removes oneself from the conversation by turning one's head outwards, away from the consciousness of the coterie within the carriage and off to the middle or far distance. It helps if one draws one's companions' attention to a thing or two on the horizon before falling utterly silent, as if having fallen into a reverie. If someone speaks during this latter period, it is important to appear not to have heard their utterance until a second appeal for attention is made. Then one must make it clear that one has no idea what has been discussed hitherto. If it sounds surprising that this simple expedient will work, just try it yourself.

I was rewarded for this deception by over-hearing an increasing number of indiscrete comments uttered in an undertone by the two gentlemen in the carriage and by the coachman and groom. This window into the uncensored male mind is interesting to me. When we arrived in town there was the usual market day crush with our horses held up behind carriages, farm carts and hand carts. After a while I realised that, despite the road having cleared, our coachmen made no effort to send forward the horses. Didier, becoming conscious of the delay, raised his cane to rap the back of the seat in front to command the coachman to move. This man, however, in a moment of perfect amity with Didier, turned to him and cocked his head to indicate that Didier should desire stasis and divert his attention beyond my side of the carriage and across the road to a young woman who was walking there.

This last, I saw out of my peripheral vision, as my gaze now was directed forwards. Didier understood the gesture immediately and whipped his attention across me to the far side of the road, nudging Beaulieu with his foot for his attention there also. The silence that followed, for some moments, paid homage to the object of all their fascination: a showy female, a dark, creole young woman in uncostly, fantastical clothes and trinkets. I could see her full well, despite my averted eye. I was arrested by her striking looks, her apparent autonomy and the depth of consciousness in her expression. As she noticed the attention of all four men, I noted there were, mingled in her look, equal measures of knowingness, shame and defiance. Finally, the spell of the homage was broken by Didier who turned away from her and muttered.

"Whore."

The homage was also broken by the coachman who laughed.

"Whore indeed! Like Madeira wine: passed around by us all and levels us all."

The young groom laughed at his conceit. Didier, suddenly choosing to assert the rule of class over fraternity said,

"Remember your place."

To this, the young groom could not resist a quip.

"Same place as your place, in relation to that harlot!"

Both horsemen and Beaulieu laughed. Didier turned pink.

"Enough of your cheek," he said, though sheepishly, "drive on!"

I was astounded, impassioned and upset. My heart, immediately, felt sympathy with the lone, young woman. As we lurched into motion, I cast a look over my shoulder and met her shameful, defiant gaze. In that moment I wished to show her respect and amity and so I smiled gravely, with a slight bow of my head, hoping that she would not take this courtesy as facetiousness. I think the spirit of my action was understood as she slightly returned my gesture. I turned my head away. I had never seen her like, and I felt a fascination and an admiration for her. Her look of defiance struck an immediate echo in my soul. Clearly, three of the four men in my carriage had known and had used that young woman intimately. They were still engrossed by her and obviously still desired her.

So why, then, did they seek to revile her? This anomaly caused my blood to rise in anger. Did they feel shame for what they had done with or to her and is that what made them spit that shame back at her? How did they all know of each other's involvement? This seemed to be an interest with the power to draw all together, high born and low born, all responding in the same way. Desire, it seemed, could lead to an activity with cross-contamination between all classes, and thus, as the coachman said, with the power to level all. The men, clearly, had voiced their experience of her to each other and had felt free to share in the details. The young woman was obviously too low and too cheap to be accorded any pretence of discretion or chivalry, and the lure of a union with her meant that none had minded what class of person had gone before. Where my brother would refrain from sharing a drinking vessel with these men, he scrupled not to share a bedfellow.

As usual I hid the sickness I felt at heart behind a dreamy facade of ignorance, convincing all the men in the carriage that the whole incident had passed over my head. In fact, my head and heart pounded. I wished I could avenge her shame upon them all. I determined to find a way to give her money enough to have some choice as to how, and whether, and with whom her person was to be used.

Finally, we drew up beside a curb. The groom jumped down to open the carriage door and let down the step. Didier leapt out of the carriage first, followed by Beaulieu who, as usual, sought to hand me down. Just as I was about to alight, my breath was caught by the sight of Aurèle across the road who emerged out of a church and onto its paved steps. Possibly he had been at his devotions. He stationed himself in the street and fell into deep discussion with the young, local curé. As is usual, at these moments, the dark clouds parted and a beam of light fell immediately upon his head, illuminating him mid-tableau, in the manner of a work of fine art. My customary presence of mind and limb immediately left me, and I missed my footing on the carriage step, causing me almost to fall into the street. Beaulieu's customary incoordination of mind and limb also left him, and so he caught me. It was while I was clasped in his arms that Aurèle looked up and across the street and straight at me. The colour immediately rose into his honest, transparent cheek and he turned on his heel and strode away.

Once again, appearances have gone against me. I feel dejected, not least because I imagine that Aurèle was in town at my behest seeking intelligence of your whereabouts, my sister.

I did our mother's shopping with the ever-present Beaulieu at my side. He was dogging my footsteps and I hoped I would not see Aurèle again while in his company. I refrained from buying several of the more expensive items on my mother's and my lists and kept the money back in my purse. Leaving Beaulieu at the door of the church, I begged a moment alone inside and handed my purse to the young curé with a note which said "Please give this purse to the young, foreign lady and explain that it is from the demoiselle in the carriage. Please tell her that she will receive a substantial sum more from me, via you, and within the next month. I thank you."

The curé looked at me as if he thought I were committing an act of great irresponsibility, but he did not refuse my commission. I determined to draw down my year's allowance to send to her as soon as was practicable. My wish not to see Aurèle again was granted and so, of course, I felt bereft that he had not felt compelled to come back for a second sight of me.

Once home, my thoughts turn again to Aurèle. I am desirous to explain the last two events to him, but I have no idea where he lives in our home. Does he sleep at the back of the house or at the front, in one of the less frequented wings? Is his room off one of the labyrinthine service corridors? The house probably contains more rooms and leagues of corridor than all the rooms and corridors in all the houses in our nearest village. I dare not ask my maid as she would ask some valet or other and then he would ask the head of the below-stairs household staff who, in turn, would enquire who wanted to know. Then my wish to know would be speculated over by all subordinates.

That evening, during the period when I knew I could not be missed by servants or family, I determined to write a note of explanation to Aurèle and take it to the forest lodge. I planned then to spy on Didier and Beaulieu. I delivered the letter with no delay and returned to Didier's apartments, most of which intercommunicate. I knew which sitting room he would choose for his evening tête-à-tête with Beaulieu. All I had to do was station myself behind the door at the end of this room opposite the door that he and the servants would be using. I could see them clearly through the keyhole. I had an idea what matter they might choose to discuss, and I was correct in my assumption: Beaulieu wanted to hear the history of the young creole woman in the market street. And so did I.

Beaulieu opened the subject.

"I need to know about that lady. Where is she from? Certainly, she is not indigenous?"

Didier snorted into his glass giving himself the air of an old rake.

"That is no lady."

"She is beautiful. If the grooms can afford her, she sells herself cheap. Has she no idea of her worth?"

"Only a tiny number of them have any sense of self-worth. That is the beauty of the transaction for the purchaser."

"And so, what is her provenance?"

"She is the grand-daughter of a Dutch plantation owner whose son forced one of his father's African slaves to his bed."

"Pleasant family. How did she arrive here?"

"Due to the lightness of her skin she did not fit naturally with the slaves but of course neither would the Dutch own her. She was sold to a Turk slaver who shipped her out to the markets of Constantinople. There, people like her exchange hands for huge sums of money. It is said she was bought by a young English Lord who was travelling across sites of the antiquities. Arriving in England he rid himself of her: bought her a passage on a free trade ship where she struck up a relationship with the skipper. That skipper maintained her for a while here in Amiens until his wife found out. Taisha was lucky to end up in a busy trading and market town such as Amiens. It can afford her a degree of latitude. This suits her mode of existence better and so it is here that she has found her niche. For now."

Beaulieu went to the heart of the matter.

"Yes, but what is she like?"

"Exquisite. Her beauty almost unmanned me. Strangely, given the nature of the transaction, I felt that to touch her would be to profane her. I would have paid ten times the amount just to gaze at her."

"Do you usually pay for this sort of thing?"

"Not if I can get it for free. But for that, one must essay among the older married ladies of the tradespeople. Pretty unsatisfactory. The married are always so vastly uneasy about being caught, and, subsequently, so short of time. It's like trying to get your leg over a mountain goat when there's a wolf about. Because of all the bother, often I must move on quickly, usually to another older married one, access being the issue with the young unmarried. What about you dear fellow?"

"Nothing much. At home it was a servant and then, at the Sorbonne, a couple of workers from the town. I suppose the busiest time was the grand tour. Each seaport has its own quartier. I have been to them all, excepting where disease was rife. My tutor quite despaired of me. He was a young fellow, hardly older than me. There was budget enough for him to indulge, but he was a curious fellow. Spent most of his time at his devotions. Pious. Refined. Reminded me of Aurèle.

What I discovered was that multiple brief liaisons are no match for one true love. Sadly, my one true love was the servant and so our love could not survive the disparity in our rank. We ran the sweet course of our passion for two intense years before our union was discovered by my family and the servant was dismissed. Since that moment I have been quietly bereft, abject in my pain. I have never been able to replace the joy and peace of that union. I am not a fellow that fits: women find me too feminine, men find me not feminine enough."

Our brother's inebriate mind was belatedly brought to faint attention.

"Uh?" he said.

53. THE CHEVALIER AURÈLE to ISABELLE AURÈLE (sent from the LEFÈVRE ESTATE near AMIENS, 6th OCTOBER 1776)

My dearest sister, my beloved parents, Mademoiselle Sophie is in danger. She is starting to look about her; she is starting to feed her vanity by allowing the attentions of a dishonourable man:

Beaulieu. Only too well do I recognise the signs. As you know, I have seen it all before with another young woman. I fear for Sophie. I fear also for myself as my passion for her is intense. My love will endure through any marriage of hers but only if she remain honest.

I am aware that her father's mooting of her marriage to Merteuil engenders mortal fear in her, as it does in me for her sake. It is this that may be providing the impetus for her attention-craving actions.

How can it be that young women are led to such iniquities? How has it come to be that the 'marriage convenience' is sanctioned by law and by the church? By forcing the union of a young woman to a man for whom she has a violent antipathy, an incitement is created for her to be tempted beyond the bounds of her marriage. Such a cruel marriage is a powerful inducement for a young woman to break faith with her husband and follow a path that will lose her the grace of God. When I see young, innocent women married to ancient or unsuitable men of wealth and degenerate habits, I fear for them.

You know I have been in love before with a woman who had escaped a cruel marriage and that my conviction was that this woman would not have betrayed her marriage had it been one of love and compatibility. Therefore, I made the mistake of overlooking the impropriety of her action. You know how devastated I was to discover she was already become habituated to petty vices and immoralities- vanity flirtations of varying degrees of seriousness. It was because of the attritive nature of these events that I lost faith in her and so did not marry her after the death of her aged husband. My heart was broken of course, and so was hers, but that was how it had to be. How could I have entrusted all my future happiness to such a one as she had become?

There is only one option for me with Sophie now. I must take her at her word and accept she will not marry me due to my lack of money. Therefore, as soon as I have succeeded in finding her sister, I must leave and make my fortune.

Sophie may be available and true to my memory when I return. There is great risk in this strategy. It has too many factors beyond my control. Sometimes I wish that instead of spending three years at the university, I had gone to war and turned my fortunes around. But, had I not attended the Sorbonne, where was her brother, never would I have met Mademoiselle Sophie. It is no use bemoaning my fate. Great careers can be made by younger brothers in the army. For speedy success in this, I must act now and place my trust in God.

In the meantime, it will not be good for me to see Sophie. The full force of my heated passion for her may lead me to implore her to wait for me and this is a dishonourable request from a gentleman. When so few options are open to her, not a single one of them must be closed. You may say I am too particular on this point, but what if I do not make my fortune and what if, in waiting for me, she turns down a suitable and loving offer of marriage? I would have condemned her to an interminable future as spinster, where her fortunes and happiness would be dependent upon the uncertain moods of her father and brother. It is more important that she has a chance of happiness than do I. I do not depend upon dishonourable people.

The more I consider her situation the more I am sure I must not meet with Mademoiselle Sophie again.

54. SOPHIE LEFÈVRE to the CHEVALIER AURÈLE (hand delivered to the FOREST LODGE within the LEFVÈRE ESTATE near AMIENS 6th OCTOBER 1776)

I must beg of you the indulgence of a meeting. I have twice seen you in the last few days and I am aware that on each occasion I did not accord you with the proper dues. I wonder whether it might be possible for you to meet with me here at the forest lodge so that I may apologise and explain myself? It makes me very unhappy to think I may have offended you.

My other concern is to enquire whether you have news of Hélène? As there has been no communication from you, I assume there has been no result from your searches. Wholly sensible of my indebtedness to you, I wish to express my eternal gratitude.

55. TAISHA MEYER to SOPHIE LEFÈVRE (sent from AMIENS, 6th OCTOBER 1776)

I acknowledge receipt of the purse of coinage that you sent to me via the curé. I do not thank you for your contribution towards my rehabilitation, however, as I cannot truthfully undertake to rehabilitate. Although I desire that you honour your promise to deliver to me more monies. Do not pride yourself for your charity; your money will more likely be spent on vice than on virtue. If you wish to lift me out of bondage and have me tread the path of righteousness, you had better lay your hands on much more than the pin money that young women in your situation customarily have at their disposal.

As it happens, I am sick of all you ladies who cast haughty glances at me from the elevation of your carriages. As regards beauty, bearing and blood I am your superior. What makes you think you all so special?

I do, however, thank you for the gesture of courtesy you paid to me. It is hard for me continually to bear the superior looks of decent young ladies who are no less enslaved than am I. Sometimes I long to shout this across the street and into their face, but my good manners do not allow me to expose their bad manners. Neither am I sufficiently motivated to rob them of the comfort they gain from treating me with contempt. I choose not to point out that they share with me the condition of slave.

I thank you for the respect you have shown me. That is the only honour you are due from me.

56. SOPHIE LEFÈVRE to TAISHA MEYER (sent from the LEFÈVRE ESTATE near AMIENS, 7th OCTOBER 1776)

You fail to interpret my intention correctly. Do not assume that everyone patronises you. You can do what you like with my money. Vice or virtue, it is all the same to me. Take what I send you. You tell me it is not enough, but it comes freely. There will be more. When I am free of my family and when I have command of my own riches, I will seek you out. You will do me a great honour if you meet with me one day.

Your beauty, bearing and blood I delight to see.

You are mistaken if you think I am not wholly awake to my own enslavement. I envy some, but not all, the freedoms you have.

I return your thanks for honouring my respect for you.

57. ISABELLE AURÈLE to THE CHEVALIER AURÈLE (sent from PARIS, 8th OCTOBER 1776)

My sweet brother, admirable as is your understanding of the condition of women, surpassing as it does the understanding of many people, still yet you judge us too harshly. You claim that your Sophie *'encourages the attentions of a dishonourable man'*. You say your previous love became dishonest through the initiation of *'vanity flirtations'*. But have you considered how these two unfortunate young women are circumstanced?

Before I lay my idea of this before you, I admit that there are women about, who, despite being in possession of independence and financial freedom, set out to trifle with the happiness and freedoms of other men and women by playing, even unto death, the games of love.

I have seen a young wealthy woman, for the satisfaction of her vanity, draw men into duelling to the death for her. I have heard of a woman with full agency and liberty encourage a man to the rape of an innocent. Also, I have heard a woman accuse a man of rape when, in fact, she had superintended each one of his advances. Although I am passionately a defender of my own sex, I am not so silly-headed as to draw a veil over consciously plotted, black-hearted actions where they are committed. I cannot be so wrong-headed as to defend my own sex in a case where probity dictates that I defend yours.

Dear young, sweet brother, as you go more into the world, I beg of you not to be so upright and unbending as to be blind to the mitigating circumstances behind the actions of unfortunates. Please recognise that what desperate people do is entirely different from the machinations of power-mongers. I will be very surprised if you do not hear of, or witness at first hand, similar events to those I have outlined.

Please write to me of events as you encounter them and honour me with an insight into your thoughts. I ask you never to withhold details of such dealings from me. I lose patience when female family members are treated as though they are jellies as will wobble off their plates at the first hint of free talk. Similarly, when relaying speech to me, please be faithful to the vernacular; I find it bizarre that swearwords and blasphemies be swept past the female ear- my ear delights to catch them! I read your letters aloud to Mamma and Papa. Their eyes are dim now. It would be possible to omit certain of your passages as I read, so I beg you, do not censor what you write to me.

In the meantime, I honour women of moral unassailability. Also, I assert that I am a woman of steadfast and honest virtue. In this last assertion, however, I do not over-pride myself as I have not ever been tried by the fire of passionate temptation or by the ice of necessity. As regards temptation, you may have noticed that lovers and libertines are not beating a path to my door; as regards necessity, I want for nothing. I am comfortably placed. Our family continues poor but not indigent. Happily, due to my plainness, valuelessness and disinterestedness, no-one wants to contract me to themselves for a lifetime of holy wedlock. Finally, and unusually for a spinster, our estimable parents are thankful for my continued existence! I am wrapped around in their love in the bosom of our childhood home.

For a brief period, prior to attaining my current perfect state of social irrelevance, I experienced the forces that operate upon a woman of high-status. It became clear to me that these forces were causing me to bend the rules of propriety to varying degrees, in order to consolidate my position. I am sure you remember that, at sixteen years of age, upon my release from the convent, our dreadful Aunt Clementine greeted me with these words:

"If you cannot find yourself a man, you will be straight back in there again, and next time you will not come out!"

I was so affrighted, I endeavoured to appeal to every man who came my way – keeping three bilious old noblemen on tenterhooks for me at once!

As we both know, women of high status are raised with a single idea in mind: marriage. The only skill we are allowed to acquire is the skill for attracting and keeping a mate. A great deal of energy and forethought is expended to ensure that as regards all other skills and trades, we remain in complete ignorance.

Your brilliant but straight mind must be able to make the leap of logic to understand that, with her main chance of survival and status depending on her ability to attach herself to a man, some women, who find themselves in a precarious position regarding their survival, may exercise some latitude with this, the only skill they have in their armoury, in the only field of play allowed to them.

As with your Mademoiselle Sophie and your previous love, Madame Celine, they are forced to a destiny not that distinct from the animals on their home farms. If ever I found myself in their place, my strict moral rectitude also might waver. I might find myself calculating to cultivate my male acquaintance and tread the thin line that some disenfranchised women tread. This is the sharp and shivering line that supports the perilously situated woman as she tries to garner the sponsorship of a man without placing herself in his power. Society waits and watches for these women to fall and then says "well, she asked for it!"

But, until we have agency and access to power, what can we do?

You, my dear brother, as a man, enjoy full agency. I am thankful for this but do be aware of the dangers in an encounter where you hold the power and the woman (for example, Mademoiselle Sophie), does not. If Sophie were to continue to seek your help, your transaction with her may become prey to dangers.

I put to you these possible scenarios: you, Aurèle, may simply help Sophie and then depart, or you may misread the signs of her need and wrongly conclude *'Sophie has an especial liking for me; I will reciprocate.'*

If you were an unscrupulous man, you may determine *'she is needy, I will take full advantage of her.'*

As for Sophie, when she steps into your sphere, she may think *'I need help, yet I am strong enough to shun this man if he threatens my person and integrity.'*

Or, she may decide *'my need is such that I may concede unwillingly to a breach of my person and integrity.'*

In another circumstance, she may think *'I can play this man to my own ends.'* In case you cannot believe this, I have actually heard a noblewoman of my acquaintance say,

'one still needs a pretext; and is there any more convenient for us than that which gives us the air of yielding to force?'! *1

I have reread your letters which concern Mademoiselle Sophie. There is some equivocation from her, whereas your love for her is in full force. As there is this disparity of feeling between you both, I whole-heartedly endorse your plan to help her and then to banish yourself from her.

It offends my sense of fairness and my intelligence to be prejudicial toward men more than toward women. Many more men are kind, upright and generous of heart than are not. Also, abuses may occur in any arena where there is a power-monger of either sex. In a position of power, the sexes enjoy perfect equality: bad women inflict damage just as do bad men.

If the stories be true, as well as King David, Judas and Cain, let us bethink ourselves of Jezebel, Athalia, Delilah -and our own Aunt Clementine. Dieu! Dreadful!

58. THE CHEVALIER AURÈLE to SOPHIE LEFÈVRE (hand delivered to the FOREST LODGE within the LEFVÈRE ESTATE near AMIENS, 8th OCTOBER 1776)

My dear Mademoiselle Sophie, you ask to meet with me, but I regret I cannot. Only when I find your sister will I offer to meet- to take my leave of you before I seek my fortune elsewhere.

It had been my desire that you leave with me, that we marry immediately and that I make my fortune with you by my side. As this plan does not meet with your wishes, I must leave in any case.

My leaving does not indicate any lessening of my love for you. I adore you; you are my heart's desire. My ardent wish is that soon we will be together. I leave so that I may make my fortune in order that I can win you as my wife.

If ever you regret your decision, if ever you wish to take up my offer of marriage, just send word and I will come.

59. THE VICOMTE DE VALMONT to M. DE BEAULIEU (sent from the HOSTELLERIE LE ST. CHRISTOPHE near AMIENS, 8th OCTOBER 1776)

My dear and strangely ineffective friend, I have decided it is best that you be not at the Lefèvre house upon my arrival tomorrow. Please excuse yourself and leave the field to me alone. You have been so little use to me, and my head is too painful from my night of drinking at the coaching inn to factor you in as well as everybody else. Your knowledge of my devices will put me out of countenance. Please stay away until I indicate to you that I need you back again.

My object, firstly, is that I assess how much Sophie is guarded, and secondly, that I shift the family aspiration and bedazzlement from Merteuil to me. If I can bring them to snub

Merteuil he will have no choice but to drop them in a fury of noble umbrage. I have more riches than does Merteuil and so they may take the bait. Should I fail in this then my jaded imagination simply must be piqued by viewing the sorry tableau of beauty and sense sacrificed to ugliness and greed.

    I must tell you about my journey to the Lefèvre district. The further I got away from Paris, the worse the roads became until the jolting of my carriage made me get out and walk. (How did I neglect to bring my own riding horse? I cursed my grooms for my oversight.) Also, I bemoaned my need for intriguing. I swear it drags me further than dynamite could blast me.

    You failed sufficiently to warn me that this inn is a mud-lagged affair.

    Upon my dazzling appearance there was the usual play-acting around the innkeeper's daughter. This time, instead of hiding her from me, the innkeeper was throwing her in my way. I was mildly surprised as she appeared still an innocent. Nonetheless, her father had coached her in the role of seductress as best he could and shoved her in my direction with all vigour. Yes, I swear he pushed her at me. I saw his leg-o-mutton arm propel her through the lobby door, her mob cap falling back with the speed of the air rushing past it. She came precipitously to my table.

    "Would ye loike more ale, Surrr? Would ye loike more cheese, Surrr?"

    The country accent, Dieu! Like the hee-haw of a donkey.

    Nonetheless I was bored, and so we kept a flirtatious charade up all through supper. It appeared that the girl was astonishingly pretty- an accomplishment, nowadays, which leaves me cold. Despite this, her lowly caste piqued my own sense of power and lent a charming mantle of ill-use to the overall effect.

    After supper, I went up to my room to await developments. Eventually, I heard a pit-patter of tiny feet up the stairs. My timing was impeccable. Just as Rosebud raised her hand to knock at my door, I opened it, pulled her inside and caught her jug of hot water as she dropped it. There was a pause whilst she recovered her breath.

    "I thought ye moight be glad of some hot water."

She said this unnecessarily.

"Did you?" I said and relished the awkward silence that followed.

In my dizzying presence she needed some moments to remember her next line.

"I thought ye moight need me for somethin'?"

"Did you?"

I was determined not to make her job easy. My back was to the door, barring her way and there followed another awkward silence.

"Um…Um…Do you need me for anythin'?"

She faltered, caught in her own toils.

"Not at all. There is nothing I could possibly need from you that hasn't already been satisfied a thousand, million times by your betters."

"Oh!" she said.

She was embarrassed, overwhelmed by the situation and desperate to leave. She took a step to the side of me to get to the door. The encounter was becoming more as I like it. I barred her way.

"It's about time you took off all your clothes."

I was determined to rob the situation of all romance. Her eyes widened. Obviously, she had been told that in the heat of my unbridled passion I would do this for her, but I was not about to pretend that the charade we played was my idea. There was another pause. I waited until I judged her ready for me to step away from the door.

"If you wish to leave, then leave. But if you have a desire to stay then I suggest you take off all your clothes."

Rosebud weighed up all the pros-and-cons and took off most of her clothes. Truly I was unmoved, but I swept her off to the bed and assumed the position of dominance. Probably she had been advised that at this point I would be a lost man, a slave to my passions and that she would have me entirely in her power. I got on with arranging our anatomy. Someone must have stopped short in her briefing as she seemed to have no idea where I was heading.

After more rummaging, I prepared to lose myself in the moment, but, as is increasingly my malaise nowadays, I was, of a sudden, overcome by an extreme ennui. A wave of complete desolation engulfed me.

I flopped entirely on top of sweet Rosebud. She craned her neck for her eyes to beseech an explanation. I gazed grumpily at her.

"Whatever are you doing here?" I asked.

There was no answer from Rosebud.

"What can you possibly hope to achieve from this situation?"

No answer from Rosebud.

"Or is it your family?"

No answer.

"What are they after? Money?"

She was in tears. Unequal to the situation, having for one brief moment believed herself heading for success. She confessed all.

"As I be so very pretty my father thought ye 'ud wish to visit me again and again and maybe set me up as yer mistress."

Honestly, this girl was priceless. I fell about laughing.

"Really! You?! Let me guess the rest. You expect me to fall in love with you and marry you. Or in the event of no marriage, you expect that I will forever keep you in my protection, despite any future marriage of mine. You expect that you, and only you, will be able to conceive, carry and safely deliver boys for me. You expect that, in the absence of any other sons, these boys will be legitimised and will inherit everything I own and that, due to my excessive drinking, you will outlive me to be the doyenne of it all."

Her silent tears were answer enough. This was exactly as her idiot father had laid it out to her. I continued; I was warming to my theme. I rested my chin on my elbow. My eyes took on a faraway expression.

"I must draw the veil from your eyes. My family is ancient. It has gained and held onto its riches by being the dupe of nobody. I come from a long line of people who have stopped at nothing to get what they want. This is true of almost all nobility. None of these riches have arrived by losing out in a transaction, or by being nice to stupid people. We are very, very rich indeed. You are very, very poor."

Rosebud continued to cry. We remained like this for a few moments whilst I worked myself up into my favourite role of instructor.

"Unless you learn to negotiate you will remain this way forever. Your father planned this night to be part of a long-term strategy to ensnare me, and so he has calculated to offer you up, this one time, at no cost. However, your father will fail in his efforts to use you to entrap nobility. Then he will throw you at the third estate and the poor. Then he will take all your earnings. I suggest if you are to choose this work, at least make sure the money ends up in your hands."

Rosebud spoke through her tears.

"How do ye call this *'choice'* when I have nothing?"

"Ah! Now you are become philosopher. As it happens, you are right. When a person is poor, very little or no choice is open to them. Death is usually the best option. Usually it arrives via starvation. However, if an impoverished person still possesses energy and health, they might take a desperate risk. One hundred and fifty years ago, an impoverished, scurvy-ridden ancestor of mine made the choice to mutiny and take control of a West Indies slave ship. Based on this theft, and on the trade of sugar, cotton and coffee, my family's fortune was made and hoarded. We paid not one sou of taxes and we gave no redress to the thousands of innocent souls who perished to make us rich. The more money we got, the more we were enabled to get, and the more we wanted to get. Once we had gouged a vast pile of wealth from the blood and toil of the enslaved, we discovered that we commanded immense respect in society. We learned from this and we entrenched our position and finally we bought our place among the nobility."

I looked down at Rosebud.

"Opportunity has not much come your family's way, but now a small chance has opened up for you. If you choose to take it, you must pitch yourself high in the market, you must refine your manners and manage your negotiations and earnings well. These accomplishments are vital because then you may become so much more than just an occasional bedfellow. Your face certainly is good enough for any level but your voice places you in the street. Unless you can change how you sound you will be selling yourself solely to drunken sewage men on high days and holy days. In which case you would be better not to try for this sort of job at all and simply give up all hope and marry a leech collector. (More tears.)

You must find a position as lady's maid and you must learn from your lady. Ladies speak beautifully and ladies read and write. You must learn to do the same. The best place for you would be in the household of an older lady whose eyes and powers are failing. It would be in her interest to teach you all her skills, including music, art and singing.

The acquisition of refinement and artistry will smooth your passage to the demi-monde. This is an alternative, high layer of society where fallen women go who have been rejected by good society. Respectable men who are a pillar of good society, may dip in and out of this place as they please, however. Free-thinkers, artists and philosophers of both sexes also make up the demi-monde. Women and men associate almost on a level. Ideas and skills are exchanged. Some of the women become great artists and thinkers. They attain a level of complete independence as to whether and with whom they consort.

If you learn all these things and are accomplished in your dealings, it is possible that you will arrive at a more advantageous position than any married woman of any station. The only people who will match you for autonomy will be men and wealthy widows. You will be almost entirely in charge of your own fortune and destiny. (More tears.)

I do not hold out much hope for you. Please understand that you have negotiated badly tonight. But do not make yourself uneasy. You will win some and you will lose some. Get educated and get wise."

Honestly, Beaulieu, I was proud of myself. Here I was, having undertaken a long, stiff journey, taking time out to educate the needy. At this point I felt that her tears smacked of pure ingratitude. I decided to buck her up.

"Oh, do stop blubbing for goodness sake. Whatever is the point in wasting tears on someone upon whom tears are wasted? Now, either get out or stay. If you choose to stay, I will show you the first lesson in one of the ways of the demi-monde."

She decided to stay. I found that we became quite pleased with each other. She was a quick learner and she asked many questions during our several hours together.

Before we parted, as she clothed herself, she unnerved me. She suddenly fixed me with a piercing look.

"I will follow yer plan," she said, "and I be certain that us will meet again. But as ye languish in yer bed imagining that the next young lady by yer side do find ye marvellous- do remember that her do this not for choice, but for survival."

I am glad Rosebud offered me this insight at the end of our encounter and not at the beginning.

(Later) Beaulieu, if your bejewelled footwear can withstand the mud, may I recommend to you a night at this tavern. You will like it; the innkeeper is always short of beds and so he will ask you to bunk with a gentleman traveller.

(Later) Beaulieu, I forgot to tell you that before I got to the tavern, I reconnoitred the estate Lefèvre. Aside from the desperate engagement of Ledoux, I note that Lefèvre has not laid out his pleasure grounds in any way whatever. There are just vast plains of grass where the gardens ought to be! I understand that Lefèvre built this great mansion five years ago and that he purchased the land for the estate twenty years ago and so he has had plenty of time. I see he has planted his woodland correctly and in advance of building (I espied at least one hundred acres of twenty-year-old timber coming on well for him) and so, the absence of gardens cannot be due to an absence of planning. The absence can only, therefore, indicate an absence of a sense of style. But really! What demand does style make of a person? In this case it would only necessitate the determination of the lay-out of the formal gardens, the water parterre, the walks, the lake, the fountains, the orangery and the positioning of the jardin à l'anglaise.

60. M. DE BEAULIEU to the VICOMTE DE VALMONT (sent from the LEFÈVRE ESTATE near AMIENS, 8th OCTOBER 1776)

My letter will concern itself with your tavern misadventure. It will prove to you that I am perfectly out of kilter with the thinking of the moment. You will read it with much rolling of the eye and with many a sigh of boredom. But long ago I reconciled myself to the opinion of all my peers that I am a fuddy-duddy.

You say you hate deflowering virgins and yet you do it all the time. What is it in your soul that leads you to such incontinence? Why is it that you bethink yourself into being such a plague to women? I can only imagine that you do it because you can. And that this is your own twisted version of noblesse oblige – which in your case is, in fact, noblesse s'oblige.

I am sure you know that for the women you prey upon there can be no redress; the low status woman has no voice against the high-status man and the high-status woman dare not lift her voice. For your fast set, long have I recognised that the hunting down of women is become a sport. But for you the sport now has become a compulsion from which you and your victim derive no satisfaction. Whatever is it that makes you choose a short, meaningless, coercive liaison over a long, sweet consensual one, when the latter is so immeasurably the better? Have you never experienced the satisfaction and joy of a long and loyal love? Is it that you have no respect for anyone, or is it that you are afraid you will be laughed at by your sportive friends if you are seen to give up the hunt, leave the field and expose your heart to lasting sweetness and delight?

I adore you, my dear frère de lait, so I tell you- beware! I am sometimes invited, by women, into their thoughts. They recognise me as no threat. I put you on notice that they, full well as we, have a high sense of camaraderie. Your conquests are numerous and indiscriminate. One day you may find that some of these women recognise you, between themselves, as their common denominator. One day you may find that they line up against you.

What happens if one of these women - just one - is a match for you and takes a stand against you? Although it is rare, very occasionally a woman may exact redress. Do not you remember Madame de Parris who was able to mobilise opinion against M. Darlin? He was placed in prison by order of the commanding officer of his regiment after his attack upon her.

My dear friend, I have worshipped and bewailed your daredevil ways since birth. I know you through-and-through. Even now I hear your voice, *'Beaulieu, you crusading ass! That wench walked into my room that night with the intention to seduce me. What did she think I was going to do: invite her to a game of pat-a-cake?'*

And in some part, I agree. Rosebud was not innocent in this. She was complicit in a long-term strategy to form a relationship of sorts and go after your money. There are many young women willingly and wholeheartedly that will try for this but there are also young women who do not wish to try for it – and some that are persuaded to by a third party. I know from your letter that Rosebud's father had applied persuasion with her, possibly coercion and that he had stopped short of explaining the full terms of her side of the deal. He had set her up as part of a bargain, the fleshly implications of which she did not fully understand.

You are a man of great discernment; all of this would have been apprised by you in a trice. Why, therefore, did you persist once Rosebud's resolve failed her? Once her wish to depart became evident, why did you choose still to dominate her? Do not you recognise that your own unmerciful, ungenerous, uncaring behaviour is the very fount of your lassitude?

Quite apart from which, once Rosebud gave signs that she wished to extract herself from the liaison, that was the moment at which it was your bounden duty to let her go.

61. SOPHIE LEFÈVRE to HÉLÈNE, the CHEVALIÈRE D'IVRY (sent from the LEFÈVRE ESTATE near AMIENS, 9th OCTOBER 1776)

Dearest Sister, every episode in my life, I revisit with reference to you.

Anxious to acquaint myself with the man over whom I intended to cast the irresistible net of my allurements, I hid myself behind the enveloping curtains of the morning salon to command the view of the sweep of the drive and to await and watch the arrival of the Vicomte de Valmont. My idea is that the Vicomte be dazzled by me into making a proposal of marriage and that our parents be dazzled by the much-publicised wealth of the Vicomte into dropping the comparatively less wealthy, though more high-ranking, Merteuil. I do not intend to have either of them. I hope this will be as when the rook bothers the buzzard to drop its kill, so that neither of them gets it.

To be alluring, as you know, I simply need to be visible. However, today, as special measures were called for, I decided that, to visibility, I would add complaisance; I would match my style exactly to suit M. de Valmont. If he were a man given to pontification, I would display a feminine character wholly gratified by pontificating. If he were a man given to punning, I would exhibit a character who recognises the ability to pun as being the epitome of cleverness. If he were a man given to... But I bore myself with this self-abnegating litany.

Luckily, I had put myself early in place for the gathering of intelligence as Valmont arrived one full hour before he was expected - at exactly the same time as Merteuil! It was interesting to see how a parade of wealth by a lowly Vicomte (these are relative terms) enabled him to eclipse the higher-ranking Marquis. It was not surprising that the Vicomte was making good time; he came flying up the sweep of the drive in a coach and six. Yes six! And this with four outriders and three postilions. It was a most impressive sight, not least because it was intended to be. This sight was thrown into grand relief by the foil of drabness that was Merteuil, who was lumbering up the drive on a great war-horse, presumably as no elephants were to hand. Merteuil was accompanied by only one mounted serving man. I imagine that the Vicomte's men mistook Merteuil for an inconsequential yeoman. They afforded him no room as they passed and this caused the hindquarters of his animal to slither down the banked verge, unseating its rider atop the dirt of the side of the road.

From this moment and on, Valmont outshone Merteuil. Valmont's lordly retinue occupied so very many of our footmen, grooms and servants that it was some while before any one of them noticed Merteuil's plodding arrival. In the meantime, Valmont exited his carriage, requiring the attendance of three servants to do so: the first to lower the step, the second to hand him his cane and hat, the third to offer his hand as support. It was during this manoeuvre that I got the best view of him. He is classically handsome and, in line with members of his class who have avoided consanguineous marriage, he has height, strength. symmetry and elegant proportions, consolidated by generations of good food and plentiful ease. He has dark hair, dark eyes and dark shadows to delineate the superb bones of his face. There is a whiff of the devil about him. As to his demeanour, with everyone and everything he looks unutterably bored. He strolls rather than walks. He has an athletic physique so when he strolls it appears more as if he prowls. He expends as little energy as possible and looks as if he has just attended an all-night bout of something.

Having prowled to the top of our great flight of stone stairs, he stood, just under the portico, arms outstretched, allowing a swarm of servants to divest him of his travelling layer and invest him in the garments and props of a most glamorous visitor to a country house. Our father, so overly sensible of all this importance, greeted him with a great obeisance, a bow so profound that his forehead nearly touched the floor. The Vicomte looked so tired that, as his host greeted him, he leaned his elbow momentarily, against one of the pillars. During this moment, Merteuil also arrived near the top of the stone stairway. He was ignored and unattended, dirtied from his fall, with dried leaves sticking to his wig. Valmont, suddenly espying Merteuil, from his vantage point, two steps above him, looked down upon him, aghast. His countenance taking on a look of wonder that such a muddied personage should infect his air.

Shaken by Valmont's evident disgust, our father's integrity as a host deserted him and so he failed to greet Merteuil and he sent no servants his way. With much fawning, our father ushered Valmont into the house and towards the grand salon leaving Merteuil no option but to trail dustily in his wake. At this moment I dashed also to the grand salon where I took my place in the reception line-up with our mother and Didier.

Up close, my sister, this Vicomte is yet more impressive. He is tall and has a sportive physique which is casually adorned with more silk, satin, lace, gold and gems than any woman I have met- and yet he remains violently masculine. I was put in mind of Ezekiel on Lucifer:

'You had the seal of perfection…perfect in beauty…Every precious stone adorned you: carnelian, chrysolite and emerald, topaz, onyx and jasper, lapis lazuli, turquoise and beryl. Your settings and mountings were made of gold.'

Merteuil, let us not forget, is of enormous frame, but his lurking self was thrown almost entirely into shadow by the black, glittering presence of Valmont, who, in any case, appears to be working with the shadows. Despite the darkness that gathers around Valmont, his influence operates in such a way that one is compelled constantly to be aware of him over and above any other entity at work in the room.

I have noticed that this is the essence of certain men and women and is less to do with their rank than their innate command - a command which is made up of their intelligence, confidence and ease and makes them the focus of all discerning attention. Regardless of age, sex or beauty, or any other personal charm, one's notice is drawn irresistibly to this sort of person and any comment one makes is addressed directly to them, or at least one makes it wholly mindful of them. So it is with the Vicomte. Even were Aurèle in the room, my attention would never wander for one second from an entity such as Valmont; the man is compelling in every respect.

Wonderfully, there are some people alive who are so undiscerning that they fail to recognise the latent power of such a person when in the society of him or her, with the result that they bumble around the awesome being, oblivious to all danger, like a fool in the court of majesty. These bumbling people are useful, as they provide a relief to the aura of intensity that surrounds the compelling one. They unwittingly inject an interesting comedy of foolhardiness into the heightened atmosphere of awe. It is in thinking of these foolhardy bumblers that my thoughts revolve neatly to the incident which immediately ensued, involving our mother.

Mamma, as you know, would never have been sensible as to the extra level of importance attached to such a character as Valmont had father not attempted to impress it upon her. But what our father has never understood is that the act of impressing upon our mother, due to her weak understanding, always has the reverse effect to the one he intended. In this instance he intended to impress upon her that we appear casually au fait with visits from nobility and that any changes we had made to our routine were coolly to pass for normal. What he had actually impressed upon her, however, was Fear, Confusion and Panic. Her nerves heightened almost to the point of failure.

As we stood in the grand salon in readiness to meet Valmont, our poor mother trembled discernibly and, on his deigning to manifest his glittering self before her, she twice voiced her greetings to him, twice asked him how he did, without once listening to the answer. In a disorder of thoughts, she too omitted to greet Merteuil. This incident was speedily overshadowed by what happened when the arresting Vicomte set his eyes upon me.

Naturally, I was last in the order of ceremony and naturally his reaction on viewing my exterior was extreme, as it always is when a man of fashion, pretension and discernment sets eyes upon me. Lest I sound arrogant in this matter, allow me to say in my defence that it is impossible for me to have my level of intelligence and not to notice these reactions. It would be like asking me not to notice that a tree had fallen over in front of me. Equally it is impossible for me to have this level of intelligence and not disguise my recognition of the homage paid to my beauty. Valmont's response was as gratifying as the best of them, which led me to rate him instantly as a man gifted in the ability to recognise and assess worth. He appeared genuinely shaken out of his composure and, stepping back quickly from me as if faced by a lightning bolt, he collided with one of the pieces of our father's new statuary, in fact the newly erected Roman bust, which toppled on its pedestal before crashing to the floor.

The monetary value of the bust was infinitesimal in comparison with the social cost of the collision as the reaction to this event exposed all our father's and our mother's arriviste insecurities and their inability to remain genteel under pressure. Their lack of manners and lack of breeding became horribly exposed as our father immediately flared up in an embarrassing outburst directed at our mother.

"Madame! Whatever possessed ye to have left that piece of ornamentation there, in the walkway, for all-comers to trip over ?!"

Mother made a predictably poor attempt to defend herself.

"Sir! I did not allow it to be left there! I had it most particular placed there, only this morning, by Jean and Gaston."

Father, reasonably trusting to our mother's ability further to implicate only herself, unfairly pressed the point in order to exempt himself from all blame.

"But why Madame, why? Could ye not foresee the accident that it was bound to cause?"

Mother, goaded into an uncharacteristic clarity of thought, managed to rebound the blame fairly and squarely with father. In the same encompassing sentence, she managed also to insult Merteuil.

"Dear Sir! I had it placed there by your own express wish! Do not ye remember? Ye requested that your most impressive pieces of art and sculpture be unpacked and be arranged, as if commonplace to we. Ye wished they be displayed in areas of prominence so that them could not fail to impress upon M. le Vicomte, our most illustrious guest!"

There followed a prolonged silence, wherein everyone assessed the extent of the damage. I looked at Merteuil to see how he took the insult; he seemed not to have comprehended it. I was inwardly cringing at the embarrassment of being related by blood to two people so prepared mutually to savage each other in public. I was surprised that there were not entrails upon the floor.

In the presence of outsiders, existing alongside my acute embarrassment, runs a deep and unshakable loyalty for our parents, a profound tie of blood and habit. It is this most primeval of loyalties that reminds me, in these discomfiting moments, how hard won is our parents' success and how high-strung is our father's desire to further it. For all their efforts I honour them and for all their disasters I feel for them. At this moment I wished Valmont a hundred leagues away from them.

My face remained sanguine which was lucky, for, as I checked the expression of Valmont, I realised he was amused and so I shared a moment of amity with him by allowing a flicker of amusement to animate my expression as our eyes met. Valmont was good enough to break the tension.

"And indeed, the bust has impressed upon me. I have the impression of it right here in my cheek."

He said this with great amiability which encouraged a general outlet of breath and an unclenching of Didier's and our father's and mother's (but not my) jaws and toes. Valmont took this opportunity to slouch across the room and fling himself into a sofa. Our mother, realising that he had seated himself before she had seated herself, landed quickly onto a sofa before his affront was noticed. I joined her to help mitigate his rudeness before the menfolk, and to help Mamma organise the servants. I could sense that Valmont's apparent exhaustion did not preclude that the full blast of his lazy, arrogant, attention fall upon me. I summoned an abashed mien and kept my eyes modestly on the tea dishes whilst calling up a maidenly blush. I had no need to raise my eyes having had more than enough time to study the man under whose scrutiny I fell.

Valmont has the charming, dissolute, devil-may-care face and attitude of body that engage all women and many men. I have heard a little about him from my brother and, in my opinion, his dedication to drink and high living has only enhanced his beauty. The exhausted pallor of his face and the lassitude of his manner heighten rather than lessen the masculine graces of his exterior. There is a huge attraction for me in a disposition that is prepared to lay to waste all inherited wealth of physique and money for the thrills and dangers of carousing. The masculine exclusivity of the act has its allure for me. Fascinating also is the disregard for personal safety- long and short term. All talents are sacrificed, all treated as worth not a whit. That such a sybarite should be clothed negligently in all the cloths, fibres, skins and gems of privilege, lends added charm. It appeals to me that silkworms have busied in Asia and that slaves have delved in Africa, that weavers and lace-makers have blinded themselves in Europe, that whalers have drowned in the Arctic, that merchants have perished of heatstroke across thousands of leagues of desert to scour for him these adornments. That he may wear the fruits of all these death-dealing labours so carelessly is captivating.

Our brother, meanwhile, shoved the great dolt that is Merteuil into the chair next to mine, whereupon he placed his great dirty foot upon my skirts in the manner of a plinth and column. Is that man so huge as to have lost all sense of peripheral vision? I made quite a show of gathering myself up and moving a good few inches away from him, which caused Papa to give me a look of warning. However, I needed to indicate to the Vicomte that Merteuil was not here at my behest. There followed an awkward silence, which I had to remember not to take upon myself to break. The Vicomte, seeming to take all his cues from me, was happy to follow suit. This left Merteuil, after a nudge from Didier, to hem himself up into a speech directed at me.

"Em, hem, Mademoiselle, hem, there will be a lawn-meet at my estate on Saturday, followed by a commanding view of the hunt from the hills above my house. I understand from your brother that you will be there to spectate?"

"I'm afraid you are mistaken, Sir. I have far too much sympathy for the hunted to admire the hunters."

At this, Merteuil appeared nonplussed. Valmont came strongly upon the alert, however, and sat up.

"Forgive me, Mademoiselle, but I remember your brother telling me you liked to hunt?"

I turned to him sweetly.

"Do you accuse me of inconstancy?"

"I admire inconstancy in a person; it lends light and shade to a character and keeps all around them on their toes. I simply seek to reconcile these two different claims."

"The explanation is simple. I do not like to watch other people relish a sport in which I can have no part. If I find myself cast in the role of the hunter, the intense thrill of the chase takes over, to the total disregard of my own safety. And the fox's. No one can persuade me this is not fair: I risk my life to endanger his."

I smiled enchantingly. Merteuil, father and Didier looked all aghast. Valmont looked all admiration. At this point Papa attempted to soften my speech.

"I require that Sophie no longer hunt."

Merteuil looked up in the manner of a preceptor reading from a treatise on the education of women.

"Hunting is not a suitable occupation for young ladies."

I agreed with him.

"That is why I went."

Another awkward pause ensued which Didier broke by directing the conversation to subjects that would flatter Merteuil regarding his estate and improvements. Valmont had much sport with this, and I found I needed to feign nothing to match my style to his. We are most perfectly matched in humour and irony.

Eventually, Valmont, to suppress laughter, moved over to the floor length window, the one that overlooks the sweep of the drive. Whilst he was positioned there, his elbow caused a curtain sash to dislodge, allowing the folded curtain to relax onto his oblivious shoulder. Father looked askance at me and then at the curtain as if depending upon me (above all servants) to understand that I must immediately set right the curtain before it betray him as being unable to be trusted with the manifold responsibilities of host. Smoothly and casually I arose, crossed the room and remedied the disaster. Valmont had no idea why I had arrived beside him, but he turned and smiled before reappraising the view.

On seeing a lone rider suddenly appear upon the drive I sensed his mood change and he made an ironic exclamation.

"I know that horseman! I would know that prepossessing equestrian silhouette anywhere; that is the Chevalier Aurèle!"

He turned his disdainful eye past me to Didier and our father.

"That man, what is he doing on this land? Is he a guest of your house?"

Father, sensing a sneer in his tone wavered in his answer, not knowing whether to publish Aurèle as friend or servant.

"Er. Yes. Well. No. He be not so much guest as part of the household staff. Er, here in our employ."

At this, the shadows gathered under Valmont's brow.

"How irregular! In your employ? His father is distant cousin to my father. How far he falls. Nonetheless, I had no idea that such a fellow as he were here."

At this, Valmont looked directly at me. My face, as usual, betrayed nothing. Aurèle was now in the near distance, within the bounds of the sweep of drive before the house. My eyes sought to read the expression on his face. It was as if Aurèle felt the heat of my attention. He lifted his gaze upward and directly to my window, whereupon, ignoring Valmont, he fixed his eyes solely and intently upon me, the blood rising to his handsome face. To my guilty heart his expression seemed to proclaim the full story of our passion.

Valmont turned pointedly from Aurèle to me and back to Aurèle again. His expression took on a darker look. Without a doubt he divined that Aurèle was more than usually struck by the sight of me.

I followed Valmont's cue to move away from the window. I was required to play piano. Just as I finished playing, there was an extraordinary moment where my eyes, through the looking glass, met the eyes of Valmont. What was surprising was that, due to the effect of the mirroring, I imagined, for one moment, that I was viewing myself, or should I say, the masculine version of myself.

Shortly after this epiphany, Valmont left precipitously and apparently in bad spirits.

62. THE VICOMTE DE VALMONT to M. DE BEAULIEU (sent from the LEFÈVRE ESTATE near AMIENS, 9th OCTOBER 1776)

In my current humour, I ignore your last letter to me. I have no need of a treatise from you on the subject of how to behave in a tavern. In any case, my whole tavern misadventure puts me in mind of the words of Fielding who narrates that his young hero *'would have ravished her if she had not, by timely compliance, prevented him'*.

My dear idiot fellow, I have just made my visit to the place Lefèvre. WHY and HOW did you omit to tell me that Aurèle was within her demesne?! Fool that you are! Of all the things of which you should have apprised me, that was EASILY the most important. How was it that you were educated into such ignorance of danger? Was it that our nurse, when you were a babe in arms, used to say to you *'Oh! Please arrest the flight of that runaway horse!'*

When you were a toddler did she used to say *'Please go and pet that rabid dog!'*

How is it that you did not descry the danger? That man is an out-and-out hero: golden, fearless, talented and true. How could you be so stupid as to think that his presence within a hundred leagues of that girl was not worth mentioning?! Manly as I am, I know he has personal beauty and quality enough to match mine. You know how I detest a rival!

Now, before you make the excuse that men are not formed to appreciate beauty in another man, and that therefore you did not apprise the danger, I beg you to turn your selective memory to your travels in the sites of antiquity. Remember your Michelangelo? I know you will tell me that the right hand of his '*David* 'is disproportionately large and that his eyes are slightly asquint but you cannot tell me that its creator was insensible of the beauties of the male form. Think also upon the innumerable representations of masculine beauty in the shape of Jesus on the cross, all carved by men. The rule of beauteous appeal, in relation to an idea of the norm, applies to men as well as it does to women: symmetry, proportion, shape, colour and expression. In any case, there is not much difference between the male anatomy and the female anatomy. We share more characteristics than we eschew.

Finally, my dear frère de lait, the time has come for me no longer to pretend that I have not noticed that you are equally drawn to masculine beauty as to feminine. Why do you so slavishly serve me, for example? I have noticed that you speak evasively whenever conversation turns to anecdotes of romantic encounter. I have noticed that you evince more than especial horror of the punishment of the crime of sodomy by burning. You will know that you may trust me not to abuse my power over you in relation to my knowledge of your sexual preference as never before have I apprised you of my understanding of it. As a matter of principle, it does not agree with me that people be punished mortally for experimenting in love. In any case, I am nothing if not a logician and opportunist and so I too wish I could find it in myself to double my field of play as do you.

Is it this, rather than your generalised ineptitude, that is the reason you have failed to warn me of the presence of Aurèle? Is it because you adore to be around him and have your revering eye rest upon his extraordinary beauty? Were you afraid I would make efforts to have him evicted from her and therefore your presence?

As it happens I have no time to terrify you further on this subject as, due to your taciturnity, I now have a much more pressing matter to consider: I have the impression that there might already be a dangerous connection between Aurèle and Sophie! I cannot explain why or how I feel this. I saw that some major turmoil was writ large across the face of Aurèle as he glanced her way. I demand of you now, with all urgency, to reveal to me if those two associate with each other in any special way. I now mistrust you on three counts: ineptitude, indisposition, idleness.

However, I must thank you for giving me intelligence of the optimum time for my arrival and for absenting yourself. Despite the family suggesting a time for my arrival one full hour after that of Merteuil, because of your information, I contrived to make an early appearance designed to eclipse his.

On the steps of the place I encountered Merteuil. What a bumpkin that man is; how does he contrive to have so little wealth on show? My equipage alone ensured that all attention was centred solely upon me. And yet, all my plans to overawe were completely laid at nought upon meeting with Sophie. Really! Should not I, more than anyone, have been prepared for that moment and been equal to it? Has not my whole life been training me to meet that sublime being with perfect equanimity? I am a connoisseur of beauty and refinement. I am sated with beauty having viewed it from every conceivable angle, circumstance, continent and country. Yet I found myself discountenanced.

It was your inability to articulate her beauty that led you insufficiently to warn me. I should have taken the hint from the young Comte who killed himself; I assumed he was being melodramatic. Now I vindicate him entirely; I could kill myself happily for her right now and possibly, in the fullness of time, I will. I ask you, however, with two such parents, where did she get that shape, that look of nobility, fire and melting sweetness? But, most particularly, where did she get that lustre and that sheen? How did two base metals produce an alloy of such luxurious vibrancy? Truly, it is an extraordinary quirk of nature that has fashioned her from them, or was some faery princeling deceived into visiting himself upon the mother?

So arresting did I find her that the first shaft from her languorous eye blast me to the core of my soul. She is perfectly, violently beautiful. I say 'violently' because, in this age of honour-duelling, immediately upon seeing her one has an idea of the legions of men one must overcome in getting her, keeping her and defending one's right to her against all-comers. Also, 'violently ', because there is a melting challenge in her glance, as if, from awareness of the extreme scale of her beauty, her eyes ask of you *'There! What are you going to do about that?'*

So, as I said, the sight of her impacted upon me as if to pin me against the nearest wall. I was knocked backwards, causing a collision with some piece of statuary or other. The thing tottered mildly on its pedestal, where, but for some malevolent daemon, it should have remained. However, defying Da Vinci's law of surfaces relative to motion, it toppled and smashed into extravagant motes upon the marble floor. In my opinion I did Lefèvre a monstrous favour; the thing looked better that way. In their anxiety to spare themselves any share of the blame for the positioning of the object, the parents immediately eviscerated themselves before me in a frenzy of recrimination and counter-recrimination, which placed them beyond hope of being able to pass in good society.

I was just beginning to wonder how long these vulgar people would be prepared publicly to tear themselves to pieces when I realised how embarrassing this must be for the maiden. I looked across at her only to discover how serenely her expression sat with the event and, since I could only have been embarrassed on her account, I decided I may as well relax and enjoy the comedy. This incident afforded me my first moment of unity with Sophie as we shared a glance of mutual regard. But seriously, how is it that the first look of that young woman caused such mayhem within my brain? Are not we men primed mentally for war and devilry? Are we not bred to walk calmly into the bursts of gunfire? Why is it that, sufficient light reflecting into our eye, conveying to us the beauty of a young woman, causes our self-command to be blasted to atoms?!

I steadied my thoughts by allowing my eye further to delight in the paintings hanging on the yellow sateen walls of Lefèvre place (bad copies of Greuze and Robert?)- and a few swagger portraits of Didier. No other ornamentation around. Really, this family is priceless.

Once we were all seated having our dish of tea, the father, in one last attempt to relieve the tension of the accident, decided to let me know that he has so many *objets d'art* that he minds not if a few of them be smashed. His silly wife, picking up but faintly on the gist of his meaning, contributed to this idea in order to further it.

"Yes," she said, "M. Lefèvre be equally easy with all of it. I often overhear his curator saying he do not know his *'Fragonard'* from his fragrance or his *'Boucher'* from his butcher!"

She followed up this rebounding attempt at promotion with a gay stream of laughter, until, noticing the chagrined silence emanating from M. Lefèvre, she ended it quickly with a faint cough. At this point the brother decided he must push Merteuil forward once more.

"Dear Marquis," he began, "pray tell, how are you getting on with the re-designing of your river?"

Merteuil, prompted to speech, looked out of his depth. Even his mouth moved awkwardly with the effort to form whole sentences.

"Oh. Well. Yes. Saw that my neighbour went to the huge expense of hiring a disciple of Argenville, to create a naturalised vista. This disciple had him re-direct his river to pass more fully before his great house. And so, I decided to do the thing on my own land myself. Re-directing the river I mean. To save the expense of Argenville design."

"And where did you put the river?" asked my lovely girl, sweetly, as if she were talking about the removal of a sewing basket.

"Oh. Well. I didn't like some cottages. They could be seen from the château and so I widened the river to take in where they were. Obliterated them."

"And what did you do with the cottagers?" Sophie asked, exactly chiming her question with my sense of the ridiculous.

"Oh. Well. The cottagers. Not sure where they ended up."

I couldn't resist continuing my beauty's line of enquiry.

"In the river maybe?"

Do you know, that lovely girl actually raised her heavenly eyes to mine, delighted with my silly joke at Merteuil's expense. A short laugh escaped her, a reward for my wit, that felt like a thousand louis.

Merteuil did not understand that we were laughing at him.

"No. Seriously. The cottagers haven't been missed. Just an ancien, an old retainer of mine. And, in the other cottage, a young widow with a mewling mound of children."

This comment drew those dark eyes of hers briefly to mine again, luring me once more to parody Merteuil.

"Oh indeed! Maybe they have removed to the woods? And living feral they would be far more in the picturesque style! I had rather see a bunch of wild-eyed gypsy children tumbling about in the loam with their young barefoot mother than a group of stuffy cottagers, suited and booted and trooping off to vespers."

"And what about the old man?" my beauty asked, more to me than to Merteuil.

I obliged her of course.

"There again! A hermit in a woodland cave is a far more interesting object than an old man slowly turning green in a cottage."

Once more, my beauty looked about to giggle. Never have I felt such gratification. Her irresistible smiles caused laughter also to rise in me, especially as her brother looked so confounded as to whether he minded my bonhomie with his sister or not. To quash my urge to laugh I moved over to the window where, in the middle distance, a cure for my hilarity hoved into view in the unmistakable shape of an undoubted rival to Sophie's attentions. I knew the man instantly to be Aurèle. No one else looks as he does when mounted. In that moment, all my geniality vanished. My mind was instantly full of alarm, *'Whatever is Aurèle doing in this région?'*

I wished him straight to hell and the devil. He rode between the gates which mark the entrance to the final sweep of the drive and headed for the steps of the main portico, a route which caused him to pass directly before the window of the grand salon where I stood in full view. At that moment, as if each sensed the presence of the other, Sophie was drawn to the window whereupon Aurèle, of a sudden, seemed impelled to lift his eyes to meet hers.

I have played the games of love since my youth. I have a genius for these games, and I can tell you that never before have I seen such a look of fierce, open, passion as I saw on the face of Aurèle during those moments. I did not need to turn to the girl to know that the beams of his eyes had entwined fully with hers. And yet, turn I did, in sudden fear, in order to read her expression. Unmistakably, despite the slight, courteous inclination of her head towards Aurèle, I read a look of disdain in her eye and my heart was made easy; no matter that the man loves the girl- the girl loves not the man.

By the time I had composed myself sufficiently to turn away from the window, her deplorable brother had started up another attempt to engage Merteuil with her.

"Sister! M. le Marquis de Merteuil has said, many a time, that he would like to hear you play at the pianoforte."

She answered decisively.

"I am tired, brother; if the Marquis can spare me, I would prefer not to."

"But M. de Merteuil has particularly asked that you oblige him."

"I do not wish to play."

Here, oblivious to the mounting tension in the room, the mother unwittingly escalated this argument.

"And how about the Vicomte? Would he like to hear our Sophie play?"

I am sure she hoped I would settle the matter by agreeing with Merteuil, but my response was designed to compound her mistake.

"Mademoiselle Sophie has said she is tired and so absolutely she must not play."

And so there! That fantastic old matron had, once more, precipitated the whole family into a crisis. The family would now have to arbitrate. Either they must offend me and have Sophie play, or they must offend Merteuil and have her not play. Which would terrify them the most, an insult to me or an insult to him? I was agog. I guessed that here was, in miniature, how the marriage choice might play out. A few agonising seconds passed while Merteuil spluttered, Didier looked cowardly and the mother looked from person to person, as though she were just realising that something was amiss. Sophie, brave girl, risking wrath, made the next move.

"Out of consideration for M. le Vicomte de Valmont's consideration for me, I will not play."

She looked directly at Merteuil.

"I am sure M. le Marquis de Merteuil would rather not oblige me to do something I had no wish to do."

Merteuil displayed surprising tactical know how. Well, that, or thuggery.

"Some young ladies play better when they are tired."

He looked directly at old Lefèvre as he said this. M. Lefèvre, aware that all onus lay with himself and aware that, one way or another, he would offend nobility, was unable to prevent his exasperation from boiling over. Losing all his little composure, he blustered.

"For God's sake daughter play. And make sure ye play well."

At that moment I surmised the Lefèvre:Merteuil pairing to be his preferred option. If this were the case, it would be the worst for Sophie. I was truly crushed. The loss of a fine spirit such as hers would pain me most keenly. I played the part of injured pride. I should have walked out on them all, but to see Sophie play was irresistible to me. She chose the saddest piece, a piece of Purcell. Technically it was not difficult, but she played it with real feeling. I wanted to watch every second of her but I had to take the part of offended nobility and so I turned my back on the scene, knowing that I could watch her through a mirror. Those lasting moments were truly poignant. I felt genuinely moved.

As the piece closed, the silence hung in the air as if the music had revealed all to all. She shut the lid on the keys and inexplicably raised her eyes to the mirror and met with my unguarded gaze. A clarity and calmness of thought shines from her. She seemed unruffled, heroic, equal to any situation. We exchanged one brief look of perfect understanding wherein our spirits recognised each other as equals.

Turning my thoughts back to the matter in hand I decided that, for now, my task regarding this young woman was done. I returned to my flippant self.

"Well, I am afraid I must break up this sorry tableau and have your valets show me and my valets immediately to my apartments."

Having already accustomed the family to the singularity of my manners I made one slight obeisance serve for them all and strode from the room, thus throwing Lefèvre, matron Lefèvre and Didier into a frenzy of worry that they had mortally offended me. I made sure that the housing of my equipage, my men and myself in their home took up all their own servants' energies for the rest of the afternoon, and I prided myself that their salon would feel empty without me.

63. THE CHEVALIER AURÈLE to ISABELLE AURÈLE (sent from the LEFÈVRE ESTATE near AMIENS, 9th OCTOBER 1776)

My dearest sister, my beloved parents, I write in confidence as ever. My love for Mademoiselle Sophie is reaching a point of infatuation. I am in danger of making a fool of myself over her. Today, on my return from my continued search for Madame la Chevalière d'Ivry, because of my fever for Sophie, I was self-persuaded to turn my horse up the sweep of the drive to the front of the house rather than via one of the back lanes to the stable yard. Against all my better judgement I did this, hoping for a glimpse of her.

    I got what I desired but in such a way as to make me wish I had not. There, framed by one of the vast windows, were Sophie and that most dangerous of men, Valmont.

    Immediately, I fell sick with apprehension; you know as well as I that he is a threat to women. In this era, where many people of our class give themselves great latitude with regard to their morality, he is unique. He delights to prey on the innocent; he delights to make public a slip or an indiscretion of the not-so-innocent. Luring and exposing women to censure and banishment is his sport. My head and heart pounded to see that such a man had been added to the venomous company surrounding Sophie.

    I had a moment of realisation that likely it had been Valmont's pending arrival that had provided the impetus for my banishment from Lefèvre society. Nonetheless, I raised my eye direct to hers. As is usual when I perceive her, my heart caught fire. I felt my passion for her blaze across my face, commixed with my anger at the injustice of *me* being barred from *their* company in favour of *him!* In return, from her, I received the blankest of stares. Doubtless she is swayed by him already. It is imperative, therefore, that I warn her about him should he be due to stay in the house tonight. Either that, or I will sleep on the floor directly outside the door of her bedchamber. I am banned from their presence but whenever he shall place himself in her company, so shall I.

I rode, flaming with anger to the stable yard, ignoring the Valmont grooms but intending to ask the grooms of the Lefèvre household what the purpose of his visit might be. However, I have always found it impossibly low to ask questions of servants about their masters and so I left that yard with no intelligence at all.

I was left to painful and wearing conjecture. What was she doing at the window with him? I had noticed also the sole Merteuil groom in the yard but surely even the crass Lefèvre style could not run two Sophie-suitor visits in parallel?

If Valmont is to stay the night, he will have a letter delivered to him, from me, via one of his retinue.

Both he and Sophie must be warned. I will send one a letter of-warning and the other a warning off.

64. THE CHEVALIER AURÈLE to the VICOMTE DE VALMONT (hand delivered within the LEFÈVRE ESTATE near AMIENS, 9th OCTOBER 1776)

I have no idea what schemes bring you here, but may I let you know that dishonouring Mademoiselle Sophie will not be one of them. I will ensure that for every night you are here, I will station myself at one end of her corridor and my man at the other.

If I catch you preying on her, I will kill you.

65. THE CHEVALIER AURÈLE to SOPHIE LEFÈVRE (hand delivered within the LEFÈVRE ESTATE near AMIENS, 9th OCTOBER 1776)

The Vicomte de Valmont is not a man to be trusted. For every night of his stay in this house, please ensure that your maid sleeps in your room, that your door is locked and that only you or Madame Lefèvre has access to the key. Although it is true that I am jealous of all male attention towards you, in this case my fear is not unreasonable.

66. SOPHIE LEFÈVRE to HÉLÈNE, the CHEVALIÈRE D'IVRY (sent from the LEFÈVRE ESTATE near AMIENS, 9th OCTOBER 1776)

I have had a letter passed to me via my maid, Victoire; it's from Aurèle who believes Valmont has dishonourable intentions towards me. This I find unthinkable, as it assumes that M. de Valmont would value me cheap.

On the other hand, I find myself in the unimaginable situation of being unable to tell whether I have made 'a conquest' of M. de Valmont or not. I saw him recognise every ounce of my worth, but how far that will carry me with him I do not know.

From the vantage point of my childhood, I watched the manners and the behaviours of the people who came into our home and who were at the convent. I made it my work to find out how they think. Never have I met an entity such as Valmont. He operates from behind so many layers of irony that only rarely must his true state of mind be glimpsed. It is true that he appeared thunderstruck by my appearance, but a good actor easily could pull off that effect.

He has the bored air of a man who has already lived his life fifty times over, so that his heart never can be surprised or exposed. He appears to have played himself out, maybe beyond recovery. He has an air that nothing and no-one can be a novelty to him, that for far too long he has been part of a set for whom falling in love is considered a joke, the amatory equivalent of falling down a drain. For this sort of man, I can imagine that the state of being in love is considered derisory: a ridiculous expenditure of effort, a heated emotion that would make him the laughing-stock of his fellows. Since his early youth I imagine he has studied to condition himself out of all idea of tenderness.

Valmont puts me in mind of the men who do not marry until they are agèd as only when their powers are failing do they allow themselves to make a genuine (if calculated) return of affection (but only with a woman a lot younger than are they). For all these reasons it would be a mistake now to marry such a person as Valmont. Since a woman must deliver so much of her being and her destiny over to her husband's keeping, she must be, if not master of him, a more subtle operator than him. No one will be master of, or more subtle than Valmont. Even I could not because, although my powers may equal his, a woman must far surpass a man to compensate for the unlevel bias in the struggle of the sexes.

We are one and the same, Valmont and I. We both know too much, and we see too much. We see right through to the core of a person's soul. From this vantage point we can weigh up and weigh into a person's heart within seconds.

Do you remember your Homer my sister?

'Come then, put away your sword in its sheath, and let us two go up into my bed so that, lying together in the bed of love, we may have faith and trust in each other.'

I know that this is how it would be: Valmont and I, set against a clashing background from the continual laying down and taking up of weaponry. Never would we reach the Homeric ideal. Never would we sheath our swords. We would be too aware of each other's powers ever truly to relax. The honeymoon period would be all too self-conscious and brief. Neither of us would be able to reach a state of bliss or abandonment with the other because of the fear of appearing derisory. Our mutual awareness of the discernment of the other would ensure that neither one of us would drop our guard. The competitiveness of each character would mean that neither one would reveal vulnerability or gentleness to the other, neither one would allow a hurt to go unavenged and the pride of neither one would allow an accession of defeat. All too soon love and passion would sink, and a prideful struggle for supremacy would begin. The only outcome of this sorry state would be a prolonged and vicious war to some sort of bitter end.

I know this from my convent-girl friendships: those whose minds are fiercely penetrative, as are his and mine, must pair only with the innocent. Although the innocent are like lambs to our slaughter, it is only our appreciation of their innocence that tempers our capacity for cruelty. Only the innocent provide us with respite from our ironical posturing. Although we never cease to abuse the trust of these innocents, at least there is a limit to our abuse, for, in deference to their *naïvité* we soften to them and show them mercy. Then, when we tire of them, the final rupture, although bloody, is quick and decisive for the gentleness of our victims prevents them from struggling with us.

Therefore, my worldly pairing ought to lie with Aurèle. His great, honest, faithful soul would act as the antidote and the balm to my deadly, all-seeing eye, my penetrating wit. Our union of opposites would endure; but for his poverty I would be with him. Because of my love for him, I try to reconcile myself to poverty, but then I recall the faces, the figures and the health of impoverished women and I remember that poverty, in the peerless form of Aurèle, cannot be visited upon me. If one day I can make a haven against destitution with you, my dear sister, and if Aurèle may make a living, then I hope, with all my heart, that he and I will come together again.

Sister, I must attempt to use Valmont to knock Merteuil out of the running. This is my only chance to leave the field clear. Our family has already slighted Merteuil for Valmont and maybe can be manoeuvred into slighting him some more.

67. THE VICOMTE DE VALMONT to M. DE BEAULIEU (sent from the LEFÈVRE ESTATE near AMIENS, 9th OCTOBER 1776)

A letter has been delivered to me from that sanctimonious Chevalier Aurèle via my valet. He thinks he has the power to limit my behaviour. I do not know why he wasted the ink on it. He is correct in his assumption that my stratagem works toward a wildly unsanctified liaison with Sophie. I will have her any which way. At present, however, I see no way to it without her full co-operation. This household bristles with men.

Regardless of these men, should Aurèle cross me again, I will spill his blood.

Now I update you on the matter of my anxiety about Sophie's attentions to Aurèle. I have mentally reprised the scene wherein they viewed each other and have satisfied myself that Sophie did not show one whit of interest in our golden hero as he entered her line of vision. I am sure his lack of wealth has rendered him invisible to her, as it should to any young woman with an eye to the main chance. And yet, and yet, and yet…is it possible that she can see that man and remain unmoved?

(Later) I have been sleeping and so I open this letter in the early hours. My mind is in a tumult and has woken me with the fleetest impression, the briefest glimpse, the merest sentiment that, as Sophie produced her look of disdain towards Aurèle, a pulse arose in her neck. I can picture the pulse now, though I took no notice of it at the time. It was excited, elevated. It betrayed significant agitation.

You must help me, Beaulieu. There is, beyond all doubt, an understanding of sorts between Sophie and Aurèle. It is an early understanding, however, as surely she would have tutored him thoroughly in dissimulation (although I imagine, in this discipline, Aurèle would prove impenetrably obtuse). His face told the story of their passion. He cannot disguise it, but she can. It was foolish of me to put my faith in her assumed mien; her blood gave her away.

Beaulieu, lax as you have been in this affair, I demand that on your return you uncover their secret. There is some way in which she is communing with him. No longer can I support incompetence from you. I had felt secure in my ability to establish pre-eminence with Sophie but now I am subject to fear. You must watch her, follow her and find her out. If you fail me in this, I swear I will make you regret it.

68. M. DE BEAULIEU to the VICOMTE DE VALMONT (sent from the HOSTELLERIE LE ST. CHRISTOPHE near AMIENS, 10th October 1776)

My dear frère de lait, where is your poise? Where is your irony? Where has fled your savoir-faire? I had not thought it possible that you show me the white of your eye and the sweat of your brow. I must request that you restore yourself to your fullest attitude of devil-may-care. Please adopt toward me your usual tone of raillery; it does not sit well with you to exhibit fear. I feel discomfited, like the dog when his master is ill. I had not thought ever to see you in this humour.

I am your slave. Although I do not approve of your stratagems, rest assured, I will do everything in my power to spring the secret of Sophie and Aurèle. I do not believe there is a secret to spring and so I say this to please you. I am spurred by the conviction that I will only recover my equilibrium when badinage be restored to your tone.

I remain here at the tavern until you tell me otherwise. I am agape at how this place discommodes one: the innkeeper is rapacious; the horses litter everywhere while the ostlers look on with blank stares; the beds are hung with dank sheets; the mattresses are laid on paillasses of straw, not feathers; the soup is broiled to extinction; the ceilings are so low as to disarrange one's coiffure at every turn.

I imagine the ceilings are unlofty because these places have been built by people who have attained un-extravagant height by not dining regularly on the heart and liver of venison. But did they not foresee that their clientele would have?

The barmaid appears to have taken your advice and has left this place.

69. SOPHIE LEFÈVRE to HÉLÈNE the CHEVALIÈRE D'IVRY (sent from the LEFÈVRE ESTATE near AMIENS, 10th OCTOBER 1776)

My darling sister, today at breakfast Aurèle and M. de Valmont set out to slaughter each other.

I will set the scene.

I arrived at the dining hall and walked across the expanse of marble to greet Valmont and our brother who were already present and stood by the sideboard. On the way in, I passed two footmen who were stationed at either side of the grand entrance. No servant was by the table to serve us and so we set about filling our dishes ourselves.

I cannot recollect how Aurèle entered the room; he must have entered via a servant-door. Of a sudden, he appeared at my left elbow, placing his person between mine and those of Valmont and my brother. Without any ado, he set about helping me to fill my dish. He seemed relaxed and uttered all the polite forms of greeting to Didier, Valmont and me, as he ought.

I cast a sidelong glance at him. He seemed perfectly at ease.

I was not at ease, however. Whenever this nobleman comes within my sphere, my heart pounds. Added to this I was violently aware of the bad blood between him and the other two gentlemen in the room. I held my breath as I waited to see how the three young men would behave. I was aware that I was the source of their problem with each other and, briefly, I wondered whether I ought to flee the room thus lowering the stakes for all. As is usual, however, I did nothing.

There fell an awful and prolonged silence.

Neither Valmont nor our brother returned Aurèle's greeting.

Finally, Didier said, "What are you doing here? You are banned from this place!"

To which Valmont replied to Didier, "Do you need this person removed?"

At this moment, Aurèle span away from me and I had a blinding presentiment that he was committed to murder. His movement, though lightning quick, to me appeared slowed expressly to demonstrate his moment by moment fluidity. The low October sun slanted through the window outlining his form and the positioning of the carving knives on the table. My mind raced, capturing each millisecond of his movement, so that I could appraise and admire him in motion. As he span around, Aurèle extended his right hand towards the deadliest carving-knife mid-table. I was sure this knife was beyond his grasp, but it appeared to leap to his palm as his hand swept near it. As the knife connected with his hand, he flipped it over, the better to wield it. His body swung round in an arc of power and grace to face Valmont. Aurèle's leonine mane followed the same trajectory. The movement of his right hand sliced through the air, straight to the throat of Valmont in an action so quick, so silent, so economical that my eyes could hardly believe what they saw, not least because in the same lightning moment Valmont also flourished a glittering knife at the throat of Aurèle. The balance of power, height, breadth and intent between these two young warriors seemed perfect, as was the detailing of light and shade. I have no doubt that these two astounding creatures would have drawn the knife across each other's jugular had not the form of our mother appeared between the doors opened by the footmen.

At her moment of arrival, Didier screamed "Dieu! Maman!"

And I said, "Gentlemen, Madame Lefèvre is arrived."

As duelling is illegal, the two young noblemen put down their knives, let go of each other's throats and endeavoured to assume an air of equanimity. Our mother reached the table. She could not fail to be struck by something in the air between Valmont and Aurèle, but, as usual, she misconstrued it.

"Ye two splendid young men must have vastly much in common, what with being noble and all! Did ye know each other from the University? How fortunate that ye be both here at the same time! What do ye plan to do today? Do ye hunt? Do ye ride out together? Do ye pit your horses and your hounds against each other's? I expect ye two will get up to all sorts of japes!"

Mamma beamed myopically from one to the other whilst a vast silence opened up between us all and whilst each man endeavoured to wipe a snarl from his face.

Father rescued the situation by entering at the far side of the room with an entourage of more young men: lawyer, steward, and clerk. Aurèle disappeared as silently has he had appeared. Doubtless, even for Aurèle, there were too many witnesses about to continue his violence.

When I examine my feelings as to this skirmish, I discover that in a dire situation I remain utterly calm. I do not know whether this is because I care only for myself and so I cannot work up anxiety about people in peril around me – even Aurèle. Or simply, I have spent so long watching men with agency and myself without, that I cannot feel I have anything to do.

70. THE CHEVALIER AURÈLE to ISABELLE AURÈLE (sent from THE ESTATE LEFVRE, Amiens 10TH OCTOBER 1776)

My dearest sister, I am losing my head. I am sure we have already decided that it is best that I do not go about killing people in front of Sophie. But today, once again, I nearly did just that. This time my victim was Valmont. He is a Vicomte and all-round villain but, despite compelling temptation, the very last thing I should do is get myself imprisoned over his death.

For my sanity, I must get away from this crazed place and calm down. As soon as the danger to Sophie has passed, I will do this.

God – how I adore her!

71. ISABELLE AURÈLE to the CHEVALIER AURÈLE (sent from PARIS, 11th OCTOBER 1776)

My darling brother, we worry about you. You take up with dreadfully circumstanced horses and with dreadfully circumstanced women. You need to break yourself of this habit. It is not one that can bring you peace or happiness. Hot as is your passion for this young woman, we implore you to find a lover who is free of encumbrances and danger.

Do not longer involve yourself in the dreadful forces surrounding Mademoiselle Sophie, we entreat you! No more contact. No more dialogue. No more letters! You said you would leave! Now leave!

72. THE VICOMTE DE VALMONT to M. DE BEAULIEU (sent from the LEFÈVRE ESTATE near AMIENS, 11ᵗʰ OCTOBER 1776)

My dear Beaulieu, I vastly endangered my freedom today by bringing myself to the point of sluicing the pestilential blood of Aurèle into Lefèvre's Limoges breakfast dishes. I found myself doing this in front of the assembled Lefvre household! Had I completed this action, I would have occasioned a change of tablecloth, and then, to avoid the law, I would have had to flee this country.

I ought, therefore, to defer the inconsequential death of Aurèle to a less public moment. Even though the heart-stopping beauty of Sophie makes any risk worth taking.

Beaulieu, I am torn in pieces over her. I'm just like the Saint Hippolytus who was pulled apart by horses. I'm torn by conflicting decisions over my beauty: I want to marry Sophie; I do not want to marry Sophie; I worry that it is too late to marry Sophie; I wonder if I can make off with Sophie; I wish I had never met Sophie.

I am sure that the various people of antiquity who have been torn apart, suffered less than I, even though it is likely that they had a jeering crowd to accompany their torture. Just imagine the comments thrown at you from the side-lines as you wait for your attendants to attach each of your legs and arms to a horse. It would be like the chanting of the school playground.

"Nerr, nerr, nee, nerr!"

As I was saying, I want that girl enough to marry her and yet, Dieu! Marriage! Her family! I can already hear the jeering.

"Nerr, nerr, nee, nerr, nerr!"

I would become the laughing-stock of all.

Therefore, as Lefèvre has no water garden for me to drown myself in, I have to find an alternative cure for Sophie. I depart the Lefèvre house tonight for the tavern. I am not in the mood for company. Do ensure you have vacated the hostellerie before I arrive there. You must return to the Lefèvre estate.

If you dare to make the faintest hint that I remove to the inn because you believe me fearful of Aurèle, I will add you to my list of people to drop.

(Later) I have had time to calm myself. I have decided that I must reprise my original plan and seize Sophie for myself. My job now, therefore, is twofold. Firstly, I must persuade the young Lefèvre to banish Aurèle from her home. Aurèle is armed and alive to my machinations; he will get in my way. Secondly, I must convince Old Lefèvre to drop Merteuil. I would rather carry her off alive than dead.

My friend, I wish that you arrive here and arrange a drinking session for us both and Didier, for tomorrow night. I will make an entrance after supper. Make sure you are present for this meeting. I need your help to diminish the reputation of Aurèle. I do not want to arrive and be told you have fallen asleep or that you have gone star-gazing with the boot-boy. For privacy, it is necessary that our meeting be held in young Lefèvre's apartments at the Lefèvre home. Didier may have other plans, but he will change them for me. It will be a bonus if I can get a letter passed to Sophie. I wish to let her know that I will do my best to break her away from Merteuil. I want her to know I do not forget her. She will understand. She has the capacity to understand everything. Your meagre faculties will be stretched to outwit her. Find out how she communicates with Aurèle. Do not disappoint me.

As regards Old Lefèvre, I will sue my business with him later by letter.

73. M. DE BEAULIEU to the VICOMTE DE VALMONT (sent from the HOSTELLERIE LE ST. CHRISTOPHE near AMIENS, 11th OCTOBER 1776)

My arrogant friend, ever since the Sorbonne where you discovered you were unable to assert supremacy over Aurèle (in any field except wealth) you have imagined yourself to have a problem with him. Like many of your notions this was a selfish one. You two, in every arena, were the over-lords of talent: fencing, equestrianism, mathematics, music, the sciences, latin and personal beauty (as adjudged by female attention).

The balance of power between the two of you was even. This is whence your problem with him derives, because you like to reign supreme.

In the matter of serious female intent, however, you forget how important a part wealth plays. In the field of wealth against Aurèle, you are out-and-out the winner.

You have nothing to fear from Sophie with regards to Aurèle. I have watched her with the jealous eye of a lover (albeit, a hopeless lover). She accords him not one jot of attention. You may be doubly assured that when I watch Sophie with Aurèle it renders me doubly vigilant. As you so rightly deduce, I am enthralled by them both.

I have no desire to see you tonight either so I will vacate this foul auberge as you suggest. Tomorrow night, in the company of young Lefèvre, will be soon enough for my eye to fall once more upon your dark symmetry.

74. SOPHIE LEFÈVRE to HÉLÈNE, the CHEVALIÈRE D'IVRY (sent from the LEFÈVRE ESTATE near AMIENS, 12th OCTOBER 1776)

Dearest Sister, we have been surprised late this night by the re-arrival of Valmont! Three days after his morning visit, he disappeared unaccountably. We were all left in limbo, gazing at each other as if to say 'Quoi?'

And now, he has reappeared! There was every indication he would return as all his servants and horses are still housed and stabled here. It was only as this night approached that I heard horsemen arrive and then I viewed him being greeted at the steps of the house by our brother and Beaulieu.

Whilst they were occupied with all the honours of arrival, I ran to hide myself in the alcove of the unused doorway of Didier's apartments, the opportunity for intelligence gathering being too great to miss. The three men settled quickly to drinking, with Valmont's opening subject for discourse being as I had guessed.

"Didier, my dear Fellow!" he cried, all chumminess and bonhomie, "Why ever do you associate with Aurèle? Always a laughing-stock when he was at the University, surely, he can be of no use to you now you are in your final year? Never more can he or his family hope to wage a place in society. Truly they have crashed out of it: no château, no equipage, no servants to speak of, all the family treasures taken by injunctions. His stock has plummeted. It is dangerous to be around such people. There is a contagion in these matters."

From my viewpoint, through a crack in the door, I could see Didier bluster. I surmised he did not want to admit his need for Aurèle's tutelage.

"But, but, his family is ancient and noble. You said yourself, his father is distant cousin to your father."

"Blood is no good without money. Without money there is a certain vestigial status but no influence whatever. Influence can be bought, but only with money."

"Oh," said Didier.

"Get rid of him," said Valmont. "Failure is catching."

There was a silence broken only by Valmont who appeared not to want to leave the subject alone.

"Do you remember what a ridiculous figure Aurèle cut at the university?"

Didier once more looked confused, as if he wanted to agree with Valmont but as if his experience of Aurèle were too awe-inspiring to be termed ridiculous.

"Um. I remember he was the best scholar in our year."

"My God yes!" said Beaulieu. "Prodigious scholar!"

Here, my sister, I noticed that Valmont gave Beaulieu a stern look. Beaulieu hastily qualified his comment.

"But he had to work like a slave for his success. Always at his books."

Valmont still seemed displeased with the way the conversation was going.

"Yes, yes, yes, but I'm not here to talk about that. I mean, do you remember the scrapes he used to get himself into? Such a fool! It seemed that whenever he wasn't on his arse studying, or on his knees worshipping, he would be out trying to effect some chivalrous deed or other, regardless of whether it was wanted or not!"

Beaulieu smiled.

"Do you remember when he was in his final year and we told him that two scholars had entrapped the sister of a fellow student in their rooms? He smashed his way in, fought off the two young men, rescued the damsel and carried her away to safety before she was able to point out to him that she was the newly widowed, young mother of those two scholars and had arrived to tell them of their elderly father's death."

Valmont picked up the tale.

"Then and there he fell in love with her. Regularly used to dine with her and her sons. Some while later, got down on one knee. Offered her his hand in marriage."

Beaulieu's smiles turned to laughter.

"She turned him down! Told him he was too young. She liked him though. Sent him a case of wine from her cellar at the beginning of every term."

Valmont interrupted quickly.

"Do you remember when that other scholar gave him that vicious horse? The animal had been so mismanaged it had turned lethal. Aurèle spent weeks with the horse, buying its feed over and above his own feed, working hour upon hour to gentle it. When he won that race on it, the scholar claimed it back. There was a lawsuit. Cost Aurèle hundreds. Now he's embroiled over his head with the money lenders. Lost the suit, lost the horse, lost all the money he didn't have. The day he gave the horse back it turned vicious again and was destroyed. Aurèle wept for weeks. Shut himself up in the college chapel and prayed for its soul in heaven."

Didier laughed inordinately at this story. But I noticed that Beaulieu's laughter was subdued. Eventually Valmont spoke.

"I heard he challenged that scholar to a duel! A Duel! Over a dead horse! Most students fight over gaming or money or women, not dead animals!"

Didier was still laughing.

"Has he ever been with a woman?"

Beaulieu chose to answer this. I noticed he did so in respectful tones.

"There is a rumour. It remains a rumour as he will divulge nothing. She was like the horse, a rescue case, an older woman who had been unhappily married but had escaped. A raging beauty. Aurèle found her and restored her to her friends. By then he had lost his heart. After the death of her husband, their love would have ended in marriage. He would have forgiven her single, original fall (the liaison that had broken her from her husband) but he found out she had been complicit in some other vices of vanity: attention seeking, flirtations- even to the point of initiation. Aurèle was bereft. She threw all her influence over him, but he would not have her. Now it is said he will have none but one true love, in the form of a wife."

Valmont snorted with derision.

"Oh, spare me! Do not tell me. He is saving himself for the right woman!"

Didier said, "You forget he is devout."

I crept away. I went straight to my chamber avoiding all areas where servants might see me. I could feel the blood surging furiously through the veins in my wrists and temple. I was moved to a passionate hatred of these self-serving scions of the rich. Unfair treatment of the innocent by bigots turns me into a bigot-hating, bigot.

In my apartment, I pondered Aurèle further and found an irksome query: why did he reject a woman he loved? His attitude towards the fallen woman was uncompromising. I felt sure there could have been more to her story. Maybe she had no option but to operate in the shady area between vice and excusable folly. The fact that Aurèle could be so uncompromising as to override his passion and reject her, might suggest a wilful refusal to recognise the nuances in a given situation. And another thing, why would he reject all love but one true love? Why does a person save themselves for one perfect soul? There is no perfect being. These are impossible ideals.

I was led to ponder Aurèle again. Is it stupid always to reveal one's feeling as he does, there written in his blood, close under the surface of the skin of his face, for all to see? Is the key to Aurèle that he be academically and physically accomplished but in all other ways foolish, the reverse of le sauvage savant:le sophist stupide?

I wondered then whether my questioning of the character of Aurèle, had arisen as the result of a primaeval impulse to herd, a wish to side with the high-status and favoured (in this case Valmont and Beaulieu) against those of low status and disfavour (in this case Aurèle). Could the herding impulse explain my flicker of disloyalty to Aurèle? I rejected this. Although I have seen herd behaviours at work, (quite apart from the horses, my sister, you remember our days in the convent?) I have only ever reacted passionately against them.

Finally, I reviewed the biggest revelation in the Valmont-Didier interaction, the revelation that delivered the greatest bar yet to any relationship for me with Aurèle: the news that Aurèle was deeply ensnared by money lenders. Now, here was the thing that could act as a permanent obstacle to any union with him. Never have I heard of a good outcome to an event like this. I have seen the childhood friends of my parents lose their homes and their every possession to people such as these. The path with them goes only in one direction: debt, compounded debt, poverty, ill-health and destruction.

Dear Sister, do you remember, young as we were, our mother, poor, undiscerning soul, taking us to visit the home of the family of her hitherto friend on the day that it was placed by bailiffs under an enforcement order? Our mother's flimsy notions of tact and delicacy were swept away by the fact that all her acquaintance was going. That our mother had been an especial friend of the people undergoing the enforcement order did not seem to register with her, but with us, it made the event all the more horrifying. There was a carnival atmosphere in the house; all former friends and neighbours had turned up for the sale of all their worldly goods.

Regardless of the feelings of the newly impoverished, there was a general scramble, during the auction, for their possessions: linen, crystal, plate, children's toys, oyster knives, shoe buckles and undergarments. Anything and everything were being sold from under the nose of the family who were arrived home from a night away to find the action in full session, unable to keep anything but the clothes on their back. The money lenders were there, the honest merchants and artisans, all anxious for their dues. I will never forget the agitation in my mind that day. I felt sick for the family involved. Their former friends regarded them with blank glee, as they scrambled over their belongings to grab the best for themselves. I never knew what had caused the unfortunates to fall into debt, whether they had fallen through good-heartedness like Aurèle, or through profligacy and gaming. Only one family member need have a compulsion in order to bring all other loved ones to ruin.

I heard that the father was taken to the debtors' prison- and that this is where, soon after, he died. I did not hear what happened to his wife and children.

(Later) I awake in the night, my sister. I am restless. My imagination is heated now that I have twice eaves-dropped on those young men. The freedom they enjoy! They ride about the countryside, they go adventuring to exotic places, they wager, they fight, they litigate, they consort with whomsoever they fancy. How I would adore to have those freedoms!

75. M. DE BEAULIEU to the VICOMTE DE VALMONT (hand delivered within the LEFÈVRE ESTATE near AMIENS, 12th OCTOBER 1776)

A nicer man than Aurèle one would be hard pushed to meet. You are not playing fair. Why do you take such delight in ridiculing Aurèle on the grounds of his honesty and his poverty? These are honourable qualities, not derisory ones! What is it that makes you stand in the way of him and Sophie? It never fails to astound me that people who have so much, begrudge an innocent pleasure to those who have so little. You have riches enough for twenty lifetimes of luxury. You enjoy the attentions of countless women. Can not you leave Aurèle alone to experience the occasional joy of being in the company of Sophie?

      In any case, what is your full intention regarding Sophie? As yet, you have done nothing. May I suggest you continue to do nothing?

76. THE VICOMTE DE VALMONT to M. DE BEAULIEU (hand delivered within the LEFÈVRE ESTATE near AMIENS, 12th OCTOBER 1776)

Not playing fair has got my family where it is today. Playing fair has got the family of Aurèle where it is today. My problem with Aurèle is not to do with jealousy. My problem with him is one of practicality: he stands in the way of me getting what I want.

      Didier is impressionable; I hope I have done enough to persuade him to have Aurèle banished. I can make no move on Sophie with that idiot hero breathing down my neck. I leave the Lefèvre home and the field now to you. Watch her. Follow her. Make sure all her movements are known to you. I need to know if she continues to meet with him. Send your news in missives to the hostellerie. I stay close by so that you can quickly apprise me of her relationship with Aurèle. If you fail me this time, I will have but a short distance to travel to point out the error of your ways.

    My full intention regarding Sophie I do not choose to reveal to you but allow me to give you a lesson in the business of libertinism: the heiress is eloped with; the non-heiress is abducted. To secure the fortune of the former, one must marry. Where there is insufficient fortune, there is no necessity to marry. There are various shades of relationship in between the two ends of that continuum.

77. M. DE BEAULIEU to the VICOMTE DE VALMONT (hand delivered within the LEFÈVRE ESTATE near AMIENS, 12th OCTOBER 1776)

You urge me, once again, to spy on Sophie and Aurèle. What on earth is it that makes me continue to do your bidding in this loathsome way?

    I feel truly that you are my brother even though, in fact, we are only frères de lait. Nursing at the same breast is still considered an immense bond, especially among the country folk. We drank the same milk, we tumbled in the same cot, we toddled in the same village dirt.

    Your crushing grip over my affections gains traction from the fact that I was born a misfit. I am a something and nothing. I am neither here nor there. I am neither man nor beast. You can have no idea how pathetically grateful we misfits are to find ourselves the tolerated companion of a beautiful creature such as yourself. Even if this means we are at the sharp end of your cruel jokes, we prefer to be in the vicinity of beauty and style than all alone with our own strangeness. Equally, we choose not to group ourselves with others who lack gorgeousness and grace as we fear this will plummet our meagre stock still lower.

It seems that beauty in a person is often coupled with disproportionate gifts of ability and daring. And so we, who have barely any idea how to arrange our thoughts, clothes and limbs, adore to be close-hand witness to the feats of strength, skill and love that you supreme beings accomplish. We watch with mouths agape; it's a virtual life where we experience the thrills of your triumphs at second hand.

You can have no idea how exquisitely lonely is the life of a misfit: no one seeks us out, no one courts our attention, no one cares if we live or die. We exist only by doing the bidding of the beautiful creatures, so that they tolerate our company.

I promise you that I will further contaminate the innocence of Sophie and Aurèle by spying on them. By doing this I have no doubt that I contaminate my soul.

I am prepared to do this for you.

I am sure I will regret baring my innermost thoughts to you. You are not to be trusted with the safe-keeping of a person's devotion.

78. SOPHIE LEFÈVRE to HÉLÈNE, the CHEVALIÈRE D'IVRY (sent from the LEFÈVRE ESTATE near AMIENS, 13th October 1776)

After writing my last, I did not sleep all night for hearing of Aurèle's involvement with the money lenders. This morning I realise I am more shocked by Aurèle's silence over his entanglement with them than by the involvement itself. If I had agreed to flight and marriage with him, I too would have been embroiled in his fatal indebtedness. Would he, before my commitment to him, have warned me of this burden? Or would he have allowed me to commit to him in ignorance? It does not make sense that such an open fellow as he would lead me blind into something so deadly. He has had many opportunities to tell me of it but not one of them has he taken.

Now that the light has started to fade in the late afternoon, I put pen to paper to write to him.

"Why did you not tell me about your debts? Would you have allowed me to leave with you and yet not have told me?"

(Later) I sealed the letter, swept on my cloak and left my chamber. I left the house discreetly by one of the ground-floor, full-height windows at the back. I crossed the lawns quickly and headed for the thickets at their periphery. It was a journey on foot of about half an hour to get from thence to the woods and the forest lodge. On arrival at the lodge, there was smoke rising from the chimney and immediately my heart leapt. Smoke meant one of two things: the spirit of a long dead woodsman (for whom my heart had not leapt) or Aurèle. I paused before approaching a window to look inside. There, lovingly illuminated by warm firelight, was the Chevalier Aurèle, crouched and pensive before the hearth. He was in a deep reverie. I viewed him for a while, making sure he was alone. There I stayed, watching the flames warm the contours and angles of his beautiful face. Eventually, I rounded the lodge and pushed open the door, allowing it to fall fully open to reveal me standing on the doorstep. Aurèle stood up and turned to face me in one smooth movement. We remained like this for a few moments until I broke the silence.

"Is there news of Hélène?"

"Regrettably, Mademoiselle, there is not."

"Why did not you tell me about the debts?"

"What about the debts?"

"I heard my brother talking. You have debts."

"None that I cannot pay off."

"If they are held with the money lenders you will never pay them off."

"Yes, I will."

"That is almost never possible."

"The debts are of no consequence."

There was a silence. I tried to find the wherewithal to contradict him, but his conviction carried all before him. Finally, he spoke.

"Mademoiselle Sophie, pray, forgive me for commenting on your circumstance. You fall under intolerable parental influence with regards to M. le Marquis de Merteuil. I am loathe to add to that burden; but why is it that you turn to Beaulieu? It is beneath me to acknowledge a rival but why are you always in the company of that man? Can not you seek support from me?"

"My brother is appointed my keeper and Beaulieu is his friend."

"Beaulieu lifted you down from the carriage the other day. I saw it, he had you in his arms."

"That was an accident, I fell. That is all. Simply, I fell."

"And what about Valmont? Why do they bring him together with you? You failed to acknowledge me when you were in company with him."

I did not answer. I had no reasonable explanation as to why I had not acknowledged Aurèle whilst in the company of Valmont. Again, I marvelled at his transparency. Had my rôle been reversed with his, I would not have deigned to question him about a rival. My pride would not have allowed it. After some moments the silence was broken by an outburst from Aurèle.

"If your intention is to evade Merteuil, why do you court Valmont and Beaulieu when you have me? Good God Sophie! They are dangerous! This is insupportable!"

His passion flared up in a way that was thrilling to me. His heated words, so revelatory of the depth of his feeling, caused the blood to rush through my veins. He may as well have thrown himself at my feet. I smiled an inner smile of comprehension and gratification. At this moment he came to me, took me by the hand and laying all his manly pride and power before me, he entreated once more.

"Sophie, please, leave with me. I love you. I adore you. I believe, for both our future happiness, it is the only way."

It is my misfortune always to be offered the one thing I desire but within moments of discovering, absolutely, that I must not accept it. My smile vanished. In my mind I braced myself to deliver a verdict that would dash all his desires and mine- again! I dreaded to make the utterance; my breath almost failed me.

"Aurèle, can you not see? This is not possible! You are a debtor! Your optimism…I find it astonishing and presumptuous. It is impossible that I submit to such conditions, much as your loveliness tempts me. And really, truly, believe me I am tempted beyond all belief, beyond almost all endurance. Doubtless you are aware of the exceptional nature of your own personal charms. As a result, you expect too much."

Aurèle was taken aback once again, as if he had received a blow. It took him some moments to recover himself. The look of pain across his handsome face deeply affected me. I was shocked to realise how much it gratified me. I too felt piercingly the hurt of our situation, but, in witnessing Aurèle's struggle for mastery over his feeling, my pain was mingled in equal measures with attraction and excitement. With difficulty, Aurèle spoke,

"Forgive me, Mademoiselle, I forget myself. I was sure that little as I offer you materially, my heart would make up for all deficiencies. I believe you would be the richer for accepting my love and all its difficult conditions than the empty comforts that money without love can buy you. All I can do now is take you at your word. I cannot believe you would throw away your life and your happiness."

Here he paused. I watched him struggle for control over his passion.

"I must accept that you cannot be mine and that once I have found Madame La Chevalière d'Ivry, your Hélène, I must leave you. It remains for me to say that, despite the constraints of the life you will choose for yourself, I will love you always, even if you marry elsewhere."

"What if you marry elsewhere?" I said.

"I will not. Not while you breathe anyway."

There was no question that this utterance of his was anything other than a statement of truth.

"I will not," he said, "if there is any chance of you."

He took my hand, lifted it to his lips and without taking his eyes from mine, he kissed it.

As he kissed me, it seemed as though, once more, he had slowed the world down. In that strange second-by-second moment I was faintly aware that a sudden soft breeze swept over me from the door as it drifted shut, lifting a strand of my hair away from my face, parting my lips and causing my breath to intake. As if by the movement of the air and my breath, Aurèle was drawn to me. He brought his face to mine, his mouth to my mouth. At the moment of his touch I felt the white heat of his passion and the blaze of it caused me to respond absolutely. Once again, his proximity, his body, accomplished what his argument could not. As his arms encircled me and lifted me, my mind and body exalted that they could give up agency. He carried me to the furs by the flaring fire where he laid me down and covered my body with his. Once again, if someone had told me these moments of bliss could be purchased only by my destruction, I would not have faltered. For the long while that we were laid there, I was wholly and utterly committed to him, heart, mind, body and soul to the death.

Now, back in my chamber, I feel as if an opiate has been emptied into my veins. I lie on my bed sated in heart and head.

Bodily, I feel as if a thirst has been raised rather than quenched. According to religious doctrine (with which we were steadfastly inculcated since our girlhood), I have sinned. I consider my sin from all sides and I find I glory in it. I recall the thrill of the moment of Aurèle's touch, the thrill that the sound of his passionate intake of breath caused in me as my body lay against his.

(Later) I remained in this state of bliss for some time, too heartful to rest or to cease remembering every word and movement of Aurèle. Eventually, I must have fallen into deep sleep because I found myself waking sometime later from a black and tumultuous dream, ice cold and chilled with fear…

I have sinned with Aurèle…and the beautiful scenes I shared with him, that my mind has thrilled to play again and again, are now become scenes of horror and devilry wherein I am ridden by him, by the hounds of hell, by incubi and worse. Steeped in religion since childhood, and according to every religious tenet, I have committed a mortal sin with Aurèle, almost the greatest sin of womankind: the sin of fornication. I have sinned to a point of exile from God's saving grace. I lie on my bed in a shaking, cowering, heart-failing agony of fear, knowing that retribution will come.

The convent has neglected my education in every way but upon the subject of sin. In this matter, however, it has been inordinately thorough. It has taught me, indoctrinated me, bullied me, cowed me, violated me with the knowledge that, by sinning, I have let the devil in.

My sister, I cannot shake off that dark convent creed. The fear of the devil hounds me. His lurking, candlelight-shadow flares up in grotesque attitudes across the walls of my chamber. He never leaves me, he is my own fully imagined, internal agent of terror. The words of Defoe resound in my head.

'Children…have told themselves…many frightful things of the devil and have formed ideas of him in their minds, in…many horrible and monstrous shapes…'

The representations of the devil that the nuns held up before us now leap before my eyes: reptilian skin, reptilian wings, horns, tusks, teeth, dragon tail and cloven feet…Bosche, Aretino, Galle, Pacher…They paint as if they have seen him.

Words from the scriptures appear as if in burning calligraphy across the diabolical images.

'…Your enemy the devil prowls around…looking for someone to devour.'

'…Satan hath desired you, that he may sift you as wheat'

Do you remember how we determined, you and I, never to give in to temptation? We determined this when we discovered that we could not seek penance through confession because our curé alerted our mother and our father to the smallest venial sin that we confessed. Do you remember how immoderately we laughed at the sin of immoderate laughter! I was so desperate to graduate from the convent. Well, indeed I have graduated - graduated from venial sin to mortal sin.

How apt for me are the warnings from the scripture of John:

'Ye are of your father the devil, and the lusts of your father ye will do.'

How apt for me are the words of God to Lucifer in Ezekiel:

'You were the seal of perfection, full of wisdom and perfect in beauty... till wickedness was found in you... and you sinned... Your heart became proud on account of your beauty and you corrupted your wisdom of your splendour. So I threw you to the earth ; ...I made a fire come out from you, and it consumed you, and I reduced you to ashes on the ground ... you have come to a horrible end and will be no more.'

I await punishment from God.

'God did not spare angels when they sinned, but sent them to hell, putting them in chains of darkness to be held for judgement.'

I await the visits of God and the devil. I imagine that, of the two, the latter will visit first.

79. THE CHEVALIER AURÈLE to ISABELLE AURÈLE (sent from the LEFÈVRE ESTATE near AMIENS, 13th OCTOBER 1776)

My dearest sister, my beloved parents, Mademoiselle Sophie is the one I will marry, her heart is pure, sweet and disengaged; she sets all my self-control at nought. She is utterly irresistible and two days ago, our passion took us to the point of consummation. She has no idea how close we came. I kept her safe, of course, but being with her drives me almost beyond myself. This young woman has a sweet, wild, adorable, unchained heart. She meets passion with passion and is beautiful and free. In our urgency for each other, we lost all sense of time. I hope she got into the house without detection. From the woods, I watched the house for a conflagration. I suspended my search for her sister, and I watched all night, but the house remained silent. I feel sure she must have got in unchallenged.

Before she left, I gave her that golden wedding ring, on the long gilt chain, the one we took from Grandmère in death. The ring is so thin with wear that it can hardly be precious, but the gold is fine, and I could see that Sophie recognised the purity of it. As we parted, I put the chain around her neck and then I knelt to put the ring onto the fourth finger of her left hand. She gave me a look of infinite regret and threaded it back onto the chain again. Finally, I persuaded her to take the ring, but she would not wear it on her finger. Even when she is fired with my passion, she will not allow me to prevail. She is ever mindful and careful.

Whilst searching for her sister, I now watch ever more closely for a letter from Sophie, each night, every night. After what has happened between us, I hope she will come away with me. What we have shared is too powerful for her to resist. I hope I have broken through her practicable heart.

Her family guards her. Poisonous company surrounds her, but I pray she will find it in herself to be with me. She is perfect and pure at heart.

80. SOPHIE LEFÈVRE to HÉLÈNE, the CHEVALIÈRE D'IVRY (sent from the LEFÈVRE ESTATE near AMIENS, 15th OCTOBER 1776)

Two days of fear and dark delirium I have endured. I prepared myself and I waited for the devil to appear to torment me, to claim me for his own. I waited and I waited for this terrifying event.

The waiting hours wore me away, my convent-tutored imagination unnerving me until the resulting disorder of my mind caused my spirit almost to fail. My family sent up servants to ask why I did not appear, and I sent back that I was ill. Daylight came and went. If my maid attended me, I did not notice her. If she brought food, if she adjusted my bedclothes or curtains, I did not notice. I was waiting for the devil and damnation.

Then a train of thought wended through my mind: damnation, purgation, salvation…these are labyrinthine ideas! Ignatius, Ambrose, Augustine and other church fathers have argued about the form of them: on death, the separation of disintegrating body and enduring soul; the subsequent and immediate first judgement of the soul by God; the sending of the soul to heaven, hell or purgatory; the souls reuniting with their arisen bodies on the last day of the end of the world, to be judged again by God and assigned once more to heaven, hell or purgatory.

It seems to me that an inordinate amount of debate by the Christian ancients has taken place to establish all this convolution.

Just before the dread fall of the third night, my anger arose, causing me violently to reject the attritive tyranny of my fear. What actuated my rebellion was my inability indefinitely to await an enemy. I remembered our father's advice in a crisis: to consult the philosophers. Our father knows not what a philosopher is; he thinks they are the astrologers of the Gazette.

My mind reached for Spinoza, Rousseau, Diderot; instantly I rallied. For this recovery I gave rare thanks to our brother as he has kept their renegade texts in his meagre library, where he has not read them, but I have. When one's spirit founders with the isolating acknowledgement of one's own transgression, the greatest comfort to be found is in communing with a like-minded transgressor. If what I have done has offended God, I need to take comfort in the words of a fellow offender. Diderot came to my rescue:

'Man will never be free until the last king is strangled with the entrails of the last priest.'

This is elegant but on reflection, the second half of the sentence does not go far enough: does Diderot reject God, or does he simply reject the church? I found I could not be satisfied with an utterance that, simply, was oppositional to the established order. For peace of mind I needed to find a thinker who has weighed up the arguments for the existence of God and has refuted them. Then I remembered Epicurus and my cure was complete.

'Is God willing to prevent evil, but not able? Then he is impotent. Is he able, but not willing? Then he is malevolent. Is he both able and willing? Then whence cometh evil? Is he neither able nor willing? Then why call him God?'

As soon as night fell, I set about excising the devil from my imagination. I invoked him. I dared to utter his name and I dared him to make his scourging visit. I had no idea how liberating this would be. Nothing happened. He did not appear. I conjured as many of his names as I could recall. I spoke them clearly and rationally: *Antichrist, Apollyon, Beast, Beelzebub, Dragon, Evil One, Lucifer, Satan, Serpent.*

I invited him, in perfectly reasonable tones, to come to me and do his worst and, since I was worn down with exhaustion, to get on with it. Nothing happened. I recollected I still had upon my walls, symbols of Godly protection: a crucifix, a picture of St Sebastian on the cross, a representation of the Virgin Mary. I took them down and invoked the devil again. He did not come. He did not hold up my wantonness in my face, and pain me with infinite tortures. And so, I determine he is a creature of straw. He will never come.

I'm released from years of the bondage of self-conditioning. There is no devil. I can now fall in with Rousseau and the other antitheists and conclude that there is no God, no heaven, no hell. I weigh up the chances of the arrival of judgement day and decide that as it has not interrupted a social event for over three millennia, then I would be unlucky if it interfered with a diary engagement during my lifetime. I'm prepared to take my chances. I am free from the all-seeing, all-judging eye and I am free from the burden of building credit for the hereafter.

I rejoice that I need not limit my earthly ambitions. I am triumphant because I live in a world where everyone is self-regulated by a superstitious and unreasonable fear. Having freed myself of this constraint, to live among a herd that has not, I will be victorious. If everyone were as liberated as am I, then the law of Hobbes' state of nature would prevail.

'bellum omnium contra omnes; the war of all against all...'

Despite my sex, by this rejection of theism I have placed myself near the top of the Machiavellian chain. For the first time in my life, I will serve my own interests entirely and without fear.

This liberation, my sister, is notwithstanding that I am in constant danger of being locked away in a very high room by our father.

81. ISABELLE AURÈLE to the CHEVALIER AURÈLE (sent from PARIS, 15th OCTOBER 1776)

My adored brother, I chose not to censor any part of your letter as I read it aloud to our parents. Now we fiercely debate the nature of your episode of passion with Mademoiselle Sophie. Father falls in with Hobbes and opines that as human existence is *'nasty, brutish and short'*, he wishes you to *'take your pleasures where you will'*. Mother says you must allow yourself *'no pleasure at all'* excepting those which are sanctified by the Holy Roman Church. I say you must *'take your pleasures where you will- but not at the expense of another'*.

Upon one thing we all agree: we do not feel your association with Mademoiselle Sophie augurs well. We beseech you to find a young woman who is available to you. We say this in the simplest of terms as sometimes we believe you to be the simplest of men.

We have never known you quite as lost as this. Excise her from your imagination. You know from the poet that what you experience is a fleeting and ephemeral thing.

'Love is a smoke, made with the fume of sighs.'[2]

If you can escape her now and stay away for ever then we believe you are in with a chance of happiness. There is danger in your dealings with her.

82. M. DE BEAULIEU to the VICOMTE DE VALMONT (sent from the LEFÈVRE ESTATE near AMIENS, 15TH OCTOBER 1776)

My dear Vicomte, by return of post you may enclose thanks to me and remuneration for my physician as I have caught a mortal chill in faithfully carrying out your instructions.

I am aware I must be trying your patience as I digress into matters of my own self when you much prefer I should be extolling yourself. I remedy this with the next flourish of my pen: you are correct in your suspicions! There is a deep understanding between Sophie and Aurèle. I will tell you how it is that I come to know this.

Earlier this evening, I realised that Sophie had absented herself from the parlour where were gathered all the family and so I sent word to her room, via her maid, that the Indian silk she had commissioned me to source for her had arrived. Was this not clever? I have had the silk for some days, but I reserved news of its arrival for exactly this occasion of finding her out. As I had not believed you to be correct in your divination of how things stood between Sophie and Aurèle, imagine how astonished I was to be told that she was nowhere to be found. The parlour overlooks the sweep of the drive, and as she was not to be seen there, I conjectured she must have departed via the back of the house. I bowed my excuses to her assembled family and hoofed to the rear courtyard where there was no sign of her.

I am aware you do not think me capable of a turn of speed, but I cantered in my embroidered shoes immediately to the rear windows of the house, the ones which lead directly onto the gardens. There, clearly marked by the absence of evening dew, was a fresh trail across the besoaked expanse of grass leading to the rhododendrons on the far side, where the trail disappeared. Fortuitously, I heard Sophie's hound yelping and scrabbling eagerly from behind the door of his courtyard kennel, clearly having sense of his mistress having just left the premises. I galloped back to fetch him, knowing he would be my guide. I clipped him onto a lead rope, and he dragged me apace, directly through the gloaming, to the same rhododendron spot. Here, he snuffled the ground for some moments, of which I was vastly glad, as my breathing was laboured and my wig askew, before he lurched off again, breaking a path through the thickly grown, snagging vegetation with far greater ease than did I. After some thirty minutes of dashing and snuffling, my speed in all this paid off as our direct route through the trees, despite tearing my costume and coiffure to shreds, had brought me to within sight of a woodland lodge at about the same time that Sophie arrived at it, she having taken, I imagine, a better made but more circuitous path.

As her hound and I came to a halt in the umbra of the skirting of trees, Sophie, after looking about her, placed some papers under a roof tile at the lowest point of the lodge's eaves. At this moment her dog, still on the end of the rope, started an anxious panting and straining to be with her. I judged it wise to allow him off the lead before he gave me away. He made a dash straight for her and she was then so busy making much of him and exclaiming in surprise at his arrival that I had time to hide myself. After she had checked the positioning of the tile, she looked about her once more and left. I remembered that you would want me to deliver her papers to you and so I waited some moments and then darted across the clearing, lifted the papers from under the tile, replaced the tile exactly as I had found it and was on the point of leaving when I decided I had better wait as some further activity surely would follow.

My dear friend, I waited for two mortal hours under the darkening, dripping umbra of the trees before being rewarded by the sound of hoofbeats. Softly lit by the hazy moonlight, glowing through a persistent evening mizzle, came the incomparable Aurèle, mounted on a steed with extravagantly elevated action. He rode quietly about the clearing, directing his penetrating gaze into all parts of the forest. As if my attire were not disordered enough, I threw myself into a dense holly bush, making myself as small as possible, my heart beating wildly, as I felt sure his powerful eye must espy me. Luckily, he seemed satisfied that he was alone as he too made straight for the tile, investigated the empty spot beneath it and then left some papers behind. As soon as he had left the clearing and put some distance between myself and him, I dared to careen across the open space to recover these additional papers. I am so in awe of his powers that I was tempted not to replace the stone correctly in my anxiety to get away. I am more scared of you than I am of him, however, and so I left all as I ought and hurried off to safety and warmth.

I have not read these filched letters as I have more scruple than do you, but I enclose them here for you.

I beg of you, if it transpires that those two are in love, do not come between them.

83. THE VICOMTE DE VALMONT to DIDIER LEFÈVRE (sent from the HOSTELLERIE LE ST. CHRISTOPHE near AMIENS, OCTOBER 16TH 1776)

Two letters (enclosed) have fallen into my hands: one from your sister to the Chevalier Aurèle and one from him to her. You will discover from them that Aurèle and Sophie have been in secret correspondence and are pursuing a passionate relationship with each other. If you value your life, I suggest you pass these letters straight to your father, rather than deal with Aurèle yourself. Your father and all his household men will have a great deal of difficulty in removing that man from your home. In case you haven't noticed, the merchant class does not usually win in a fight against the warrior class. That young warrior will die rather than leave Mademoiselle Sophie unguarded.

To limit damage to life and limb, furniture, paintings. wall hangings, china, silverware, and glassware, may I suggest you dose the supreme Aurèle with hefty opiates?

It would appear that in accordance with the convention of tragic romance, the correspondence has been interrupted at the very point where the lovers would have reached a perfect understanding of each other and then eloped in the night. By ensuring that their letters did not reach each other, one may assume that Aurèle and Sophie remain in ignorance of the perfect unity of their desires and plans and therefore that all is not lost with regard to putting them asunder and effecting the reclamation of Sophie. I am sure I do not need to urge you to banish Aurèle WITH IMMEDIATE EFFECT.

84. DIDIER LEFÈVRE to M. LEFÈVRE (hand delivered within the LEFÈVRE ESTATE near AMIENS, 16TH OCTOBER 1776)

Sir, I have long told you that Sophie has a corrupt and vicious streak and that Aurèle abuses your hospitality. Please find enclosed their letters which show how irrevocably they steep themselves in vice.

You Sir, will need to remove this young upstart from our home.

May I suggest opiates?

85. SOPHIE LEFÈVRE to the CHEVALIER AURÈLE (hand delivered to the FOREST LODGE within the LEFÈVRE ESTATE near AMIENS, 15th OCTOBER 1776) (now enclosed within the hand delivered correspondence of Didier Lefèvre to M. Lefèvre)

Since I saw you last, I have come to an understanding of myself which has led me to the decision that I would like to live a lie with you. This you may not appreciate as you are devout.

My realisation is that while I wish to remain accepted by good society, I do not wish to fulfil any role it offers to a young woman of my status. I do not wish to: marry, beget children, enter a convent, become a governess, become companion and amanuensis to my family members as they age.

With my sister missing, the only legitimate societal role that is attractive to me is that of the young widow. However, I have no wish to fulfil the prerequisite of marriage or endure the suspense of waiting for the untimely death of a husband.

My foremost wish, therefore, is that we may be together without my submitting to marriage or to childbirth. After the passion of our last encounter I feel this last condition places an impossible constraint upon our union. If, however, you could love me and live with me childless and unwedded then I would agree to flee with you as of this moment. The peril regarding your debts would be bearable for me with these conditions in place, as I would not acquire responsibility for them. Our poverty and my imperilment would be lessened by the absence of pregnancies and children.

The lie is that we would live among strangers and give the appearance to them of being married.

This letter does not speak of my love for you nor of how my imagination is fixed upon you. I have no time to write of these things although the impression I carry in my heart of your beautiful looks, words and touch engrosses to delirium all my waking and sleeping thoughts.

86. THE CHEVALIER AURÈLE to SOPHIE LEFÈVRE (hand delivered to the FOREST LODGE within the LEFÈVRE ESTATE near AMIENS, 15th OCTOBER 1776) (now enclosed within the hand delivered correspondence of Didier Lefèvre to M. Lefèvre)

Mademoiselle Sophie, my darling love, where are you? I must have news of you. I must see you. I think of nothing but you. Now that we have experienced such bliss how can you bear for us not to be wed? If you are afraid of childbirth, then I will keep you safe. I do not want you to live in fear and I do not want you to be unhappy. I would rather wed you chastely and have you forever for my own than never have you because of this fear. Do not you see that if we create a sanctified but careful, perfect love, then we can be together? If you do not wish to marry me, do not allow this to keep us apart. My love for you will accept any condition.

With my promise in place there can no longer be need for us to delay. I love you to distraction. Come with me. Be with me. I will live with you under any condition. I adore you. Let us leave now!

87. M. LEFÈVRE to SOPHIE LEFÈVRE (hand delivered within the LEFÈVRE ESTATE near AMIENS, 16th OCTOBER 1776)

When this letter were pushed under your door, ye may or may not have heard the key turn in the lock. This turning of the key to the locked position is to remain the permanent orientation of it until the day of your nuptials to a man of our approving. I have no need to explicate nothing more to ye, as persuasion be not necessary now that ye be captive. However, to prevent a flurry of querying letters from ye, I point out that ye will have your meals in this room, that ye will perform your toilette in this room. There will be no reprieve and no escape. Do not think I will relent because I will not.

My irrevocable decision have come about as a result of reading your lewd and wanton letter of yesterday, addressed to the Chevalier Aurèle. This letter were intercepted well before the Chevalier come for it and 'tis now in my possession. I be certain that by ensuring he did not read it I have done ye a favour as it do contain notions of such profanity and irreligiosity, couched in such insouciant language that no man under God's skies could find the woman what could pen such ideas to be anything other than a monster.

Never did I imagine it possible that a young female such as ye could have sprung from my loins. It be like as if I had nurtured a snake.

88. M. DE BEAULIEU to the VICOMTE DE VALMONT (sent from the LEFÈVRE ESTATE near AMIENS, 16th OCTOBER 1776)

By the way, to forward your stratagem vis-à-vis Sophie, I suggest you hire cannon and troops; the action you took of alerting Sophie's menfolk to her subterfuge with Aurèle has resulted in her being placed under lock, key and a double guard in a very high room. Did not you foresee how this would play out? You have placed her beyond even your reach. They plan to force that bull-elephant Merteuil upon her now as a matter of urgency.

89. THE VICOMTE VALMONT to M. DE BEAULIEU (sent from the HOSTELLERIE LE ST. CHRISTOPHE near AMIENS, 17th OCTOBER 1776)

Do not under-estimate me. I have prevailed against greater obstacles. The way in is not through the wall but through the maiden. Please desist from opening your letters with the words 'by the way'.

90. THE CHEVALIER AURÈLE to ISABELLE AURÈLE (sent from a RUINED COTTAGE within the LEFÈVRE ESTATE near AMIENS, 17th OCTOBER 1776)

Today I find myself face down in deepest forestry with every bone of my body battered to breaking point. I have been evicted from the Lefèvre home. From what I see of the disturbance in the loam around about where I lay, I believe I have been dragged to this spot.

 Somehow, I have survived and have hauled myself into some kind of forestry hovel.

 You will wonder how it was that I was overcome, and I am ashamed to tell you that I believe I was easily duped into accepting a drink laced with opiates. The last thing I remember, in any case, is my evening drink being brought to my room. As you know, I am housed in an out-of-the-way and unfrequented wing of the Lefèvre mansion. No amount of howling from there could carry to the ears of rescuers.

 After drinking, I remember crashing dizzyingly from wall to wall, straining to remain upright. I remember seeing the great upright clock in my room, fall to the ground, open its maw and start snapping at my legs. I remember my table falling onto its back in order to cast its four dagger point legs skywards for my impalement. I remember the windows imploding showers of tearful, wet droplets all over my head. I remember the candles overturning, setting light to the papers on my floor, the flames leaping high, each one creating burning images of the stricken faces of anyone I have ever loved. I remember a numerous, surging onslaught of men hanging from my arms and my legs by their teeth like great, black boars, until I flung them into the walls and up to the ceiling. I remember roaring like a wounded bear, shouting Mademoiselle Sophie's name over and over.

And then, I remember nothing.

What I do know is that the beating I have endured is in retribution for my latest written proposition to Mademoiselle Sophie that she elope with me. There was a letter near where I lay, from her father, which explained this. I understand her father's pain. If someone tried to steal my daughter I would react violently. In this case though, his marriage plans for her are murderous. And so I am wholly justified in my deception of him.

By allowing me to live, he has made a terrible mistake. Nothing now will stop me from breaking back into his house and making off with his daughter.

I enclose the letter he left lying beside me after he dragged and dumped me in this forest.

Do not worry about me. I am fine.

91. M. LEFÈVRE to the CHEVALIER AURÈLE, OCTOBER 16th 1776. Letter placed by the body of THE CHEVALIER AURÈLE in forestry within the LEFÈVRE ESTATE near AMIENS

If you recover consciousness to find this letter - which I leave beside your stricken body - you will wonder how it is that you find yourself face down in a wilderness. I delight to inform you that I have removed you from my home. I stopped short of your death as I do not wish to damn my soul over you.

The abuses ye have heaped upon my house are come to an end. Ye has snatched away the innocence of my daughter and ye has corrupted her mind. Earlier today I was handed your twin correspondence. The sentiments my daughter do express in her letter, as a result of your dark influence, be anti-religious in the extreme. Therefore, I saw fit to show you no mercy. I hope God will do the same.

If you ever find yourself in a fit state to try to breach my premises, the marshalcy will be called. Also will be called the men of this house. I have trebled the guard. They have orders to patrol my premises in threes and fours. If they meets with resistance from ye they have orders to horse-whip ye til your skin be flayed from your bones.

Do not drag your carcass back here for your chattels. They are at the bottom of the horse pond.

I pray that your twisted soul now leave your twisted body and go straight to the Devil.

(Later)…My hand will not sign off this letter! My blood is up! It do pulse out of my fingers, through my pen, into my ink and onto the page!

If you are alive to read this, read on! I have more to say about your type!

I be sickened by the high-handed way ye young noblemen do make free with the generosities offered to ye by people of my station. Do not ye forget, 'tis the people of my rank, the third estate, who pays the taxes what powers this country and not the people of your estate. That ye nobles seek to rob us of the chastity of our daughters and of our reputation be loathsome in the extreme!

Do not imagine that the people of my station fail to notice that ye nobles do bankrupt this country through your attachment to extravagance, intemperance and war. Ye expect us lowly people to finance your self-aggrandising plans. Ye expect to extort our money for yer faulty schemes.

I warn ye, noble young Sirrah, the day comes when us do not choose to starve us-selfs for the honour of underwriting the vainglorious follies of ye privileged few. Do not imagine us to be so endlessly silly as to allow ye pampered people the means to continue in your irresponsible ways.

The day dawns. Attend!

92. SOPHIE LEFÈVRE to HÉLÈNE, the CHEVALIÈRE D'IVRY
(sent from the LEFÈVRE ESTATE near AMIENS, 17th OCTOBER 1776)

My dear Sister, everything is deathly quiet here. When I have read about young women being locked in their room, I have thought it exciting. But I can tell you it is not. The lock has been turned on me for just two days now and already I go mad with restlessness. Unlike the romantic heroine, I see no way out. My mind is entirely taken up with thoughts of Aurèle and with the hope that I have not endangered him. It is to my eternal regret that I was not more circumspect before leaving my last letter to him. It is the interception of this letter that has me placed indefinitely behind this oak door. My heart is gripped by a chilling dread that I may have imperilled him.

I find myself praying for his wellbeing, which is strange given my new-found apostasy. Old habits will not die. It takes a great effort of will in a crisis not to resort to superstitious rituals.

If my letters ever reach you now it will be a tribute to the assiduity of Aurèle in finding you and in establishing contact with my maid.

This morning my door was unlocked, and our mother entered. With my mind oppressed from imprisonment and with my heart full of Aurèle, it was sickening to me that she should bring up the subject of Merteuil. Here is how the conversation went:

"Sophie child, M. le Marquis de Merteuil already be seen on the estate and 'tis necessary that ye prepare to meet him. Ye must be dressed. I have alerted your maid."

"Mamma, please send word to M. le Marquis that I am ill"

Our mother's horror was comical.

"Child! Ye cannot be ill! Not on this day of all days!"

"But I am."

"Impossible!"

"How ridiculous Mamma, why cannot I be ill today."

"Because your father says ye must meet the Marquis and hear what he do have to say."

"Cannot I hear it another day?"

"No, Sophie, your father have said today and so today it must be."

"Mamma, have you ever followed father thus?"

A sudden weariness clouded our mother's face.

"My dear daughter, I do not know why always ye set yourself against your father. 'Tis not the normal way for a girl child to go. Please understand, in this world, a woman be as a reed. Unless her be prepared to bend, her will surely break."

I had not ever thought to hear our mother so profound.

Over the years Mamma has come to realise that her best option for getting me to do as our father wishes is not to involve herself in an argument about it. Simply now she delivers his edict, leaves me and sends in the maid. This expedient works. Generally, I co-operate with the plan for want of having a better one. On this day, I wanted to get out of my chamber. My maid brought in a new powder-blue, silk dress; I looked astonishing in it. I am used to looking at my beauty as an everyday event but, on this occasion, I was taken by surprise. I removed it and put on my old yellow sateen, the one that matches the wallpaper.

When Didier and two footmen came for me and unlocked my door, I walked, under guard, the interminable walk to my father's study. As I entered the room, three men turned to face me: M. le Marquis de Merteuil, father, lawyer. An excited air hung about them of business having been concluded; the room vibrated with the energy of it. I felt uncomfortable at having six pairs of male eyes upon me, even though three of them were only servants and two were of our own family. Our mother ought to have been in the room but she was probably hiding. Whenever a situation becomes too difficult for her, she runs away from it. This is a useful manoeuvre which I have yet to adopt; it will be a life-preserving moderation to my current habit of standing in the way of trouble.

Our father stepped forward, took my arm proprietorially and did not notice that I did not wish that anyone take a proprietorial hold of me. M. de Merteuil made a low bow before me. What a sham these politenesses are; what possible courtesy can make up for an enforcement to marriage? I returned his courtesy although I felt like pointing out that their obeisances were not making me feel better about being in their company. Father spoke first.

"Your brother and M. le Marquis de Merteuil has suggested a drive in the great park and I has requested that your mother, brother and M. de Beaulieu do accompany ye."

Here our father turned to M. de Merteuil.

"I beg ye would excuse us, Sir. Most regrettably, us has other business what must be attended to."

Father bowed deeply and left the room; the lawyer and one footman followed. Didier, M. de Merteuil and I stood about awkwardly and then filed towards the door where there was a tussle between Didier and M. de Merteuil as to who should steer me through it. It is interesting to me that women are domestic captives but that the parade of niceties about us maintains the charade that we are higher status individuals than the men who surround us. Clearly this is a palliative to our subjugation.

I was surprised to see that father had ordered the barouche for me and M. de Merteuil. It would afford far less privacy than an enclosed carriage. Mother, it appeared, was to ride in it also. Beaulieu was to be horsed alongside it and our brother primed to race around it in a new curricle, driving off the bit and the whip and working his animal into a lather. Two of the usual coachmen were driving the vehicle and a groom was riding on the footplate at the rear. This was going to be a thickly attended proposal of marriage. I decided that father must highly rate my powers of defiance to put these many men of the household around me.

I climbed into the carriage. Father had suggested that we drive out to the great park to view the progress of his new timber plantation there. This, as you know, is an excursion that takes three parts of an hour. I wondered how I would manage such a long trial and how the proposal would take place. Our mother sensed the depression of my spirits and took the burden of the conversation for the first part of the drive. I sat back whilst our mother chatted about the difficulty of finding and keeping good servants. I contemplated the man before me. Overall, he was lumpen. His eyes, the windows to his soul and to his intelligence, were small and so pale that it was almost impossible to distinguish between the pallidity of the pupil and the surrounding yellow-white of the eyeball. The great overhang that was his brow further obscured his eye, as did the bulging, bullock bones of cheek and jaw. His clothes, although bespoke, were yet too small, as if the tailor had not trusted to the extravagance of his measurements or had simply run out of cloth. This meant that the great packs of muscle across back, neck, arms and thighs strained the material of his apparel at every flexion. The overall picture was of various large cuts of prime beef on the bone, arranged massively into the shape of a man and then clothed.

    The character of M. de Merteuil was as obscured as his eye. Was he a gambler? Did he drink excessively? Did he make use of unfortunate women? Even after his marriage to our discreet and honourable sister, we do not know. I have only ever seen him on a handful of straitened social occasions.

    I contemplated the irony of my having to debate for the second time that week whether to attach my fortunes to a man. Since my young years I have studied men and women. There is not so much difference, it seems. Men appear as flawed as women. How ironic that my only chance to weigh up this man came during the one private conversation engineered for me by people who intended that I should agree to spend the rest of my life with him.

    I made a plan, other than a flat refusal, which I would use only as a last resort, I would convince M.de Merteuil that it would be against his better interest to have me. I decided to behave ill towards him in order that his dread proposal would not take place. The trouble with a plan like this though, my sister, is that, for young women like you and me to be impudent before a man, we must overcome years upon years of our strict conditioning. If you consider, our whole lives as girls are spent in training for compliance: obedient first to our nurses and our mothers; obedient then to the sisters and to the Abbess of the convent; obedient ultimately to our brothers, our fathers and to all other menfolk of rank.

Was I brave enough to be rude to M. de Merteuil, knowing that everything I did would be reported back to our father, if not by him, then certainly by the carriage driver or by the grooms? Before, when I have risen to rudeness, it has been directed at my brother and always with the help of a flare up of temper. The sudden rush of blood that accompanied this thought came to my aid, and so, with a surge of impulsion, I cut across the chatter of our mother.

"I hear, Monsieur, that you are scouring the market for a new…er…"

I paused here, *'scouring'* was disrespectful but I wanted M. de Merteuil to wonder whether I would say *'wife'*.

"…horse," I said.

As I finished this sentence, I heard our mother breathe a small sigh of relief. M. de Merteuil showed no such discomfort.

"Yes, Mademoiselle, you have heard correctly. Both of my riding horses have pulled up lame and so, as you can imagine, my need is urgent."

I forced myself to continue in this vein.

"And do you have a preference as to a mare or a gelding?"

By the way that our mother sucked in her breath again I imagined that the mention of sexual differentiation in horses had hit the mark of indelicacy. M. de Merteuil, however, evinced no feeling.

"I have no preference."

I ploughed on.

"Unusual. All the men in our family complain about mares. They find them temperamental and, in some cases, as difficult as an entire."

This time I had overstepped the mark. I had heard the grooms refer to stallions as entires and I knew that this was not a polite term on my lips. Our mother drew her breath in again and held it. The Marquis' expression remained perfectly bland.

"I cannot say I have an opinion on the matter. Mares or geldings are all the same to me. As long as the animal is sound."

I could not help but admire his composure; not a flicker of sentiment did he betray. Either he is the most boring man on earth or the best tactician. Possibly he knows he has me secured and so will not risk an argument. Maybe he does not have the wit to argue. At the expense of my mother's nerves, I decided to try him again.

"And what about women?"

I nearly laughed; if our mother sucked her breath in any further, she would faint and fall out of the carriage. I continued,

"Many men swear by the company of their own sex, running from their wives and sisters at the first opportunity."

M. de Merteuil allowed himself a polite simper.

"Mademoiselle, you could not but expect me to side other than with the fair sex, especially when in the company of two such fine exemplars of it."

He smiled. His teeth were edged with moss. Relieved at his unwillingness to be drawn, our mother laughed rather too heartily at his gallantry.

"Ye are too kind M. le Marquis, I know ye men very quickly tire of our inconsequential chatter."

This last was uttered with a meaningful glance at me. I leaned back in my seat. I would give up for now and try again when alone with him. I knew that sooner or later some contrivance or other would occur to throw us both together. As if on cue, our brother hurtled alongside, cutting through his horse's mouth in his attempt to bring it down to the pace of our carriage.

"Mamma, you must have a spin in this new vehicle, it gives one the smoothest ride imaginable."

I viewed our brother with ever growing distaste. I recalled his comment, regarding my capability of '*bagging the glittering wealth of the Guyenne Comtes*' and I found I was beginning to loathe him for the part he was playing in my life. I decided to intervene.

"You cannot expect Mamma to ride with you, Didier. It is not safe."

"I will drive slowly."

"I still do not think it a good idea."

Our mother was already out of the carriage, however, clambering into the unsteady curricle, despite her horror at the horse's rolling eye and heaving sides. She must be truly desperate to help father in this business, I thought, as I watched them careen off. Beaulieu also drew away.

Excepting the two coachmen and the groom, my proposed husband and I were now alone. I was more aware than ever that at no other time in my life have I been alone in the company of a strange man not of my choosing. I felt momentarily disadvantaged. How did one negotiate with such a man? I had no clue. A tense silence fell. I willed my courage to rally. Twenty minutes of the journey had passed. The greater part of the ordeal was to come.

"At last," he said, "the October rains have eased."

I nearly laughed at the incongruity of this comment with my siege-like frame of mind.

"My God," I thought, "we will be discussing the roads next."

The Marquis continued, "Thank heavens the roads are drying up."

This time I did laugh. All my nervous energy came out in one brief burst.

"Forgive me, Sir, but you are so dull!"

Unmistakably provoked, still he managed to neutralise the conversation.

"What would you have me talk about, Mademoiselle?"

A very urgent desire to jolt him swept over me. I had nothing to lose.

"Either you have a gift for the inoffensive comment, Sir, or you have a very real desire to hide your character. Which is it?"

His rejoinder was as smooth as glass.

"By my comments my character is revealed. I have never liked confrontation and I have no wish to argue with you."

"But the situation you have me in is confrontational."

"How so?"

"Because you bring me here to propose marriage."

There was a silence whilst the Marquis cogitated.

"It is true. I have viewed you these past twenty months. I have always judged you as having the best conformation of all women. Since first I saw you, I have desired to have you for my own."

'*Conformation*'! This is how the physique of a horse is termed! Also, by this speech, he demonstrated he had not the sense or tact to remember that his claim to desire me coincided entirely with the time he had spent as husband of our adored sister. I was disgusted. In two rehearsed, self-absorbed sentences he was presuming to gain a lifetime of mortal risk from me.

"Does it not trouble you, Sir, that you would have me under duress? If I were to accept, you know it would be out of coercion. What is worrying is that you would be happy to have me on those terms."

"How do you know I would?"

"Because without the benefit of one single conversation with me you have fixed the financial and legal aspects of the union with my father. Does that not show a certain bravado, a certain carelessness as to my opinion?"

"Forgive me, Mademoiselle, but that is often the way that this business is done. Our families make a good alliance, our land is contiguous, and the terms were already in place from your sister. From your father's point of view, it would be best for you to help him salvage something from this most unfortunate situation."

I allowed my anger to flare.

"My sister! My dead sister! How dare you speak to me of her and of the land deals to do with your union with her, as you try me for your wife! It is you that destroyed her! Here is the crux of the matter: since I was a child and watched the domestic world about me, I have been afraid of death in childbirth. You are a man of massive size so I am afraid that if you have me, I will perish. My sister and I are far too slender of build. It's like putting a great Charolais bull to a little Guernsey heifer. What you need is a wife commensurate with your size. You need a tall, wide-hipped female of Amazonian extraction."

M. de Merteuil looked justifiably dumbfounded; my utterance sounded deranged even to my ears, but it was what I thought, and it was how I felt, so I continued,

"Besides, it does not appeal to me to be a unit of currency between the one side and the other. I am not sorry to disappoint you as this dialogue should never have come about. However, I am sure that if economic considerations remain foremost in your marriage plans then you will find I am interchangeable with any other young woman of fortune. As there are many of these about, your pride will not for long be wounded."

M. de Merteuil took a few seconds to recover. The moments passed in heavy silence. Finally, he spoke,

"Out of consideration for you, Mademoiselle, I will not trouble you on this matter again today. I know that many young women find it immodest to accept an offer when it is made for the first time. I have anticipated this event and so, out of delicacy for your maidenly modesty, I will not make this offer again within the next forty-eight hours."

My answer was quick and venomous; there is an exhilarating freedom that comes when all barriers of politesse are down.

"And how, pray, will the passing of another forty-eight hours wreak such a miraculous change? I do not like you today and I will not like you tomorrow or the next day or any day. I cannot admire that you demand so much for so little. You have shown that you have no consideration for me and so I need show none to you. My answer, therefore, will ever more run counter to your expectation."

The rest of the journey passed in a silence that was not agonising for me. The plantation came and went. I barely looked at it. I felt no embarrassment or shame. I blamed our father for disregarding my objections. I blamed Merteuil for causing us this discomfiture. Anyone less presumptuous would not have engineered a proposal of marriage to occur in an enclosed space from which there was no escape.

Our mother joined us for the last mile of the journey and, mistaking my flaming face for a sign of my assent, chatted happily away to herself for the remainder of the trip.

At the steps of the house was a reception party: father, brother, lawyer. As soon as the carriage pulled up, I made sure I was the first out. I rushed past everybody, which I imagined was what they would have expected me to do in any event. Didier and two footmen caught up with me and I was accompanied to my room. I felt suddenly sick with apprehension; M. de Merteuil, it was clear, was due to go straight into a meeting with those men, a meeting that I knew could only have been arranged to sign off the land transfers and settlements. As my guardsmen locked me in my room, it struck me as curious that, in the matter of agreeing a financial settlement for a proposed wife, the bridegroom-to-be must also face the spectre of his own death (but with a lot less apprehension of real danger than his bride) - and make a monetary provision for his wife in case of it.

I felt a sudden shiver of fear. In one decisive interview I had defied some very powerful men - men with power over me! I dread what might be the consequence. I wonder whether the impassivity of the Marquis will remain intact. He is so superior in rank to all the other men involved in this deal. Will the reporting of such a rejection be embarrassing to him?

No feeling he can muster, however, will come close to the mortification that our father will feel on learning that I have defied him. He will have assured Merteuil, upon his honour, that I was to be depended upon, that the asking of my permission was simply a formality. How such a proud and insecure man as our father will stand to be undermined by his daughter in front of such people I do not want to imagine.

I am again locked into my room. Through the window, I see the carriages leave: first that of the Marquis, then that of the lawyer, then the riding horse of the steward.

A silence of terrifying intensity settles on the house.

(Later) My sister, four hours passed and then I heard footsteps in the corridor. It was our father, who has never come to my chamber before. As he stepped into my room, he commanded that the door be locked behind him. He was a study in mortified pride, the very picture of the angry cockerel. He strutted around and around my room, his gizzard jerking in and out, venting his spleen, whilst I stood in the middle of the room, my head following his arc in order to show respect. I did not want to look at him at all. I only turned his way to do my duty and take my punishment.

"WHAT!" he spat," Rejected as ye be by a Comte, WHAT gave ye such idea of your own importance as to think ye could turn down the suit of a Marquis?! What life do ye think ye destined to lead that makes ye think ye too good for a Marquis? Is only a Prince to suffice for Sophie Lefèvre, the daughter of a merchant? And be there enough Princes in the country for ye to pick over? Or is it that ye think yourself marvellous enough to tilt for a Duc? Whatever is it about yourself buried here in the campagna of Amiens that makes ye think ye so unparalleled? Please do not run away with the idea that 'tis your uncommon allure what do draw these young bucks. 'Tis my money they be after and NOT your face; a barmaid could have your face and they often do! 'Tis the dowry what I settles upon ye that attracts they. Ye could have the face of a poxed pig and still them would come. Lest ye forget, your face and your person belong to me. I made ye, I raised ye and believe me, I will dispose of ye."

There was the most awful pause. The silence was resounding. He started up again, his wattles wobbled, and flecks of spit flew about as he spoke.

"Or is it that ye set out to humiliate me? Ye must have known when I entrusted ye to his society that I was entrusting ye with the safe keeping of my honour, my self-consequence and my pride? He do tell me that not only did ye turn him down but that ye was unwomanly and offensive in your manner of doing so! Unwomanly! Offensive! HOW DARE YE! Have ye any idea how this do reflect upon me?

So, now, listen. This is my decree. Your duty, absolutely, be to accept M. de Merteuil. I have assured he that this match will proceed. Until ye recognise my sovereignty over ye in this matter there can be no escape for ye. If ye defy he, ye defy me, and I swear I will see ye dead than defiant."

He wrenched the door handle to fling the door open and slam out of the room. He kept snatching at the door until I reminded him that he had commanded it be locked. When, finally, he effected his exit, I was left to weigh up whether he would carry out his threat of my murder.

As it would be a matter of honour, I decided, on balance, that he would.

93. THE VICOMTE VALMONT to M. DE BEAULIEU (sent from the HOSTELLERIE LE ST. CHRISTOPHE near AMIENS, 18th OCTOBER 1776)

My God Beaulieu, I go mad with frustration!

Never have I found a household so impenetrable! Their doors are closed to visitors; the demesne is littered with burly, farmyard hobble-de-hoys and the domestics will not take a bribe! I can only assume their purse is made too heavy by old Lefèvre. How typical of a poor-man-made-good that he reward his household so well. But for his talent for trade, he would have been one of them himself- or dead of starvation. If only this were the château of a grasping nobleman. I would have bought my way up to her chamber and made off with her a thousand times by now. Dieu! How my desire is thwarted! If only you had urged me to act sooner!

94. M. DE BEAULIEU to the VICOMTE DE VALMONT (sent from the LEFÈVRE ESTATE near AMIENS, 19th OCTOBER 1776)

I am glad you fail in your enterprise. You tarry too long between honour and dishonour. The beauty of the girl unmans you. Never before have I seen you so unavailing. Your wild admiration for her at once is your impetus and your impotence.

By the way, Merteuil proposed to Sophie two days ago.

95. THE VICOMTE VALMONT to M. DE BEAULIEU (sent from the HOSTELLERIE LE ST. CHRISTOPHE near AMIENS, 19th OCTOBER 1776)

A less effete man than you would pay for your last letter with his life.

    It is of no matter that Merteuil has proposed. To spite you, Beaulieu, I have rallied. You are premature in your assessment of my failings. I have not yet petitioned the maiden direct. I have yet to put her to a trial.

96. SOPHIE LEFÈVRE to HÉLÈNE, the CHEVALIÈRE D'IVRY (sent from the LEFÈVRE ESTATE near AMIENS, 19th OCTOBER 1776)

My dear Sister, I take up my pen again. Three days have passed. No one comes for me. All the usual communications have ceased. There has been no visit from our mother, no fire lighting or clothes arranged by my maid, no summons for supper. Nothing. I have not been able to get a letter to Aurèle and he has not been able to get one to me. I do not know if you are found or still lost to us. You never leave my thoughts. I fear for you and now I fear for myself.

    This episode is accompanied by an eerie silence throughout the house. It is this silence that wears my nerves the most. My maid hands my food to me on a tray through the door but I note she is not allowed custody of the key; a footman is at her side for the unlocking of the door. My thoughts and imagination, flooded with Aurèle, cause me to rail at myself for not having left with him. The triptych of Aurèle, Poverty and Hardship is now a vision from heaven. Aurèle was right. I should have fled this house with him.

    I know he is there, somewhere out in the estate waiting for me. After our passion, how could it be otherwise? He has ever been in my thrall. During the rain-lashed night of last night, when the sky momentarily was lit by a lightning flash, I was sure that the figure of a cloaked man was briefly outlined amongst the trees. Sometimes, when my hound is allowed up to me at night, she will rush to the window, eyes, ears and nose alert, and so I am sure Aurèle is there. I spend my days trying to make him out. I tuck myself against the stone reveal of the window, peeping through the leaded glass, looking for Aurèle. I do this so often that our brother has been moved to come to my room.

"Sister, parading yourself always before that window is immodest. The groundsmen comment and snigger. It is unwomanly that you display yourself in this way. With one sister gone wild and you showing the same wayward tendency what would you lead me to? Would you have me chain you by the wrist to a post like I did my hound bitch? Except that you, same as she, would probably chew through your own paw in your avidity to get with your mate."

I stared at Didier in contempt. The poor hound probably chewed through her paw because she was being starved.

"I have no idea what you are talking about. I can only assume, brother, that to speak as you do, you must be terribly fearful of Aurèle. And so you should be. He could fell you with one blow."

Now Didier has sent men to put extra locks on the doors and windows of the house. I look at him and laugh.

"What?! Do you think I have extraordinary powers?"

(Later) I have woken in dread. Because of my vigil at the window, I have alerted Didier to the possible continued presence of Aurèle! By this slip I have made my imprisonment more secure and I have put Aurèle in danger. There are so many young men and hunting dogs about here now. If only I could alert Aurèle to flee!

97. MME. LEFÈVRE to SOPHIE LEFÈVRE (hand delivered within the LEFÈVRE ESTATE near AMIENS, 19th OCTOBER 1776)

My dear child, I must beg that ye make your will more pliant to the will of your father and your brother. Ye have been encumbered with a bold nature but please remember, as ye look towards becoming a wife, what one of the prominent men do say:

'A clever wife is a plague to her husband, her children, her friends, her valets, everyone.'[*3]

I does not deny that us women do be capable of thought, but our reasoning be unprincipled: a woman feels, a man reasons. Where nature have made us think that us do 'know' a thing, in fact, us do 'feel' a thing. Us do be all sensibility. I do wish ye would learn that us must not provoke but please our men. Us do have strength but it do lie in our charms and not in our challengings. T'would do ye good to prime your mind to accept this now. Please do accommodate your ideas to those of your father and your brother. The house will be a happier one if your efforts in this direction do meet with success.

98. SOPHIE LEFÈVRE to MME. LEFÈVRE (hand delivered within the LEFÈVRE ESTATE near AMIENS, 19TH OCTOBER 1776)

Mother, I know better than do you the writer to whom you refer, it is Rousseau that famous muddle-head. He is not certain of his own mind regarding women. He lists women who have shown greatness:

'Zenobia, Dido, Lucretia, Joan of Arc, Cornelia, Arria, Artemisia, Fulvia, Elisabeth, the Countess of Thököly…'

He writes,

'…all proportions maintained, women would have been able to give greater examples of greatness of soul and love of virtue and in greater number than men have ever done if our injustice had not despoiled, along with their freedom, all the occasions manifest to them in the eyes of the world.'

Dear Mamma, by contradicting you I do not wish to denigrate you but to honour you with my reasoning.

Do you want to lose another daughter to this Marquis?

99. M. LEFÈVRE to SOPHIE LEFÈVRE (hand delivered within the LEFÈVRE ESTATE near AMIENS, 19th OCTOBER 1776)

Child, I have conferred upon ye an expensive education, and I be confident that ye be sensible of my liberalism in allowing ye latitude to read modern philosophical thought. I did this in order that ye be raised as fitting mate to a gentleman of high-status. On pain of lasting punishment, do not make me regret this decision.

    I have consulted with your brother on your recent incompliance and he do direct me to direct ye to draw upon the fruits of your education and remember, generally, the precepts of Le Brun in relation to the placement of women in society and the words of Rousseau, who your brother do assure me be one of the foremost thinkers of our day. Your brother do advise me of a passage what he do say be found in *'Julie'* or in *'Heloise'* or in *'Emilie'* or in one of Rousseau's other treatises entitled with a girl's name.

    Women exist *'merely to nurture and to comfort men…Always justify the burdens you impose upon girls but impose them anyway…They must be thwarted from an early age…They must be exercised to constraint, so that it costs them nothing to stifle all their fantasies, to submit them to the will of others.'* They must be kept, *'closed up in their houses'*.

    Rest assured, if ye do not choose to understand Rousseauan injunction in all matters pertaining to your sex, ye will be brought fully to understand this last one.

100. SOPHIE LEFÈVRE to HÉLÈNE, the CHEVALIÈRE D'IVRY (hand delivered within the LEFÈVRE ESTATE near AMIENS, 20th OCTOBER 1776)

In the meantime, I work on my maid, Victoire. She is a country girl and long ago I established my authority over her above any other member of my family. It has always been my instinct that one day her loyalty may be essential to me. Always have I been generous with her and always have I been careful to assert myself. Country people are particularly superstitious, not only believing in the power of God and the devil but also believing in all manner of bumpkin lore: ghosts, bad luck, bad omens, witchcraft, curses. It is by this last that I asserted my potency.

In the days when I could ride out with other young women, I encountered the daughter of a neighbour, an arrogant, young heiress, who for a brief period had been the barbarous, pettifogging mistress of my maid. It was my maid's running away from this foul female that caused her to come into my father's employ and therefore to me. One day, soon after her arrival, as my maid helped to lace me into my riding habit in preparation for another mounted excursion with the abhorrent female, she was moved to confide in me her hatred of her former mistress.

Laughingly, I promised my maid that I would curse the malevolent one on her behalf, and then I thought no more about it. Luckily for me, before the end of that day, the young, mean heiress was carried back into my home on a gurney. My maid was called to attend her and was delighted to discover that the despicable one was layered lavishly in mud and that she had leaves in her ears, a broken arm and hoofprints on thigh and torso. Not only was this young heiress humiliated, but so too was her family embroiled in a dangerous and litigious action, because, before her horse had bolted away with her and dumped her, it had had the forethought to lash out with one miraculously placed iron-tipped hoof at the unimaginably valuable racehorse of the son of a nobleman, somehow smashing its metal mouthpiece into two pieces and embedding one of the broken shanks into the magnificent horse's eyeball.

I need hardly mention that this fortuitous calamity, on the day of my curse, prompted my maid to an awesome fear and admiration of my powers. Fortuitously this fear is tempered by a genuine friendship, fostered, ironically, by my innate generosity. In the months following the equine event all I needed to do to reinforce her opinion of my powers, was to use my privileged access to information to tell her, every now and again, that I had cursed such and such a person. Of course, my curse would be issued shortly before it became public knowledge that the poor unfortunate had suffered a seizure or some such thing.

Once a day now my maid is allowed into my room for my personal linen (footmen left outside for this) and so I work on her. For example, can she get me a key? I believe her when she says this is impossible and not even I am naïve enough to suggest she attempt the charming of two pious, unimaginative and grizzled footmen. I explored with her the possibility of getting a letter to the forest lodge but while she is willing always to do my bidding, she is so fearful of forestry (ghosts) and so genuinely unable to understand directions (left from right, north from south) that I have judged that sending her off there would likely bring more sanctions upon me as she would surely fail and be discovered.

It occurs to me, even if Victoire can get a letter to the forest lodge, what then is Aurèle to do? Unless he can smash his way into my house, slash his way through all the household men, smash through my door and slash his way out again, a letter would be of no use.

101. THE VICOMTE DE VALMONT to M. LEFÈVRE (sent from the HOSTELLERIE LE ST. CHRISTOPHE near AMIENS, 20th OCTOBER 1776)

I was honoured to be a guest at your home four weeks ago. I am curious as to the state of affairs that is rumoured to exist between your daughter, Mademoiselle Sophie, and M. le Marquis de Merteuil. I am reluctant to declare an interest in that quarter unless the path be clear.

If I knew that your daughter were free, I would happily meet with you to discuss matters.

102. M. DIDIER LEFÈVRE to M. LEFÈVRE (hand delivered within the LEFÈVRE ESTATE near AMIENS, 20th OCTOBER 1776)

Father, please do not apprise Sophie of the news that she has made a conquest of Valmont as this will give her airs and hopes above and beyond M. le Marquis de Merteuil. I would go so far as to tell her that Valmont, despite approaches, does not choose to speak for her. This will serve to cut down her prideful opinion of herself and soften her up for the approaches of M. de Merteuil. I hardly dare calculate how much MORE money, land and property we would have to commit to transfer Sophie from M. le Marquis de Merteuil- where the arrangement is in place- to M. le Vicomte de Valmont.

103. M. LEFÈVRE to the VICOMTE DE VALMONT (sent from the LEFÈVRE ESTATE near AMIENS, 21ST OCTOBER 1776)

I am wholly sensible of the honour ye does me in your alluding to making a union with my family. I hope ye do not find me overly cautious when I observe to ye that your letter be full of 'woulds', 'ifs' and 'mights' and that ye stop short of anything substantive.

Your reputation precedes ye as being a young man of immense independence who is not desirous of marriage. I be fearful of entering an hypothetical debate with ye regarding my daughter simply for it all to come to nought. I respectfully require that ye furnish me with proofs of a much more solid interest before I overturn the serious intent shown toward my daughter from our noble neighbour, M. le Marquis de Merteuil.

I cannot help but feel that, were ye serious, by now ye would have made me a visit to discuss terms.

I anticipate that Sophie will be married to the other suitor before the next moon.

104. THE VICOMTE DE VALMONT to M. LEFÈVRE (sent from the HOSTELLERIE LE ST. CHRISTOPHE near AMIENS, 22ⁿᵈ OCTOBER 1776)

I fail to see how it is that you could have made money in business. Your desire to trade runs blind. Having thrown away one beautiful daughter on that oversized, wife-breaking aristocrat, I am amazed that you prepare to do so again. In this deal, you will be the loser; what you will gain by her marriage, you will lose by her death.

105. M. LE MARQUIS DE MERTEUIL to M. LEFÈVRE (sent from the CHÂTEAU OF **** ****, 22ⁿᵈ OCTOBER 1776)

I do not mind admitting that I was shocked by the mettlesome humour of Mademoiselle Sophie during my proposal to her. I was discommoded, almost to the point of abandoning all idea of wishing to make her my own. Her extraordinary beauty carries all before her, however, and I take heart that a wife is a very much more biddable thing than a missish maid. I do understand that in these matters, young, single women feed their vanity by enjoying being applied to more than once. Considering the excitable temperament of your daughter, I wonder whether my suit had better be sued by letter next time? I admit to a certain reluctance to meet face-to-face with your daughter again until the day of our nuptials. Her nature, at present, is high and haughty and I would prefer that my next dialogue with her be from the vantage point of husband than of petitioner suitor.

106. M. LEFÈVRE to M. LE MARQUIS DE MERTEUIL (sent from the LEFÈVRE ESTATE near AMIENS, 23ʳᵈ OCTOBER 1776)

I be vastly sensible of the honour ye do me with regard to your patience in the matter of my daughter. I thank ye for your willingness to try again for her hand. I can answer for the fact that her response next time will be in the affirmative. I vouchsafe that Sophie will make a pliant and easy wife. Her be an intelligent girl who have no real wish to overthrow the prescriptions laid down for her sex by society. Her temporary incompliance be due only to the commonality of behaviour of young women during this narrow period in their life when they flatter theyselfs that them have choices and so them exercises what power them believe theyselfs to have with regard to marital decision-making.

      Once the path be made clear to them, they do put their theyselfs under the yoke and become quieted as to their lot. I have reminded my daughter of the control I have over her. I will prepare her for your next proposal which ye may securely make in person, within the next few days.

107. THE CHEVALIER AURÈLE to ISABELLE AURÈLE (sent from a RUINED COTTAGE within the LEFÈVRE ESTATE near AMIENS, 24th OCTOBER 1776)

    Dieu! From the woods, I watch the Lefevre house in fear! I need to spring Sophie from that place and yet still my strength will not return to my body. My injuries are too numerous. I fear I fail my Sophie. I fear she may any day be forced to wed Merteuil. I espy Merteuil visiting daily. I espy the servants of the bank arrive with outriders and the little chest, the casket of the nuptial jewels of her dead sister. I fear that by some infernal way they have worked upon her to gain her consent.

108. SOPHIE LEFÈVRE to HÉLÈNE, the CHEVALIÈRE D'IVRY (sent from the LEFÈVRE ESTATE near AMIENS, 23rd OCTOBER 1776)

My sister, Valmont has made his move. I have had a letter. It was pushed under my door this morning by M. de Beaulieu. Through the thick oak, I heard Beaulieu ask both footmen to run a short errand for him. They refused to leave their post but during their heated exchange of words this letter appeared, possibly shunted by the foot of Beaulieu.

109. THE VICOMTE DE VALMONT to SOPHIE LEFÈVRE (sent from the HOSTELLERIE LE ST. CHRISTOPHE near AMIENS, 23rd OCTOBER 1776)

Occasionally a young woman will conceive the idea that she inhabit the trope of the tragical heroine; almost always her menfolk are happy to co-operate with her in this. It is of no surprise to me, therefore, that you find yourself locked in a room. The role of *antihero* comes easily to me and so I tell you I am prepared to offer you rescue. Fervently I wish I had offered this succour earlier. If you can break out of your house, I will undertake to have armed men, horses and a carriage waiting beyond the estate walls to carry you away. It is a matter of fact that in many abductions there is a degree of co-operation from the damsel.

    I recognise that the terming of myself as *'antihero'* may put you on your guard. I understand that the phrases *'prepared to offer you'* and *'I will undertake'* may sound insufficiently passionate. I am sure you will understand why when I point out that, away from the pages of a romantic novel, arranging for four armed men, four large horses and a carriage to remain concealed from all eyes, fed, watered, compliant, unriotous, undetected and yet close to your family home will tax all my powers of stratagem and forbearance when one factors the all-day and all-night vicissitudes of weather.

My incentive for undertaking this enterprise is the extreme nature of your allure. And this is where my not casting myself as hero can be explained.

If this were a literary escape, the way in which it would be effected is that, whilst undertaking to carry you away from your family, I would falsely promise to marry you, the false promise of this serving to persuade you to entrust yourself to me. After an extremely testing passage of time, you, the tragic heroine in the romantic novel, would come to realise that my designs upon you be not honourable. Despite much heroic resistance on your part, you would, eventually, be undone and I would be the author of that undoing. In all likelihood, your death would ensue.

As it happens, in this matter, I prefer honesty to mendacity and so I tell you that once I get you away from your house, I will NOT marry you. At the point where you leave the protection of your family and step into the carriage with me, you will be unmarriageable, ruined in the opinion of decent society. Your bargaining power, along with your status and stock, at that very moment, will plummet. In relation to you and your dispossession, my own power will be in the ascendency. This means I will have no need to marry you and I will find that I am in a position to do as I wish with you.

In this eventuality, however, you have my word that I will treat you with respect. I will undertake no indecent act against your person, and I will set you up in an independent, high-status household entirely of your own. What you do after that is your own affair but of course I hope that you choose to take me as your consort. Naturally, if you accept these conditions, you will find yourself entirely beyond conventional 'good' society and at the very pinnacle of 'bad' society. I promise you that this is the better place to be as it is where all the fun and freedoms are to be had. It is true that you would not be accepted into certain venues, houses and events of 'good' society. It is also true that you would have to stand by and watch the man or men that you might consort with, enjoy full acceptance to all the venues at which you are barred. However, within the demi-monde, you would be the equal of many men. You would enjoy more freedom than do the women of most marriages. Socially you would stand to gain at least as much as you would lose.

I flatter myself that you could do no worse than take me as your love. I offer this more as an observation than a compulsion. The fact that I make you no false promise of marriage means, I hope, you will find yourself able to trust all the other things I promise you. Still, you may ask yourself, why would this man settle money and independence upon me rather than simply force himself upon me and leave? For this I would remind you I am a prideful man who is passionately and powerfully drawn to you. Where you are concerned, I would prefer a long, voluntary, sweet liaison than a short, violent one. Since I am being honest with you, I tell you this is not always the case.

110. SOPHIE LEFÈVRE to the VICOMTE DE VALMONT (hand delivered via Victoire to Beaulieu from the LEFÈVRE ESTATE near AMIENS, 23rd OCTOBER 1776)

Your offer insults me; I am tempted almost beyond resistance to accept it.

I admire you and easily can I picture how harmoniously we would exist together in the demi-monde were all things equal between us. However, in the scenario that you put before me we would not be equal, despite your best intentions. The reality is that I would be in your thrall and, at some point, despite great bonhomie, a quarrel may arise between us and you may be driven to exert power over me.

I am sure you know the utterance of Diderot:

'There is no kind of harassment that a man may not inflict on a woman with impunity in civilized societies.'

I believe I might have been prepared to take my chances with you, in the manner you describe, were it not for a deep and abiding reluctance in me to put myself beyond the pale of *'good'* society. Sincerely, I wish I could throw off the shackles of this prejudice as I am sure that this is where, speedily, I might attain almost perfect freedom, (notwithstanding the possibilities it would offer me to attain perfect slavery). I admire the few women I see who have been brave enough to cross that invisible line. Despite my imprisonment, I do not yet feel emboldened to join them. Sincerely, I thank you for your offer. Regretfully, I decline.

111. M. LEFÈVRE to SOPHIE LEFÈVRE (hand delivered within the LEFÈVRE ESTATE near AMIENS, 23rd OCTOBER 1776)

Daughter, M. le Marquis de Merteuil will wait upon ye again within the next few days. Prepare yourself for his proposals and perform your duty with good grace. If ye defy me once more in this matter, it will be the last thing ye do.

    Do not allow your impure hopes for Aurèle to bedazzle ye. Nor should ye raise hopes to Valmont. I have made an enquiry in that direction and he shows not the slightest interest in ye.

112. THE VICOMTE VALMONT to SOPHIE LEFÈVRE (sent from the HOSTELLERIE LE ST CHRISTOPHE near AMIENS, 23rd OCTOBER 1776)

I find it impossible to persuade myself out of an interest in you. Passionate turns of phrase do not come readily to my tongue and so I tell you that while I endeavour ceaselessly to talk myself out of my engrossment with you, I cannot foresee an end to it. I am heartily sorry you will not cross the line with me into the demi-monde. Together, we would have found that world wonderfully diverting.

    I wish you good luck with whichever you take of the limited choices now open to you. None of them seem hopeful to me. Fervently, I wish you good health as without it I will fail in my ambition to meet with you again (whenever it may be that people desist in their habit of locking you inside a room). I look forward to a time when you may have some relative freedoms. I put you on notice that I am intent on trying you again, in the future, for a liaison.

I hope Beaulieu gets this letter to you. I congratulate you on your inventiveness in getting your letters, via Beaulieu, to me. I imagine you have motivated your maid into complete devotion to you. I hope one day that I may serve you just as devotedly.

113. THE VICOMTE VALMONT to M. DE BEAULIEU (sent from the HOSTELLERIE LE ST. CHRISTOPHE near AMIENS, 24th OCTOBER 1776)

I assume Sophie now will be forced to wed Merteuil. So long as she remains alive in that marriage, I will still be in with a chance. You cannot have forgot how many wives of other men I have enjoyed by breaching the flimsy bounds of the *'marriage convenience'*. Well in this case, this marriage is VERY *'convenience'*. After she has spent a few months as wife to the hoofing beast that is Merteuil, I will appear as a veritable demi-god. Sophie will have tasted the very worst that love has to offer and so will be primed to recognise and value the best (me). Before aspiring to partner me, I find it suits me that she become accustomed to the strange attitudes and all the worst aspects of the act of love.

At least she soon will be at one remove from old Lefèvre. From a tactical and practical point of view it is far easier to access the wife of a man than the daughter of a man.

(Later)…Dieu! Beaulieu! I cannot escape the idea that I have failed my Sophie. I had thought to reconcile myself to the idea of her wed to the animal that is Merteuil, but in truth I cannot.

Do not write to me. Do not crow over me. Do not seek me out. I am in no mood to allow further flippancies from you to go unavenged. Her situation is hopeless, beyond rescue. There is nothing more that can be done.

114. SOPHIE LEFÈVRE to HÉLÈNE, the CHEVALIÈRE D'IVRY (sent from the LEFÈVRE ESTATE near AMIENS, 24th OCTOBER 1776)

My dearest sister, I am sure I am pregnant. To avoid incarceration in a convent, I need a husband as a matter of urgency.

Two days ago, I realised that my monthly règles had not arrived and for this reason I am cold with fear. I know from your gentle instruction to me, my sister, during your pregnancies, that an absence of règles could indicate the conception of a child in the female body. I know, from you, that this results from male bodily contact with the female. You know that I have experienced contact with Aurèle.

Aware that the household laundry maids and washer women have become familiar with my calendar, I have managed to produce linen with a little blood drained from my own finger. My problem is pressing. As a matter of urgency, I need either immediate confirmation that I am not pregnant- or a legitimate father.

I weep with rage at my own fear, ignorance and weakness. Why did I not make it my purpose to gain knowledge and control of my body and why is it that my body, heart, soul and senses have betrayed me to such danger?

Do I resent Aurèle for his part in my downfall? No, I adore him. How can I blame Aurèle for finding me irresistible? How can I blame him for his passion for me? How can I blame Aurèle for discovering that my proximity takes away all his powers of self-control? No, my estimation of myself is far too high for that. And yet, violently, I resent that nature has conspired to play this trick on me, to implant his child in me before the time that I have chosen. Why is it that I cannot be left free to love Aurèle and love myself? Why is it that I bear punishment for my love? Why did nature give this passion to man and woman only to have the result of it put them asunder?

Sometimes I am calm, and I remember that if I were a young savage on a tropical island, this baby, likely, would be a boon. Even were I a peasant girl in this country, this baby might be a boon. It is only within a family where a legitimate conduit, a pure vessel for the passage of wealth is perceived necessary that this baby will be viewed as the issue of vice and sin and have me banished.

It is imperative that I consider, with all clarity, with whom I might be better off in this state: Valmont, Merteuil or Aurèle. Valmont cannot be trusted, Merteuil brings opulence but I dread him, Aurèle brings poverty but I love him.

I will write forthwith to Aurèle and ask if he can see any way of effecting my rescue. People in romantic novels manage prodigious feats in this area. Truthfully though, I cannot see a way through for him. The proposal is so dangerous that I can hardly bring myself to suggest it to him. I will not tell him I carry his child as it would endanger him were I to lay too great an obligation upon him. He is the sort that would take the ultimate risk for love.

115. SOPHIE LEFÈVRE to the CHEVALIER AURÈLE (hand delivered within the LEFÈVRE ESTATE near AMIENS, 24th OCTOBER 1776)

I have imagined, many a time, that it would be worth purchasing a moment of bliss with you with my own destruction. Now I find myself prepared to realise this wish.

I have finally prevailed upon Victoire, my waiting maid, to employ the services of her brave little dryad-urchin sister to attempt to deliver this letter, and the latest bundle of my letters for Hélène, to you, following the normal route through the woods to the Lodge.

I write to ask you for help although this is what I had fervently hoped not to have to do. My father, as I am certain you must know by now, has published his idea of my infamy by locking me into my room. By doing this, he hopes to make me agree to marry M. le Merteuil. He has posted two footmen as permanent guards in a rota outside my door. These footmen are bachelor brothers, faithful retainers who are well paid and secure in their employ. They are pious, hoary, realistic in their imaginings. They cannot be bought or seduced. They are the keepers of my key. I see no way around them.

If you can think of a way to bring about my rescue, I would be very grateful. I am prepared to marry you now. It is the least disastrous option available to me. My state of mind is such that I prefer to endanger myself with you than with any other person.

It is said in the Bible that no man may put asunder two people joined in marriage. Even a clandestine, defiant marriage, therefore, would place me beyond the reach of my father and all other men- a trip to the alter being irreversible. I understand now how it is that fortune hunters get away with making off with heiresses. I imagine that, quite often, an heiress might marry the young, handsome fortune hunter of her choice in order to evade marriage to a raddled old aristocrat not of her choosing.

My love for you is such that I prefer that my life should be in danger rather than yours. If you cannot think of a peaceful way to rescue me from this place, then please do not make an attempt. I beg of you to undertake no action that carries risk of violence to yourself.

116. THE CHEVALIER AURÈLE to ISABELLE AURÈLE (sent from a RUINED COTTAGE within the LEFÈVRE ESTATE near AMIENS, 24th OCTOBER 1776)

Mademoiselle Sophie has written. Regardless of my physical state, now is the time to act. My fear that they try to force her into marriage is well founded.

    From watching the house, I have worked out the internal positioning and route to her room.

    Tonight, I will acquire fast horses by whatever means necessary.

    Tomorrow night I will break my Sophie out of that place.

I send this letter to you by express rider.

I put you on notice: Mademoiselle Sophie and I may arrive with you soon.

117. ISABELLE AURÈLE to the CHEVALIER AURÈLE (sent from PARIS, 25th OCTOBER 1776)

Oh! Fie! fie! Disaster! All three of your letters have only just arrived with us today! Only now do we know of the danger you are in.

This is a command from your Father and your Mother: DO NOTHING! Do not go near the Lefvre house. Do not go near the Lefvre young woman. We send a rider immediately to speed this missive to you.

You are one man against many. Leave that place now!

We are all certain of two things: firstly, that this young woman does not wish to be rescued; secondly, that she does not wish to be rescued by you. We are put in mind that you have rescued women before who would have preferred to be left as they were.

If this young woman had loved you half as much as do we, she would have fled with you long before now. As it is, she cannot make up her mind about you. In the long run, you will be happier alive with us than dead with her.

Do not endanger yourself. We love you. We fear for you. We weep for you. We beg of you, come home!

118. SOPHIE LEFÈVRE to HÉLÈNE, the CHEVALIÈRE D'IVRY (sent from the LEFÈVRE ESTATE near AMIENS, 25th OCTOBER 1776)

My God! My God! Aurèle is come for me! The fighting rages all over the house! I knew he would come! I knew he would triumph! My God! I hear the yelling of the multitudinous young men! I hear the vicious clash of metal on metal. There is no one can defeat him. There is no number of men can overwhelm him. My God! I must throw what few belongings I have into a saddle bag and be ready to fly!

My Helène, soon we may both be free and together again!

119. THE CHEVALIER AURÈLE to ISABELLE AURÈLE (sent from ROUEN, 26th OCTOBER 1776)

I am the loser in all this but not so much as Sophie. I have failed her.

Knowing that extra men had been placed at all points of the house and yards, I decided to take a chance and so, in the dead of the night, I simply strolled through the great portal that is the front door. It was as I had divined; under Didier's hopeless commandeering, he had forgotten to lock it. Trusting to its forbidding architecture, he had left it unmanned.

My presentiment proved correct, but my timing was catastrophic. As I stepped through the great portal, I walked straight into the path of Old Lefèvre. He was alone, making his way to his study in his embroidered night robe and fez cap. It was due to him that I made my mistake. In that moment, in cold blood, I should have slashed him down in revenge and left him silently to bleed out across the marble floor. Then I could have made my way undetected to the part of the house where is her room. Never, though, have I cut down a life in cold blood. In most circumstances, it is unholy to cut down a life created by God and rarely do I feel the need. Quite apart from which, history has proven that one does not win heart, mind and legal possession of a young woman by wading to her through the blood of her father.

On seeing me, Lefèvre looked as though he viewed a ghost. He shook with fear and I knew then that he believed he had left me in the forest for dead. To my everlasting shame, I mistook his fear for surrender and so I did not to capitalise on my undoubted dominance. I decided to follow chivalrous form and petition him for his daughter. I was sure that this quaking man would agree with all I proposed. In the manner of a knight-of-old therefore, I sank to one knee on the marble floor (where his blood should already have been spreading) and, with my sword arm across my chest, my hand on my heart, I urged him for a hearing. He politely and shakily requested that I remove my sword, which I gave word I would do as soon as we had retired to the privacy of his room, away from the public hall. As the balance of all power lay with me, he agreed to retire. Like the fool that I am, I thought he did this out of respect and that a coming to terms was inevitable.

We entered the sanctum of his study. He stood himself to the left of the blazing fire near the bell pull for the servants. I allowed him to remain there and handed him my sword before retiring a few steps and bowing deeply. I knew I could take my sword off him at will. By giving it to him I assumed it would allay his fears and help him to agree to any terms. With surprising presence of mind, however, he placed my sword into the cradle of the flames of the fire. His spirit fired up after this move.

"This be an unorthodox arrival Sirrah!"

I was furious at his duplicity. I kicked the sword out of the fire and onto the hearth stone.

"Sire, I come for your daughter. No man in this world can love her as truly as do I. I am of an ancient and noble family. There is no shame for you in joining her name with mine, in mingling her blood with my own."

"Ye cannot afford her, Sir, and providence did not endow her with such a face and figure and fortune to be given away for nothing."

"I bring lineage, nobility of blood."

"Aye Sir, and can us shelter under your heraldry and blazons? Can us eat your coat of arms? Where be your money and your land? Where be your rents, jewels, horses, carriages, servants, society and connections? Where be all this? Hmm? Where?! If ye had all this Sir, ye could have had her! As 'tis, ye have nothing, and besides, her have not spoke for ye, her have spoke for M. le Marquis de Merteuil."

"You lie! This cannot be true!"

"Do you dare tell me ye doubt me?"

I was instantly ablaze with anger.

"You are no gentleman! You lie! You force her! You imprison her!"

"Believe me, Sir, she will marry M. de Merteuil of her own volition. I must ask ye to give me your word that peacefully ye will leave."

"I will not give you my word, Sir. I am here for your daughter, with or without your permission."

With this, Lefèvre reached for the bell pull. Naturally I stopped him, but his ensuing shout brought men running through doors to left and right. My sword had cooled and so I flicked it up to my left hand with my foot. Then, I grabbed a fire iron, wheeling around to catch the first comer a blow across the wrist. Before his weapon hit the floor, I had it caught and in my own power. I now had a sword in each hand and so the fight came relatively easily. There were only two men of the company who gave me any trouble; the others were only as bothersome flies. I inflicted as much injury as possible before gaining the door and attempting the stairs. More men came running from the landing and I engaged with them mid-staircase. Others ascended the stairs behind me. After some time of holding them off in front and behind and with more advancing from both sides, I judged my chances at nil and dropped over the banister into the hall. With men advancing now through the main portal, I ran to the back of the house where farmhands and grooms came flooding into the courtyard. These men fought with far more savagery, strength, courage and commitment than the company of gentlemen and household men. I had a great deal of trouble to get past them with my life. I slashed to left and right 'til my arms became leaden. Finally, I cleared my path and fled into the outer darkness, howling in my soul for my failure.

I leave now for École Militaire in Paris. The next time you hear from me, I will have enlisted in the army.

120. SOPHIE LEFÈVRE to HÉLÈNE, the CHEVALIÈRE D'IVRY (sent from the LEFÈVRE ESTATE near AMIENS, 25th OCTOBER 1776)

… I am bereft…Aurèle made his move…Somehow he failed. I am abject in my misery and in my fear for him.

Victoire tells me that it has long been suspected that Aurèle has been here by night, in the grounds. The dogs have been agitated indoors but when let out have become quiet. Victoire tells me there has been a frisson of fear in the household and that regularly men have been sent to rout him but that the hounds will not hunt him down. Extra men have been brought inside to guard the house and all doors and windows have been sealed. Often, Didier has invited a company of young gentlemen to stay, to drink late into the night.

Tonight, in the late hours, interrupting the sound of Didier's young carousers, I heard an almighty commotion, dogs, men, yelling and the clash of metal on metal. I knew that Aurèle had revealed himself. The violence was prolonged and vicious; it raged about the house. As I heard ever more men come running, I felt horror at the peril that Aurèle was in. After lengthy bouts of fighting, I heard the affray progress to the rear courtyard of the house. Desperately, I hoped that Aurèle had fought himself out of danger. I ran to my window and became sick to my soul to see him standing against an onslaught of young men. The affray was extended and fierce. The moonlight highlighted only Aurèle and his flashing blade, the other men appearing as a cordon of ever-lunging creatures from the shadows. It seemed a hopeless cause. With so many men committed against him, I was reminded of the pack of hounds upon a single fox. Miraculously, Aurèle's bright sword, shoulders and head remained elevated above all-comers, the action of his blade steadfastly flourishing. I judged that he must be exhausted but at no point did his golden silhouette buckle to the weight of the savagery. After an age, a break appeared in his dark opponents. Aurèle saw the opportunity and still slashing about him, he ran from the scene. The relief I felt at his deliverance from danger sank me to my knees.

When all had quieted, I was released and taken downstairs by two household men. I was warned that windows and doors were secured once more. I was strangely delighted to see how much damage Aurèle had wrought in his attempt to get to me: the banisters were broken; wall hangings were torn down; chandeliers and mirrors smashed; tables, chairs, all ornamentation shattered beyond recovery. My relief at Aurèle's escape, entirely reconciled me to my imprisonment. Never could I have forgiven myself had I been the cause of injury to him.

I am recognised as the only effective nurse in a crisis. My mother, father and the maids cannot deal with quantities of blood, splintered bone and raw tissue. When a surgeon is awaited, the initial care falls to me.

I was directed to the kitchens. Didier was laid out on a scrubbed table, bleeding faintly onto it. The other men, Didier's gentlemen friends, household staff, farmhands and grooms suffered varying states of injury, with one, a hay swain of sorts, in quite some danger, stretched out on the floor and bleeding freely in a rivulet onto the tiles. The surgeon had preceded me this time and although Didier was squealing like a pig, the surgeon had assessed that this last silent patient was the one that needed his immediate attention. He commanded that Didier be carried away from the scene (and his hearing) into the drawing room, where I was to apply bandages to his wounds. This I did with Mother, a weeping and wailing Greek chorus, all the while. I finished speedily and under Didier's direction, he was soon elaborately swathed from head to foot. Father was giving voice to his agitation.

"Good God Didier! How is this?! All ye young swordsmen, men of the household, men of the stable and farmyards and still ye was unable to detain he!"

"He is freakishly, prodigiously the warrior! There is nothing can be done about him!"

"But this is humiliation! It is insupportable! And ye! Where be your pride? I feel the failure keenly and yet ye be content to lie under the yoke of it! Better ye be dead than a cowering, jibbering craven! There be so many young men here at your command! All ye young men! We be a laughing-stock!"

Didier pointed at me.

"Why blame me? It was that bitch in season he came for!"

For once, our father was not to be deflected.

"Ye had a household of men and a company of young gentlemen; how did ye not prevail? How be it that so oft us do fail for the amusement of all our neighbours?! All the région soon will learn that they may take our name in vain and that there be no redress! How is it that one single man can best a company so numerous?!"

"Father I am hurt! Perhaps mortally. You must spare me tonight at least!"

Didier lay on the sofa whimpering while our father paced up and down, seething and storming, until he had gathered enough thought for his next tirade.

"Of all them young men what have marauded about my house this night, he, Aurèle, if the truth be known, be the one I would choose for my son. Not ye, ye puling, milksop of over-mothered, kitten-flesh! What a shame the Chevalier Aurèle be too piss-poor to contemplate! Of every young buck what has come howling for my Sophie, he be the one I would choose! I tell ye what Sirrah, if he could have been the one, I would have disinherited ye in a stroke of the pen, for I would stake more on the blood of he mixed with she than of anything ye will muster as issue!"

My God, my sister! How close our father came to the truth! As he spoke of the comingled blood of mine and Aurèle's, I felt he could see through my clothing to the beginnings of our child in my belly.

He continued.

"As 'tis however, I cannot have him for my son and so he be my sworn enemy. Oh, if only ye, my boy, was made of the stuff of my girls! I would command ye to go get him and to bring him to justice or death! As 'tis, simply I must look upon ye and despair!"

My God, my sister. Aurèle and I have lost our chance to be together. Now I know I should have fled with him as soon as first I saw him. I should not even have bothered with "Hello". Simply, I should have said, "Let's go!"

I am abject.

121. SOPHIE LEFVÈRE to HÉLÈNE, the CHEVALIÈRE D'IVRY (sent from the LEFÈVRE ESTATE near AMIENS, 1st NOVEMBER 1776)

Aurèle is gone and the dogs turn their throats up to the sky and howl for him. It is their inexorable opinion that all is now lost.

They are right. I have agreed to marry Merteuil. There is no other choice: my father tells me that unless I marry him within the next se'enight, he will hunt Aurèle down and have him killed. In any case, I am pregnant. I am locked in a room. The clock is ticking. All that is left for me is the convent, or Merteuil.

For fear that I might change my mind and that my agreement is a feint, our father keeps me yet under lock and key. Our family has scrambled quickly. A marriage license has been got so that the banns can be waived. The trousseau of our dead sister is dusted down; her jewels are brightened.

M. Le Marquis de Merteuil has come again to plight his troth. I believe, after last time, this was almost as dreaded an occasion for him as it was for me. I was led downstairs to the morning salon by both brother and father and two footmen: a Praetorian guard. They do not trust me to hold steady to my course. M. de Merteuil was already in the salon with our mother. We joined them both. Platitudes were exchanged and then a poorly enacted pantomime ensued whereby our father, mother, brother remembered each some pressing reason which drew them from the room. As they left, the footmen turned the locks in the doors. I was left with M. de Merteuil and he hemmed himself up to a speech. I could not have been less happy or less interested. I cut him off mid-utterance.

"My answer is yes. Please do not trouble yourself further."

"Ah. Oh. Glad about that. A young woman usually comes around to seeing sense."

We both remained a long while in silence as if sitting for our portrait in oils, until relieved by the return of our parents.

122. ISABELLE AURÈLE to the CHEVALIER AURÈLE (sent from PARIS, 1st NOVEMBER 1776)

My darling brother! We three who adore you are overjoyed that you have escaped with your life. Father, Mother and I are unutterably thankful that you are released from the dangers surrounding the place Lefèvre.

As regards the unfortunate young woman with whom you have fallen in love, she is beyond your reach now. For this we feel relief.

We do not rejoice that you enlist in the army. It seems that we must reconcile ourselves to receiving letters from an heroic young man who courts danger at every turn.

Please be mindful that we live our life through you. Upon your happiness, your life, your breath, depend ours.

123. THE CHEVALIER AURÈLE to SOPHIE, the MARQUISE DE MERTEUIL (sent from the ÉCOLE MILITAIRE, PARIS, 14TH NOVEMBER 1776)

I ought to term you, 'Madame' or 'Marquise', however, I will address you 'My darling Sophie'. You can see from my direction on this letter that I am apprised of your marriage.

I am bereft that the chance of having you for my own has gone. At first, I felt that the desolation raging in my soul could not abate for me ever to function again. I thought that my tears over my lost chance with you would never stop flowing.

I have rallied with the idea that one day you may become free and that you may seek me out. This will only be possible upon the death of your husband and as I fear God too much to wish for the death of another man, I have left. I have fulfilled my long-postponed plans of joining the army.

Please memorise the enclosed direction of my sister in Paris. If ever you need me, send word to her and she will inform me. I will not forsake you.

I enclose a letter from your sister, Hélène. I discovered her whereabouts. She had been taken in by a woman of low repute and was dwelling in meagre rooms in Amiens. I have delivered her to the convent of the Ursulines. For this it was necessary to negotiate with her husband, the Chevalier, for his permission. The man is a brute. Your sister is well away from him.

It is forbidden that Mme la Chevalière correspond from the convent, but she is desperate with desire to communicate with you. It does not sit well with me to subvert the convent rule or a decree of the Holy Roman Church, but she was in such a dangerous and febrile state when she begged for this indulgence, that I had no choice but to comply.

I have delivered, to your sister, via your maid, your considerable bundle of letters and from now, if you send your maid weekly to the convent for a basket of dried lavender and herbs, Hélène, with Victoire's help, will secret letters in and out for you.

I will never forsake you. I love and adore you and I always will. Send to my sister if you need me.

124. HÉLÈNE, the CHEVALIÈRE D'IVRY to SOPHIE, THE MARQUISE DE MERTEUIL 14th NOVEMBER 1776 (sent from the CONVENT of the URSULINES, enclosed within the preceding letter of Aurèle)

My darling sister, Aurèle has rescued me. How aptly is he given the golden name borne by saints. On his finding me, he appeared like a haloed vision of goodness and, in his goodness, he carried me to safety at the convent. Here I will recover. The Ursulines are unsurpassed in their care of the sick. I have asked to have the same room which housed me as a novitiate. Please do not grieve for me. Gladly I submit to my permanent incarceration here. At last I am at peace and at rest.

When I have recovered strength, I will tell you my story. It is a lengthy one and I will need better health to write of it. For now, I can tell you that had it not been for the bravery of a young, creole, streetwoman named Taisha, I would have perished in abject circumstances. Taisha saved me and then, when she learned I was your sister, her loyalty to me was boundless.

I am devastated to learn of the death of our darling sister, our Jeanette. I fear now for how your own future will be arranged. I pray for you hourly.

125. SOPHIE, the MARQUISE DE MERTEUIL to HÉLÈNE, THE CHEVALIÈRE D'IVRY (sent from the CHÂTEAU DE **** ****, 15th NOVEMBER 1776)

My darling sister, never more am I moved to thank God for his mercy and so the thanks I offer up for your rescue, are all directed toward Aurèle. How gratefully, how fervently will I honour him if ever again I find myself in his presence.

I am full of anxiety that you have not the strength to write more to me. All I can do is send to the Ursulines for assurance that you will recover speedily from your trials. Then I will await assurance from your own hand.

I am happy for the delay in hearing your story as I fear it will greatly sadden me. I will stifle that feeling better if you tell it me when you are restored to perfect health.

My own tale is a long one and I am confident that all the letters which recount it have been delivered to you by Aurèle. I have just heard that he conscripted into the army shortly after my marriage. This news has distressed me in the extreme.

I am now married to M. le Marquis de Merteuil. I will tell you of my nuptial day another time.

Aurèle tried to rescue me from this marriage but all his efforts came to naught. He was at once my rescuer but also my captor - as I thought he had got me with child. In my ensuing terror, I needed a husband and I chose the only one to hand: M. de Merteuil.

As it happened, I proceeded up the aisle a virgin. True to my oft proven appalling judgement in a crisis, the full knowledge of how the body works in reproduction, gleaned from our father's veterinary books, was apprised by me but too late. Aurèle, I discovered, had kept me safe. There had been no earthly chance of a pregnancy. True to the vindictiveness of Mother Nature in this matter, the erroneously termed 'monthly' proof of this appeared, also too late, on the day after my nuptials.

I have been carried off to the dismal mansion of M. le Marquis de Merteuil thence to begin the next chapter of my life as the reigning Marquise. My main occupation here is to nurture a secret, seething grievance against men. The only exception I make is for Aurèle, even though he is in part to blame for my being in this predicament.

My father, my brother, my husband, their lawyer, their curé, their steward, agent, manservants and all the other men I know have used me ill. Also, they have used my sisters savagely. My heart is twisted with hatred for their species.

In my new role as Marquise, I acquire freedoms, charms and powers.

I will use these, to enthral men and avenge myself upon them.

The End of Volume 1

Sophie, Valmont, Aurèle, Merteuil, Beaulieu, Didier, Mme Lefèvre, M. Lefèvre, Hélène, Rosebud, Taisha Meyer, the curé, the grooms and several new characters will be back in Volumes II and III in this, *Dangerous Liaisons*: *The Prequel*.

*1. Pierre Choderlos de Laclos, *Les Liaisons Dangereuses (letter 10)*   *2. William Shakespeare, *Romeo & Juliet*   *3. Jean Jacques Rousseau, *Émile*